T0196517

UPSHUR 1877

PARIS, TEXAS, A TOWN ON FIRE

OTIS MORPHEW

IUNIVERSE, INC.
NEW YORK   BLOOMINGTON

UPSHUR 1877
Paris, Texas, a town on fire

iUniverse books may be ordered through booksellers or by contacting:

iUniverse
1663 Liberty Drive
Bloomington, IN 47403
www.iuniverse.com
1-800-Authors (1-800-288-4677)

Because of the dynamic nature of the Internet, any Web addresses or links contained in this book may have changed since publication and may no longer be valid. The views expressed in this work are solely those of the author and do not necessarily reflect the views of the publisher, and the publisher hereby disclaims any responsibility for them.

ISBN: 978-1-4502-5710-7 (sc)
ISBN: 978-1-4502-5631-5 (ebk)

Printed in the United States of America

iUniverse rev. date: 9/13/2010

Dedicated to my wife, Connie, and all my children

PROLOGUE

William (Billy) Upshur was first and foremost, a gunfighter,...a Shootist, some would say. But if you were to ask him, he would say he was only lucky! Luck, however, had nothing to do with his ability to kill a man, as his talent was a natural one. He would also say, that he was only as fast as he needed to be to survive,...which in his mind, could very well be so. But whatever it was, Upshur's ability with a gun proved him to be the best there was, an exceptional gunman, his was the quickest of reflexes,...he had an insight for danger beyond that of other gunmen.

Upshur never wanted to be what he had become, what he was. He was always his father's son, a farmer!...And after the war, with the help and love from the people of Paris, Texas, he lived his dream. He was a farmer, a husband and a father. For a gunman with a past, however, fate sometimes plays a different game,...and anyway you look at it, a man's destiny is already pre-written, and must be carried out!

So it came to pass!...Billy Upshur was not a farmer anymore, and a gun had become a part of his life again. But his love for family and friends never wavered, and that love continued to direct his life. But, in so doing, would also lead him into many dangerous adventures to protect them, allowing nothing to deter him from his happiness. That is, until his beloved Paris was destroyed!...The very town, and people that had risked their own futures to give him a new life, were experiencing destruction. Those same people that had lied to protect him, were now homeless,...and in the aftermath of a devastating depression!

This is possibly my last novel on Upshur, and perhaps his last adventure! This will culminate his exceptional life, at least for us! There is nothing else to interfere with his way of life now,...unless another accident occurs in the mountain sometime in the future. But if it does, I will surely try to write about it. But now, he helps his town rebuild the only way he can. He aids in the capture of renegade Raiders that took advantage of a helpless Paris in its time of destruction and need. So what possibly could be left?

My rendition of Paris, and the city's struggle with the first great fire of it's history, stemmed from articles my little brother, Bill found in the archives at the Junior College Library. However, none of the stories gave me anything other than the appropriate facts pertaining to it, only how it started, what it burned, who and why? It did give the names of a few establishments, and names of pertinent people involved, but ultimately, not much else. Therefore, I began working my story around what information I had, placing businesses around the square where I wanted them to be, etc. After all, this is only a novel!

I have depicted Cantrell's Raiders akin to that of Quantril during the great war, Cantrell himself being a Mormon Minister whose family is assassinated by the Mormon Church as a tactic to force him into silence, a tactic that only resulted in retaliation! This is a novel, and does not in any way seek to portray the Mormon Society in any capacity other than that!...It is only fictional food for a work of fiction. It is, however true that the Mormon Church was a powerful entity in the eighteenth century, and at times flaunted it!...but by what means, I haven't a clue.

Billy Upshur will go down in fictional history as the fastest gun that ever lived! How do I know,...I wrote it! He will never know the fame of a Wes Hardin, or Bill Hickok, because he was relatively unknown,... and he had no dime novelist to write about him. But I would venture to say, that if Upshur had ever met one of those famed gunmen of history, and was forced to fight, that gunfighter would not have found his niche in the history books!...Fictionally speaking, of course!

But Upshur will live on,...he will hold his friends close, and his family closer. He will nurture his mountain of wealth with it's alien mysteries and myths,...and he will continue using his gun to protect it all. But mostly, he will just be happy,...loving to live, and living to love!...Thanks,...Otis!

Be sure to look for my two unrelated novels, "The rippling storm, a time odyssey" and "Dancer" Out sometime next year, or 2011.

CHAPTER ONE

For the most part, the Recession in America was all but over. Paper money was almost worth its full face value again, thanks to the new Gold Standard of the Hayes Administration. People were once more spending previously hoarded-up dollars, and Merchants were finding ways to reopen their doors for business again, able to restock depleted merchandise with goods from reopened mills, and eastern factories. Men all over the country were slowly being put back to work after four long years of Depression, near starvation, and absent wandering.

Farmers were planting their crops again in fields that had become overgrown with weeds and brush from the lack of attention. Millions of bales of cotton, at last were being sold, shipped by rail from warehouses and Depot platforms where they had sat for three long years,...sold at less than half the previous market price, but sold never the less, as one by one the great iron horses were put back into operation. The country was entering the throes of recovery which, according to the newly elected Rutherford P. Hayes, would be only a memory in another year's time. Hayes' administration was already being credited with saving the country from complete ruin.

Thousands of homeless families still roamed the Nation's countryside's, however, out of work men with gaunt, starving loved ones to support, forced to take them along in his quest for a new start. But at last, there came a bright side to it all as many of these wanderers, having seen the beginnings of change, were returning to their home states as more and more news of recovery began filling the papers. Those that were not putting down new roots elsewhere were leaving

1

with renewed hope for a future, and that hope was flickering in hearts of those so long without it.

But that, too, became a tragedy for many of them as outlawry was still on the increase across a devastated country. Unlucky families were being robbed, their women raped and children abused as roving bands of these men took their meager belongings, sometimes wagons and teams as well, leaving them with nothing,…sometimes not even their lives. The tragedy was that the law was still without proper manpower to stop it. Cattle rustling was a booming business, especially in Texas as herds of stolen steers were driven across the Rio Grande to be sold in Mexico. However, it was becoming more difficult, as the Texas Rangers, coupled with Cavalry patrols were instilling burrs under the thieves saddle blankets.

Stagecoaches became a favorite for many outlaws, but in reality, they always were, as these coaches had always been in danger from Highwaymen, even before the Recession. But coach robberies had escalated three-fold now that money and gold was once more being shipped to banks, and in greater quantities than before. Trains were being more frequently held up as well, though mostly in the northern states and this, by the way, kept the renowned Pinkerton Detective Agency, who had been hired to protect against such activity, quite busy especially in the Missouri, Arkansas area where the James gang was most active. But there were other men even more ruthless to contend with,…the bank robbers. Bank robberies had steadily escalated and now, banks that were only just beginning to recover and become soluble again were being hit hard, especially the Federal Reserve Banks, as these establishments had the most readily available funds,…and these outlaws were quite brutal when robbing them.

Now that Reconstruction had been abolished, Martial law had also been lifted from the Southern states and with it Federal control, and it's involvement in state and city Government. This allowed Town Councils the responsibility once again to run their own town, pass new laws, and to enforce them,…this however came with an option. The Government, though out of the picture completely, could still be asked to step in, if needed,…otherwise, it could not, and would not interfere without meaningful cause,…which, in reality, could cover a lot of territory! This arrangement gave extra meaning to local lawmakers, who took precautions in their efforts to do their jobs right the first time. No one wanted more Government interference.

Local lawmen had their permissive shackles removed, giving them free rein to enforce the peace. United States Marshals were stationed in larger cities, appointed and controlled by Federal Judges, and had jurisdiction anywhere in the country,...and with lawlessness so rampant, had their hands full.

City taxes were being paid again, even those in arrears levied on business establishments, farms and ranches. They were finally slowly becoming able to ship produce and cattle to out of state markets again. These taxes allowed the hiring of more peace officers for town and county patrols. Civil and County Judges were once again becoming busy as more criminals were arrested and brought to trial....At last, America was on her way to recovery, but would not be able to celebrate fully for some time to come.

CHAPTER TWO

Paris, Texas had not suffered as severely as it's counterparts, this mostly due to the Farmers' and Merchants' Bank. Mister Horace Bratcher not only had instigated the joining of forces with other lending establishments, but he had enough faith in his city's future, and people to see they survived. It had paid off, too, and now the outstanding loans were slowly being repaid,...and with the least possible interest.

Stores and shops around the large square, most having been closed to business, were slowly able to reopen, having received their first shipments of goods from Mills and Factories in more than three years,... and because of Horace Bratcher, were able to pay for those goods. A few stores around the square, and even some in the outlying areas had managed to stay alive, both by monies saved, and living frugally,...and because they had diligently paid premiums on expensive, and largely inadequate insurance policies. But these stores, too, were not fully solvent and needed some help from Bratcher.

Paris had been able to retain Marshal Jim Stockwell, and one of his deputies throughout the lean times, but Sheriff Gose had not fared as well, having had his job put on hold. However, the good Sheriff had recently been reappointed to his former post, by Judge Bonner, as well as two of his deputies,...thievery in the county having dictated the necessity. John Rucker's State Militia had been cut to a minimum of only four men in '75, and could not cover the county and it's needs. But according to the Government, his force of a dozen men would be restored by the following year's end!

Many businesses on streets just off the square had to be repaired, or completely remodeled due to the plague of break-ins, and vandalism since the recession started, half of which was blamed on the hoards of vagrants, and homeless families,…and during this time, residents inside the town's limits had been warned to stay at home when possible,…and to arm themselves accordingly, as law enforcement could be hard-put to respond in times of need.

It had only been four years, the last two being the worst, but to most, it seemed like a lifetime of misery they had been forced to endure,… having to do without the things that had once been readily accessible. But lean times most always makes a man appreciate the good ones and in most cases, prepare for the bad. As such, Paris, Texas was able to survive the worst of those times.

Men were once again being hired by the city to clean up the littered, unkempt streets of town, the paper and debris taken to a cleared-pit on the outskirts of town and burned. Shops, Markets, and even houses were being freshened with new paint and much needed repair. Vegetable gardens were cleaned and reworked, preparing the soil for planting. Although still reasonably broke, residents could sense that the worst was behind them, because they were slowly being called back to their jobs, and actually earning money again. However, it would take some time before their lives were back to normal,…but men were working again, crops were in the fields, and the large square would soon be crowded with produce venders in the coming fall,…something not seen in a while! Paris, Texas had survived the worst economic National disaster since the war between the states, and it's residents were so relieved and elated, that they were not prepared at all for the very worst.

*   *   *

The country's financial panic had yet to be felt in the Choctaw Nation, as life there continued at it's everyday usual pace. The Choctaw had no way of knowing what went on in the white man's world,…and most cared even less. They had always been self-dependent, and continued to be, raising their own beef, planting their own crops and gardens. There was no money to be had, but needed none, although it did make meager living much easier when they had a few dollars to spend. But when all was said and done, the Choctaw had no idea that a National Financial

Depression had devastated the Nation and if they had, would not have had a clue as to what it was all about.

Those families who were industrious enough did make an extra dollar by selling produce, hides, honey and sometimes beef and cured pork to the Trading Post at Upshur's Mountain,…but most times, would end up trading the items out for needed supplies like sugar, salt, baking powder, etc., items not readily available elsewhere,…not without money to spend. The Trading Post had also employed a couple of Choctaw women to work in the store. Business, though slow at times, was thriving,…and was the only place in many miles to give the Indian a fair shake when it came to spending the few accumulated dollars.

Wandering families could purchase fresh supplies at very reasonable prices, what little they could afford to buy, and those with no money at all could still get a meager grubstake. Families from farms, and even remote ranches in Arkansas made the trip to restock supplies at Taylor's Trading Post, drifting cowboys as well. Oh, they still had run-ins with men outside the law, men on the run, bands of men,…even a gunfighter now and then. But the visibility of heavily armed Choctaw Police, and the prominence of a Federal United States Marshal's office, deterred any thoughts these men might have of any wrong doing. Taylor's Trading Post had become quite renown in it's short existence.

Devil Mountain, a name still feared by the Choctaw because of it's association with the mysterious Ancient Ones, was now known as Upshur's Mountain,…and that alone, coupled with the knowledge that Man-with-glass-eyes kept the mountain's evil spirits at bay, served to ease some of that fear and would most surely become a thing forgotten in years to come. But not so with Man-with-glass-eyes, Billy Upshur would forever be revered by the Choctaw, as the only man who could do battle with spirits, and conquer the evil in the mountain,…this alone made them unafraid to do business at the store.

Peter Birdsong's Light-horsemen had now made such a difference in the Wilderness, that most policemen only rode routine patrols in the mountains anymore. However, there were still occasional acts of drunken killings, or rustled cattle, but these were usually recovered before they could be driven out of the Nations and the guilty arrested, or killed when they fought back. Not even the notorious Thomas Starr saw fit to venture into Choctaw land.

Rodney Taylor was content to leave Peter in charge of keeping peace in the wilderness, while he expanded his patrols to include the Cherokee, Chickasaw and Creek Nations,…sometimes working with Bass Reeves to bring in, and transport wanted criminals to Fort Smith, Arkansas. However, they were still barred from venturing into Thomas Starr's country,…the reasons for it still unclear in both their minds.

Bass Reeves had regained the use of his left arm, but it would never have more than half of it's previous strength, and it did pain him quite often, especially in cold weather,…and each time it did, he would curse Maxwell Loughmiller all over again. The deranged killer would forever rest heavy on his mind, as the only man he never brought to justice. Never the less, Bass Reeves was still considered the best U.S. Marshal ever to work the Territories, credited with more arrests than any other lawman there.

Rodney Taylor had become quite adept at using his sidearm now. He was much faster on the draw, and quite good at throwing a hunting knife, thanks to both, Billy, and Peter, all having spent countless hours with him on the practice field. He had more confidence than ever before, and had developed a little of Billy's sixth sense when it came to gun fighting. But the one thing he could not do, was outdraw Billy Upshur,…and as hard as he tried, he could never quite clear his holster before looking down the muzzle of Billy's drawn pistol. He never considered that he would ever be able to actually out draw his best friend, because in his mind, no man could do that!…He only wanted to be his equal, and he knew that he could not! However, he was still confident that he could now hold his own with any other gunman.

Life at the mountain had become almost routine as well, and was sometimes quite boring to Billy Upshur, who spent his time around the trading post, or riding in the mountains with Willy, and sometimes with his whole family, but that was when he was not busy baling the tall, luscious prairie grass and storing it in the barn and of course, Willy would help him do that, providing he was not busy with his schooling. Billy was still having thoughts of farming the area of the old battlefield, but somehow, the thought of disturbing the treasure hunter's graves disturbed him,…and he did not know exactly where the army had buried them.

Him and Connie had made only one other trip to Denver since her ordeal with the Mason Flood gang, and this one had gone unmolested, as they delivered three hundred more pounds of the extraordinarily pure gold to the Mint there. But because of the shortage of Government money, they were forced to stay another three weeks in the mile-high city before returning home, this trip taking them almost four months in the lumbering freight wagon. They were informed while there, not to bring any more for at least another year, as the bank would not be able to purchase it. Mister Greene, however, did say that once the economy became stable again, he would happily accommodate the shipments.

CHAPTER THREE

August 2, 1877...'Looks like rain' thought Billy Upshur as he pulled the heavy door shut behind him and thumped the spent Durham into the yard. Breathing deeply of the fresh morning air, he walked the length of the long porch to stare up through the trees at the tall, man-made fence hiding the entrance to the hidden valley,...this was an every morning ritual before going down the steps and on to the corral to check the horses. He scanned the towering fence as he stopped at the edge of the porch, noticing again that the giant Firs, the Choctaw had planted in front of the structure, were beginning to grow ever taller and full-bodied,...and each day he would think that it wouldn't be long before the fence would all but be hidden from view.

Sighing, he turned and walked back across the porch and down the steps, stopping just long enough to tie the holstered pistol to his leg before continuing up the grade to the corral,...and hearing the Roan's greeting as he walked up, reached a hand between the rails to pat her on the neck then seeing they had plenty of hay, turned and walked down toward the trading post. He'd taken only a few steps when he saw the large footprints, and grinned as he stared down at them. Their elusive friend was still hanging around!

Looking up, he scanned the rear of the store-room which, on Connie's suggestion, they had converted half of it into a kitchen and lunchroom. He knew that her and Lisa were preparing food for the day and hurried on down the rock-strewn slant and around the front side of the building, only to stop when he saw the two tethered horses at the hitch-rail,...and that's when he felt the tell-tale tingle on the back of his neck and was instantly suspicious. Cautious now, he jumped up just high enough to sit on the end of the porch, brought his legs up then got to his feet,…and slowly walking the length of the porch, he could see that the large front door was open and once there, stopped and leaned forward enough to peer into the store.

He could see into the Marshal's office from there as well, but saw no one at either one of the desks, but at that moment, he heard a man's angry voice and leaned out until he was able to see farther into the store. One lone gunman was holding a pistol on the two Choctaw Policemen, while another was holding a large potato sack open with one hand and with the other, holding a gun on Connie and Melissa while forcing the Choctaw woman to fill the bag with supplies.

Both men had their backs to the door, so he took a deep breath and moved inside to slowly walk up behind the man watching the guards. He pulled the pistol and quickly laid the cold barrel against the man's right cheek, bringing a startled gasp of surprise from him as he cut his eyes around,…and when the man opened his mouth to speak, Billy put his forefinger to his lips and cocked the gun.

One of the Choctaw quickly reached and took the man's gun from his hand, taking him into custody as Billy moved away toward the other one.

"Get a fuckin' move on, you cow!" Spat the man when the woman dropped a can on the floor. "You can move your fat ass faster'n that,… fill th' God damn bag!"

Billy took that moment to crack the gun's barrel on the side of the man's head, felling him with a gushing grunt from surprised lungs.

Billy grinned at the woman's expressionless face then and shrugged. "You can restock that stuff now, Mildred."

"Thank God, you're here, honey!" Breathed Connie as she and Lisa rushed around the end of the counter to help Mildred.

"It was my pleasure, Ma'am!" He grinned then stepped aside to holster the gun while the Policeman hoisted the would-be thief to his feet and picked up the fallen weapon. The Choctaw nodded at Billy then ushered the man toward the large opening, and down into the Marshal's office.

"We were worried one of the children would come in," Said Connie somewhat breathlessly as she placed canned goods on the shelf. "No telling what might have happened!"

"Well, it's okay now!" He nodded. "They take any money?"

"All we had in the till." Nodded Melissa shakily.

"I'll get it." He nodded. "Don't guess breakfast is ready yet?"

"Billy!" Gasped Connie. "We were just a little busy here!" She stared angrily at him for a second then shook her head when she saw him smile. "Trouble comes in small packages, Mister, so be careful!...And yes, breakfast is ready, if the potatoes aren't burnt."

"Good,...then I'll be right back."

"The children up yet?"

"Still in bed." He shrugged again, and went on toward the jail area.

"Come on, Lisa," She sighed, getting to her feet. "Just another day at the mine for him!"

"Well, I'll be shaking for the rest of the day." She shuddered, and followed Connie back around and into the kitchen.

Billy looked back as he stepped down, and still grinning, he saw the downcast expressions of the light-horsemen and became serious. He knew that both were ashamed at having been caught with their pants down, so to speak, and so walked on to stop in front of them. "How'd this happen, Jonas?" He asked as he stopped and watched the other guard lock the cell door.

"I am sorry, Mister Upshur," Returned Jonas, his eyes still on the floor. "We did not expect trouble from these white men."

"They asked for Marshal Taylor," Said the second guard, as he also stared at the floor. "But, when they came inside, one man was hidden behind the first with a gun in his hand....We were not prepared, Mister Upshur!"

"It could a happened to anybody, even me, so don't worry about it, it turned out okay!...A man learns from his mistakes, remember that." He gestured his head at the cell door then. "They took money from th' till out there, Henry, will you bring 'em out here, please?"

Nodding, Henry turned back and opened the door again before stepping aside.

"You two men get on out here!" Said Billy sternly, and when they were standing before him. "You took some money from th' till in there, hand it over!"

Both men glared hatefully at him for a second but then, still holding his aching head, that man pulled currency and coins from his pocket and gave it to him.

"While you're at it," He nodded. "Both of you empty your pockets on th' desk there, gun-belts, too!" He waited while, grumbling, the two would be hold-up men complied,…and when they were done, he stepped up and went through the items, pushing pocket knives and well-worn watches toward one of the policemen, who placed them in a desk drawer then picked up the ragged wallets, finding nothing with their names on it.

"What's your name?" He asked of the man he had clubbed.

"None a your fuckin' business!" He growled, still holding a hand against his head. "We ain't got a tell you nothin'!"

"You're right, you don't!" Sighed Billy. "But when th' Marshal gets back, I'd advise you to level with 'im,…might go easier on ya, if you ain't wanted anywhere….Besides, this is his store!"

"His name's Buster Cates." Confessed the second man suddenly. "I'm Norvell Smallwood. We're just broke and out a luck, Mister,… and in jail, now!"

Nodding, Billy turned to Jonas, who had already taken wanted posters from the desk and satisfied, nodded again at Henry. "Lock 'em up!" And while that was being done, he went back and stepped up into the store again, leaving the policemen to their jobs.

*   *   *

The rain started right after the noon meal, and Billy, the women, children, and the Choctaw Police were gathered on the long porch of the trading post and watching the downpour in silence, when one of the Choctaw brought their attention to the vague shapes of approaching riders, almost indistinguishable in the rain.

Billy thumped his spent smoke into the mud, and was standing by the post when he recognized the black horse and it's rider. Peter Birdsong waved in passing and continued on to the hitch-rail in front of the office as Jonas and Henry hurriedly met him there. He dismounted and gave the reins to Jonas, and while the policemen took charge of the prisoners, he came on up to the porch and shook Billy's hand.

"Had a little luck, I see!...Where'd you find them two?"

"I find them stealing cows near Pine Mountain," He shrugged. "They did not fight."

"Hi, Uncle Peter?" Said Willy as he came to join them. The joyous greeting was echoed unanimously, as Christopher and Angela also came to grab his arms.

"Do not get so close, little ones," He laughed. "I am very wet!" He reached to touch all three of them, and was grinning widely as they went back to join the women.

"The children make me feel happy." He said, looking up at Billy. "It is good to be an Uncle, I think!"

"Yes, Sir, it is," Grinned Billy. "Be even better when you're a father."

"Yes, my friend, maybe,...I am thinking on this as well!"

"Anybody in mind?"

"Yes, maybe." He smiled and stared out through the rain, not wanting to discuss the subject any further.

Getting the message, Billy grinned. "When you gonna start your house, Peter?"

"Soon," He shrugged. "But now, my friend, what has happened here, while I was gone?"

Billy told him of the robbery attempt that morning, and of how the guards had been caught off guard by the gunmen, and he could tell the tracker was upset by it when he finished,...and while Peter mulled it over, he rolled and lit another Durham.

"I will talk with them," He sighed. "This should not have happened, and will not happen again!"

"Don't be too hard on 'em, my friend, they were tricked,...besides, it could a been a lot worse!...It ain't hard to get too relaxed when nothin's goin' on, we ain't had a customer all week,"

"Yes," Nodded Peter. "But they must not relax, never,...they are Light-horsemen!" He turned and looked back at the drooping animals. "I must tend to the horses, my friend."

"See you at my house later, for supper?"

"Yes,...I will be there!"

"What about th' other patrols, they comin' in?"

"No,…I think, maybe they will be at their homes tonight."

"Then bring Henry and Jonas with you tonight."

"I think, maybe it is better I bring them food, they must keep watch!"

"You're th' boss,…see ya tonight." He watched him until he led the three horses around the building then went back to his chair and sat down again.

"Were those men prisoners, honey?" Queried Connie.

"Rustlers,…said he caught 'em at Pine Mountain."

"Sure is a lot of that going on." She sighed.

"Always has been, always will be," He replied. "Nature of man, I reckon."

"Well, I wish Rodney was home!" Sighed Melissa as she hugged Cindy against her. "He's been gone a week already. He could catch his death of cold in all this!"

"Now, now,…Rod's got savvy enough to get out a th' weather, Lisa. He's learned a hell of a lot these past few years, got scars to prove it!"

"I know, Billy," She sighed. "He's wonderful, but he's not bulletproof,…and I worry about him!"

"I know you do, sweetie,…I do, too!" He had thumped the butt into the rain as he spoke. "I look for 'im home today, though."

"God, I hope so!"

"Well, I'm all for locking these doors and going home!" Sighed Connie.

"Not in this!" Returned Billy. "We'd never climb that grade,… maybe I'll build a fire in th' fireplace here, you gals can fix supper here tonight, how's that?"

"Then would you do it now,…I'm getting chilled out here?"

"You bet'cha!…Son, watch for Peter to come back, tell 'im th' change of plans for supper."

"Yes, sir."

*   *   *

They were sitting down to dinner when Rodney arrived, having first deposited a prisoner of his own in the cell before coming through the store to the dining room, and as he stopped in the wide doorway, Cindy

14

yelped and cried, "Daddy", causing everyone to look up as he entered, then came on to lift her in his arms.

"God, I'm glad you're home!" Exclaimed Melissa as she got up to hug him.

"No, no," He laughed, putting Cindy down. "Let me get out a this wet slicker first!" He shucked the rain gear and went back to hang it on a peg, then came back to hug and kiss her. "I'm glad to be home, too, baby!...Just in time for vittles, too!" He nodded, turning to smile at everyone,

"Hey, Billy, Connie, you, too Peter, how are ya?"

They all exchanged greetings then Connie set his plate at the table as he sat down. "Miserable weather, ain't it?"

"That's a tolerable word for it," Grinned Billy. "That beard does you justice, by th' way!"

"Don't feel like justice to me,...more like punishment!"

"Why didn't you shave then?" Fussed Melissa. "You had a razor."

"No time, darlin',...chased a bank robber down! Took me two days to catch 'im, and another to return 'im to McAllester." He sighed then as he filled his plate. "Been in rain all day, today, bringing him in."

"Anybody we know?" Queried Billy.

"Walter Evans." Said Rodney as he chewed. "Says he's from Kansas."

"Any trouble?"

"Had to wing 'im,...got 'im doctored up in McAllester before comin' home." He looked at Peter then. "I see you've been busy, too."

"A little, my friend, but Mister Upshur caught two of them."

"Oh, yeah,...how'd that happen, Billy?"

"They tried to rob us!" Said Melissa. "Almost did, too!"

"Billy got here in time, though." Smiled Connie.

"Nobody hurt?"

"They were just scared," Returned Billy. "Couple a drifters, down on their luck. First timers, I think,...dumb as hell!"

"I'll say," Laughed Melissa. "They let Billy sneak right up behind them!...Sure scared us, though."

"I'm glad you was here, man,...where was the Police?"

"My Light-horsemen allowed these men to take their weapons." Said Peter sadly. "I must teach them some more."

"Well, it turned out okay," He said, filling his mouth again. "That's th' main thing. I wouldn't be too hard on 'em, Peter, everybody gets suckered now and then." He grinned at Billy then as he reached for more potatoes. "I'm a professional on that!...You tell Peter what we talked about yet?"

Billy shook his head. "We'll do it after supper, if you're up to it?"

Rodney nodded, and they all kept up the small-talk until the meal was over, and then Peter and Willy took plates of food to the jail for the policemen, and the prisoners....When they came back, while Willy carried cups and the pot of coffee back to the jail, the women began clearing the table as the men and children retired to chairs set up in front of the large fireplace in the store.,...and once they were seated.

"Peter," Began Billy, as he rolled and lit his Durham smoke "As you know,...me and Rod bought this mountain because of the evil, White Buffalo told us about,...and because we didn't want anybody to find it and set it free,...and with White Buffalo gone, they would have, too!... Anyway, we had no choice, but to buy it and live here!...You know all this, right?"

"Yes, my friend,...you have told me this!"

"Well, there's somethin' we didn't tell you, my friend, and I sure hope you won't be upset when we do."

"Yeah," Broke in Rodney. "Remember when you asked me why Billy went to Denver?"

"Yes, you said to sell the gold you had left,...I remember."

"Well, I lied to you, Peter, and I hated doin' it!...Truth is, White Buffalo gave us the gold for helping fight those treasure hunters."

"There's a gold mine in there, Peter." Said Billy. "Half a that whole inside wall in there is pure gold. That's why me and Connie went to Denver this last time, too, to sell more of it."

"Yes, my friend." Nodded the tracker. "My Light-horsemen have seen you bring pack mules from there."

"Are you saying, you already knew about the mine?" Blurted Rodney.

"No,...but I think, maybe it is gold."

"Why didn't you say something?" Queried Billy.

"The mountain belongs to you, my friend, not to me, not to the Choctaw. The gold belongs to you, also."

Billy and Rodney looked at each other in disbelief, each shaking their head in astonishment.

"And that don't upset you?" Asked Rodney.

"No, my friends. You have been good to the Choctaw, to me also. You show us respect." He shrugged then. "If you did not buy this place, the gold would be there forever, because no Choctaw will go there,...and if you do not own the mountain, one day more white men will come, and they will find it. I think, it is much better that you have it."

"Peter," Laughed Rodney. "I don't think I have ever met a man with more savvy than you. How did you figure all this out?"

Peter shrugged. "If other white men find this place, the white man's Government will take our land again, and we will have to move again. I do not want this, it is Choctaw land!"

"You humble us, my friend, thank you....And now that we've eaten Crow," He immediately saw the expression on the tracker's face when he said that, and cleared his throat. "Uh,...Peter, that just means we embarrassed ourselves." He explained.

"Yeah," Breathed Billy. "What we're wantin' to say here is that, starting now, tonight,...when we sell gold from this mountain, part of it will belong to you, and the Choctaw."

Peter peered narrowly at him. "Why do you do this?"

"It was yours to start with." Said Rodney. "Besides,...it's the way we want it!"

"When we sell more of the gold, you'll get ten percent of the money it brings." Informed Billy. "You can distribute it out anyway you like!... The only thing that worries us, is what Chief Bryant will say, or do if he finds out about it. After all, it was him that sold it to us."

"Chief Bryant is no longer Chief of the choctaw, my friend." Grinned Peter. "Coleman Cole is now Chief,...and he will not know, because my people will not know! Only myself, and Joseph,...he will distribute the wealth....Besides,...all Choctaw knows that Chief Bryant has kept much of your gold for himself,...because their lives were not bettered."

"Coleman Cole is Chief?" Queried Rodney. "When did all of this happen?"

"Most of three years ago, now."

"Man alive,…news sure travels slow up here!…Nobody said anything to us."

"It was not so important, I think," Shrugged Peter. "He is much the same as Chief Bryant,…there is no difference."

"Then it's settled!" Sighed Rodney. "And I got a tell ya, I feel better about it now.…I don't like lying to a friend!"

"Myself also, my friends, thank you."

CHAPTER FOUR

It was raining hard by the time the group of riders stopped in the trees, and they were only visible because they all were wearing long, gray rain-gear, their soggy hats hanging loosely over their faces. All but two of them were grouped silently behind the three men in front as they stared down through the trees at the fast-moving Red River, and the seemingly deserted river-front, shipping port on it's shore.

The man on the center horse was slouched slightly in his saddle, visibly disgusted with the weather, and the discomfort it was causing him. "Okay, Mitch," He growled, turning to look at the man on his right. "You know this country, what's that place down there?"

"That, Jarvis, is what used to be Jonesboro, Texas!"

"Used to be?"

"Yeah, look at it!...Damn place looks deserted. Last I was here, it was a wide-open shippin' port,...hell, there was steam ships in th' river!"

"Well, it's a fuckin' ghost town now!" Commented the man on the left.

Jarvis Cantrell was not a tall man, nor was he short, that was left to his sometimes, short disposition. He was a man with a short fuse for a temper, and could explode at the slightest provocation,...and kill even quicker. He was a man of the cloth, turned killer, a gunman who could draw and fire a pistol in a whisper. He had been a Minister his whole life before, and during the Great War, a Mormon man of God who had four beautiful, young wives, and seven children, a man of power in the Mormon community. He was a Holy man whose words carried much weight with the Elders in the Mormon Church,…a man whose words could sway votes and sentiment.

But this was all before someone in the Society, one of the Elders, sent an Assassin to murder his family, meant as a warning and at first, he believed that it had been Brigham Young himself who gave the order, but Brigham Young had multiple wives, and children, so he had been sure it wasn't him. That left only one possible answer, the ones responsible were surely those behind the movement to abolish Polygamy in the Society,…a secretive movement, that when it came to his attention, he had spoken out against on occasion, and because he did speak out, the movement was in danger of failure before it could gain it's desired momentum.

Regardless of who was responsible, his family was dead, and he had grieved long and hard before finally relenting to the hatred. From that day forward, Jarvis Cantrell rejected his religious beliefs and began a murderous quest to find the man, or men responsible,…a career that would in time, surpass those deeds performed by the Society's Assassins,…and because of his efforts to find these men, had become a marked man himself! No one seemed to know who had given the order, nor who was leading the secret movement to abolish Polygamy, that, or they were all lying. Either way, not telling him what he wanted to know earned them the death sentence as well.

He was a man possessed by now, but he had known from the onset that he might never know who had killed his family,…and eventually realized that he would have to gain an audience with Brigham Young himself to get his answers. But before he could get to Young, Union Soldiers had arrested the top man, and were then in pursuit of him,… as were the Mormon Assassins, fatefully leaving him with only one alternative. So, taking his hatred with him, he reluctantly left his beloved Utah, and as the war raged continued his own war, eventually recruiting a small army of his own. Thus began Jarvis Cantrell's reign of terror as he raided and killed from Utah to Missouri, and from Tennessee to Arkansas. So fierce were his raids, that many times his misdeeds led authorities to believe it was actually Quantrill they were after.

Now, thirteen years after the war, and Quantrill's demise, the Jarvis Cantrell Gang of Renegades were being hunted relentlessly, and to the point that a safe haven became something to be wished for. They had run out of a place to hide, no place was safe from the Government forces, or law enforcement,…and both were tireless in their efforts and now, in his feverish mind, his only sanctuary was in Mexico. He was tired and out of options, and still a long way from the Mexican border,…and it was raining!

He looked at Gator Malloy with distaste for a second before nodding. "That was very observant of you, Mister Malloy,…and a ghost town is exactly what we need right now,…I'm tired!"

"Yeah, well th' Army ain't that far behind us, Boss, you forget about that?"

"I do not forget anything, Mister Malloy, nor do I forget that you are becoming a pain in my ass!…If your desire is to keep running, then by all means do so,…and take your vulgarity with you!"

"Awww, Boss, that ain't what I meant, you know that!"

"Then stay in your place, Sir,…let me do the thinking!" He looked back through the downpour at the gray waterfront buildings below them, and suddenly felt sorry that he had unloaded on the man,…and wondered why?…Then sighing heavily, looked back at him.

"Mister Malloy,…you must forgive me, I'm feeling very old today. I have bunions that hurt like hell when it rains. I have a rheumatic back, and aching joints. I have a short temper, and I hate the use of vulgarity,…so please refrain from using it in my presence?"

"Yes, Sir, sorry, Sir!"

"Well,…that being said,…yes, I know the Army is not that far behind us, but they also can not track us in this storm. We lost them two days ago when we turned north in that swamp!" He sighed again then. "They might cut our trail again, in maybe a week,…but they'll lose it again, too.….There are times when rain becomes your only ally,… remember that!"

"A few days rest wouldn't hurt me none, Jarvis." Added Mitch Kelley. "What do you think, Sir,…if it's deserted, that would be a good place for it?"

"I believe you're right, son. Let's go." He spurred his mount out of the trees and down through the drenched maze of a forest, and was closely followed by nineteen men as they rode toward the once notorious outlaw haven, and shipping port of Jonesboro.

*   *   *

It is a believable truth, that without people, or some form of human activity, man-made structures will age multiple times faster than otherwise. Such was the case with Jonesboro, a very old river town,… and though its buildings and thick plank boardwalks were old, they had been well used for decades and had seemed to withstand the constant bombardment of man and the elements,…until now.

Buildings along the riverfront were nothing but warehouses where, in it's day were always filled with bales of cotton, feed, and other items for shipments East, and North, and constantly being loaded onto barges and Steamers,…while at the same time other items were unloaded and warehoused to be picked up by freight wagons for shipment overland. The almost three quarters of a mile-long boardwalk stretched it's width all the way from the warehouses across to the shipping docks and ramps, almost fifty yards of heavy, wide planking held in place by eight by eight timbers that crisscrossed beneath the planks. The walkway was a sturdy structure held off the ground by a hundred or more upright support posts.

But now, after only three years without man, this wide expanse of platform was already a creaking, rotting mass of treacherous footing, and the warehouses,…a leaking, dark mass of damp emptiness that reeked of rotting timbers and animal excretions. The two saloons were the last to finally close their doors to business, those, and the rickety old ferry at river's edge,…a ferry that now lay half submerged in the muddy waters of Red River. All of the shops and eating dives that once lined the street along the Texas Road were long-closed and boarded up, and most had already collapsed, or were in the throes of collapse.

However, life along the mighty Red had not completely gone away, there were occupied shanties built on stilt-like log poles out over the water, weathered structures with fishing nets draping down from the shack into the murky water beneath it. There were shacks along the opposite shore as well, and were occupied by poor whites and several Choctaw families who also depended on the river for their primary food supply, that along with few vegetable gardens that stretched in rows behind the huts.

The bulky paddle-wheelers had all but stopped using the river to freight goods anymore, and the few that did venture in now docked at Fort Towson, some few miles west of there in Indian Territory.

Jonesboro had indeed become a ghost town in only three short years, it's buildings now occasionally used by outlaws, and men on the run as a place to hide for a time, and rest. There was a marker on the Texas side at river's edge, and close to where the old barge rested. It was a painted sign, placed there by the Army Corp of Engineers, stating that a bridge would be built there in the near future, to join Texas with the Choctaw Nation.

Cantrell raised his hand in the rain to stop the riders coming up behind him then cautiously urged his horse up onto the platform before dismounting to inspect the old planking,...and he was peering through the downpour at the dark buildings still farther along the way when Mitch led his horse in beside him.

"This whole platform was loaded with hundreds of bales of cotton when I was here, Jarvis,...a hundred men working, too!"

"When was that?" Queried Cantrell loudly, to be heard over the drone of water against the old boards.

"I don't know, ten, twelve years, I guess,...I was barely out a my teens!"

"You joined up with me ten years ago!"

"Eleven or twelve then,...I don't know exactly!"

"A running horse would fall through this thing easy, I think." Nodded Cantrell. "Might anyway!...Where's the best place to hold up?"

"Saloon, I guess,...got a fireplace in it, if it's usable. We can keep th' horses in there, too!"

"Let's go then,...and we'd better walk, I don't trust this thing,... tell the men, son!" He led his horse across the partially loose, and water-logged platform toward the warehouses while Mitch gave the orders to lead their mounts, and twenty minutes later were leading them through the wide doors of the one-time, Murphy's Saloon and Gambling Hall.

Cantrell gave his horse to one of the men and watched them lead the animals to a rear room and through the door then sighing, he stretched his aching muscles and surveyed the debris. The long bar was still intact, but fairly scarred and mildewed from years of humid weather. Broken tables and chair parts still littered the floor, along with animal dung, rotting paper and broken glass. The walls were warped in places, as well as was the ceiling, but the floor was dry, and it surprised him that the roof was not leaking,…but that suited him just fine, he was already sick of the rain!

Mitch brought his bedding and rifle to him, placing them atop the bar then leaned his back against it and also scanned the room's wreckage. "At least it's dry, Jarvis." He said, taking off the dripping slicker and draping it across the bar. "We ought a be okay here for a while."

Cantrell slipped out of his rain gear and placed it atop the bar as well. "Mitch," He sighed. "I am quite tired of this,…all of it! The killing, robbing, all the rest….It don't make sense like it used to!…I have not had a night's sleep in years."

"You're right, Sir,…time does seem to be runnin' out for us.…We can always quit, Jarvis,…do somethin' else,…hell, I wouldn't mind it!"

"Too late for that, son,…I've had the Devil on my shoulders for too long!…This whole God-forsaken country knows who I am now,…and what I look like."

"You're right about that!…Think Mexico's gonna be any better?"

"No,…I don't. Not with an army of men around us,…we'll draw too much attention." He looked at Mitch then. "With all these men around us, I have my doubts we'll ever reach Mexico, son." He sighed heavily then. "That's why I'm thinking of disbanding, sending them all packing.…You and I might get there on our own, Mitch."

"Jarvis, you're th' fastest man with a gun, I ever saw,…I can't see you bein' able to quit, there'll always be somebody forcin' a fight,…and you won't back down!"

"I know, boy," He sighed. "But I'm of a mind to try."

"You was a preacher once, weren't you?"

Cantrell nodded. "Once,…yes, I was once a devout man of the cloth, son,…a man of God. But that was before I found out he didn't exist!…I'm reduced to this now,…I have become the Devil's Deciple!"

"I don't know about that, Jarvis,…but whatever you decide you want a do, I'm with you." He pushed away from the bar then. "But right now, I'm gonna check out that fireplace, get a fire goin',…I'm hungry." He grinned at the older man and walked off toward the opposite wall as the men filed back into the room with their saddles and gear.

Cantrell motioned Gator over, and when the Cajun Killer stopped in front of him, nodded at the room. "See if you and the boys can clear this place out a little, Mister Malloy,...break up the wood for the fire and bring in what supplies we got left."

"You got it, Boss!" He nodded and went to talk with the other men.

*   *   *

The rain had stopped during the night and they were all having their morning meal in the trading Post dining area again, and when he was done, Billy leaned back to roll and light his morning smoke while the rest finished eating.

"When you leavin' out again, Rod?"

"Not for a while, I'm gonna take some time off, I think!" He sighed, reaching a cigar from his shirt and lighting it. "Lisa wants to go see her folks. What about you all, want a go?"

"Matter of fact," Grinned Billy. "I was about to ask you that!...I need to check on Doc and Mama,...Ross, too, see if they need anything."

"That'll work!" Nodded Rodney. "When do we go?"

"After it dries up some, maybe in a week?"

"Week, ten days, whatever. Sounds good to me." He nodded. "What about you gals, that all right?"

"Of course!" Smiled Connie, then laughed because her and Melissa had said the exact same thing, at the exact same time,...and it had also been rivaled by a chorus of "Yeas" from the children.

"How about it, Peter?" Queried Rodney. "You up to takin' over for a while?"

"Yes," He nodded. "I will place extra police to keep watch."

"Thank's man, that's great!"

"Say, Peter," Said Billy in a serious tone. "Think you can bring in a couple a carpenters again,...I damn near busted my butt on that slick-ass clay hill this mornin'. That stuffs dangerous when it rains?"

"Of course, my friend, what would you like?"

"I'd like a walkway from th' cabins down to th' store here, maybe some steps, or somethin', I don't know....But I'd like 'em to look good, like they belong there,...somebody's gonna get hurt like it is."

"It will be done." Nodded the tracker.

"You're gonna need a cook while we're gone, too, th' police have to eat, prisoners, too….You think Mildred can do all that and run th' store?"

"I do not believe so, my friend. I will ask the carpenter to bring his wife, she is a very good cook, and she will help Mildred with the store as well."

"Speaking of Mildred," Said Connie. "She should be getting here, I'd better open the store."

"If she's not too rattled from yesterday?" Sighed Melissa, also getting up.

"I hope not," Came Connie, and hurried out through the store.

"I'd better go help with the shutters." Sighed Melissa, pushing her chair in. "It's still plenty dark in there." And she hurried off in pursuit.

"Can we go play, daddy?" Asked Willy as all four of them got out of their chairs.

"It's too dark out to play, you can't see anything, and you know what'll happen if you get muddy….You best stay inside to play, or on th' porch, okay?"

"Okay, come on, you guys, let's go on the porch."

Grinning, Rodney watched as Cindy ran after the older children then turned back to look at Peter. "Did you get all the information we need on th' men you brought in?"

"Yes, I am ready when you are."

"We'll fill out the reports this afternoon,…and maybe take the prisoners to Fort Smith when I get back, that sound okay?"

"That will be good, yes."

"When you going out again, Peter?" Queried Billy.

"Maybe tomorrow, I think,…I will go for the carpenter….I will have him here in one week's time, his wife as well. And I will also go to the Fort."

"What are they now, Peter,…six months behind on our pay?"

"I think, maybe six months."

"We should get it pretty quick now, the McAllester paper said that paper money was good again, and that was a quote straight from the mouth of our brand new President!…It also said this damn recession was about over, if you can believe that?"

26

"Could be," Nodded Billy. "That wire from Ross last month said he finally sold th' cotton. Said he'd be pickin' again this fall, too! That means he's already planted th' crops, or about to."

"Sounds like it," Agreed Rodney. "About time, too!...All right, tell me this, now,...you ever heard of a telephone?"

"Nope, what is it?"

"According to the McAllester paper, it's a new version of the Telegraph, except,...instead of dots and dashes, people can talk to each other with it, over long distances, too."

"You believe it?"

"Ain't seen one yet, don't know, but Alexander Bell invented it, even got a patent on it....I'll say one thing,...if it is true, we could sure use one!"

"Whatever happened to your plans for a Telegraph?"

"The way it looks, the Telegraph could be obsolete by the time I get the okay for it!...Course, it said the Telephone would be using the same wires as the Telegraph, except that it would take electric current to transfer someone's voice from one destination to another,...and it won't take as much electricity as they first thought. In fact, Mister Bell used iron and magnets to make the electric current he needed."

"That don't make sense, neither!"

"No, it don't,...but the Telegraph didn't either at first. He invented that, too."

"You know for a fact, he did?"

"Nope, but he invented this one, and all he was trying to do was improve on the Telegraph. The Telephone was an accident!"

"Billy shook his head and grinned. "If there's one thing I've learned these last few years, it's not to question things I don't know about!"

"Amen to that!" Grinned Rodney. "How about that, Peter?...One day you might be in Fort Towson and need to tell me something,...and all you'll have to do is use the Telephone and talk to me right here."

"I think, maybe, I will wait to see if this is true!"

"That makes three of us!" Laughed Rodney. "But that's not all I read about!...It seems that the words "Open Range" no longer means what it used to,...because there won't be any! Ranchers in Montana and Wyoming are fencing off some of their grazing lands with something called "Barbed Wire"!...Can you imagine not being able to ride somewhere because there's a fence in your way?"

"What is this, "barbed Wire?" Queried Peter.

"There was a drawing of it in the paper. It's a thick, double wire with sharp barbs twisted into it about six, or eight inches apart. Something like that could cut a horse up real bad, a cow, too!"

"A man, too, he gets tangled in it!" Nodded Billy, and grimaced at the thought. "I can see where somethin' like that would lead to war, too!...Gonna be a lot a fence cutting goin' on."

"Not counting the senseless killing!" Added Rodney.

"Okay!" Smiled Connie as she and Lisa returned. "Clear out of here, we have to clean up and start lunch."

*   *   *

"Okay, Rod," Sighed Billy, leaning to lift the wagon's wheel upright. "Hoist it up!" Once the wagon was high enough, he worked the wheel forward enough to slide it onto the greasy axle and replace washer and nut. "That'll do it!"

Rodney let the wagon down, removed the pry-pole and returned it to the barn before coming to take the stump away. Billy had tightened the nut down and keyed by then, and was wiping the grease from his hands.

"I guess we're ready." Commented the lawman as he leaned against the end-gate. "What say, we put th' gals a rocking chair in there this trip, they both complained last trip with their legs hurting?"

"I guess so," He grinned. "They ought a have a slidin' good time in 'em."

"They might at that, guess we better ask 'em first."

"That would be th' best….Your in-laws on your place yet?"

"Oh, yeah, last October,…had to close up, so they went ahead and moved in."

"What about th' deal to sell it?"

"Had to take less than what they wanted, but yeah,…it belongs to Mister Kress now, whoever he is?...Why,…you thinking about th' gold?"

"We need to do somethin' with it, Rod." He said as he leaned against the wagon beside him. "I was thinkin' we could maybe crush it up and divide it between Lisa's folks, and mine….They could sell it off a little at a time as they need to!...At any rate, it ain't doin' anybody any good where it is, and we don't need it."

"I agree,…but I think we should confide in Mister Bratcher, sort a prepare 'im for it,…maybe he wouldn't ask too many questions that way….Hopefully, he wouldn't!"

"And tell 'im what?"

"I don't know, tell 'im we're doing a lot of prospecting on our land!...The folks won't have to sell that much at one time, maybe a few ounces a year. We tell Bratcher we're bringing what we find to them, to see them through the hard times!...I don't know, maybe a dozen ounces a year."

"We'll try it, then, can't hurt nothin'!...But we need to get it out a that barn." He heard Willy shout at them then and looked up to watch him slide to a stop beside them. "Whoa, son, what's all th' rush?"

"A man's comin' in, Daddy!" He panted. "Mama said hurry."

"Comin' in from where, son,…which direction?"

"Down th' valley,…from Arkansas!"

"Well, that can't be an easy chore!" Chuckled Rodney.

"Okay, son, thanks,…now go on back and keep th' kids inside, tell mama we're on our way."

"Okay, Daddy." He turned and ran back toward the trading post, purposely sliding his way on the spots of slick clay and mud, only to disappear around the corner.

"I used to could do that." Laughed Rodney. "Busted my ass a lot, but it was fun."

"Let's get washed up, Rod, could be a payin' customer."

"That wouldn't hurt nothing, been few and far between here lately!"

They washed their hands with soap and water from the pump behind the store, and were just rounding the end of the long porch when they saw the slow-moving rider and stopped to watch him.

"Don't sit the saddle like a cowboy, does he, Billy?"

"He ain't a cowboy, Rod,…too stiff in th' saddle,…you better go on down with th' guards." Rodney nodded and made his way to the steps, and once on the porch walked off the other end and into his office.

Billy stood and continued to watch the erect figure of the man, his body moving with the motions of the horse as the animal slowly worked its way toward the store in the almost knee-deep mud and water of the narrow valley,…and he could feel the tingling on the back of his neck, the longer he watched him.

He knew the man was watching him, too, because the challenge was unmistakable. He was a gunfighter, he was sure of that! He continued to watch the man's approach, his valiant horse having to forcefully lift each leg high before taking another sinking step in the mire. At that moment, movement in the store's open doorway caused him to look up and see Willy also watching the man. He walked on to the steps and up to the porch, causing Willy to retreat back inside when he saw him,… and grinning, turned back to watch as the rider urged the tired animal up onto more solid ground then reined it up, and onto level ground toward the hitch-rail in front of Rodney's office. As he stopped the horse, his cold eyes were still on Billy, and he sat the saddle for a long minute just watching him.

"Something I can do for you?" Queried Rodney loudly as he stepped out onto the boardwalk.

The gunman slowly brought his eyes around to look him over, and then the two armed Light-horsemen beside him. "Didn't expect to find any law out here." He responded in a low voice.

"I'm a U.S. Marshal for this area, Mister,…?" He left the question hanging.

"Storm," Said the man, flicking a quick glance back at Billy. "Morgan Storm." He turned to peer back at Rodney then. "And No, you don't know me, Marshal!"

"You're right, I don't!" Nodded Rodney. "If it's supplies you need, step on down, the store's open for business,…if not, tell me what you do need, and I'll try to help you?"

Storm seemed to relax a little then. "That's real neighborly, Marshal,…in fact, I am in need of a few things. But first,…who is the man on the porch there?"

Rodney looked toward Billy then, seeing him slowly walk along the porch toward them. "That's Billy Upshur, he owns the mountain there behind us, and we both own the Trading Post, including the swamp you just swam through!...Why do you ask, do you know 'im?"

"Uh-uh,…not who he is,…but I know what he is!"

Rodney grew a little tense, then, afraid that if he didn't do something to intervene, there could be trouble. "And do you find that threatening, Mister Storm?"

"No,...not at all, Marshal," He looked at Rodney and grinned as he said that, false, though it was. Because even Rodney could see that Storm's steel-gray eyes did not reflect the gesture. "I never feel threatened!" He suddenly lifted his left leg up and swung his foot over the horse's neck, and using his right leg, lowered himself to the ground, his eyes flicking back again to size Billy up as he stepped forward to loop the animal's reins over the top-rail.

Morgan Storm was about five feet, ten inches tall, but he was a slender man in his lightweight, black waist-jacket, and pale blue trousers. But what held a man's attention the most was the silver-plated, bone-handled Remington conversion pistol, and silver-studded black holster and belt around his slim hips. He wore black, almost knee-length boots over his pant-legs, and he smiled slightly at Billy before turning to Rodney.

"Don't guess you sell cigars, do you, Marshal?"

"Oh, yeah,...cigars, tobacco, and even a pipe, if that's your fancy?... But, there's something I have to tell you now, Mister Storm....If you're here to do business with that gun, I won't tolerate it!"

"Oh," Smiled Storm. "That is the farthest thing from my mind today, Marshal, I assure you!...But now, I have to tell you something.... If that was my intention, you couldn't stop me. You," He turned his eyes back on Billy then. "Or your Mister, Bill Upshur there!"

"But then, I'd have to tell you, you'd be wrong, sir!...Now,...if you want supplies, I'll be glad to assist you. Anything else on your mind will get you arrested! Is that clear, Mister Storm?"

"You think way too much of yourself, Marshal," He grinned. "Truth is, I'm used to going where I want, and leaving when I'm ready,...and that's what I intend to do here!" He saw Rodney flick his eyes toward the store's porch then, and quickly turned, his hand dangerously close to the Remington, and watched as Billy came down the steps to stop in front of them,...and then to shake his head at Rodney.

"Take it easy, Rod." He looked back at Storm then, and their eyes clashed again, each knowing what the other was, and each feeling the challenge between them,...but then, Billy grinned widely to break the tension.

"Do I know you, Sir?...Or better yet, do you know me?"

"No, to both questions." He stated, still looking Billy up and down. "You carry yourself like a gunfighter, Bill Upshur,...but on second glance,...you sure don't look like one!"

"That's because I'm not!...And I want to apologize for starin' at you th' way I did. I knew what you was by th' way you carried yourself, but what really threwed me, was th' way you dismounted just then,... why'd you do that?"

"I don't turn my back on anybody!" He replied, still curiously eying Billy up and down his slender frame, and then he suddenly shook his head.

"I'm not usually wrong about a man, Bill Upshur,...and you sure wear that pistol like a gunfighter would....So, if you ain't, you're either a good liar, or you are fooling me good and proper!"

"That was th' plan!" Shrugged Billy. "We get a lot a rough-lookin' characters out here, and well,...if I look like I can use this thing, it changes a lot a minds when they come lookin' to rob us. In fact,...Th' Marshal there can shoot circles around me!"

"Name's Morgan Storm." Nodded the gunman as he held out his hand.

"Bill Upshur." Grinned Billy and shook the hand firmly.

"Marshal," Said Storm then turned to look back at Rodney. "I am right sorry for my actions here, but it's hard for me to trust anybody,... and I'm sure you can understand why?"

"I can, yes, sir,...and it's not a problem. Now,...you still need them supplies?"

"Sure thing, lead on!" He looked up at Billy as they both fell in behind Rodney and climbed the steps. "I saw a boy in the doorway a minute ago, he yours?"

"Name's William," Nodded Billy. "We call 'im Willy, for short. His brother's name is Christopher, and his sister, Angela."

"A family man." Sighed Storm, shaking his head. "I think I envy you." He stopped on the porch to look out at the canyon's muddy floor. "What about your folks, Bill,...they live up here, too?"

Billy shook his head. "They was killed when I was a kid,...River Rats!"

"Sorry to hear it,...lost mine when I was six." He sighed. "I don't think they're dead,...I just don't know where they are,...or who they are?...We got separated, that's all I remember!...Anyway," He said grinning up at him. "I consider a family, a luxury that I can't very well afford."

"Have you tried?"

"Thought about it,...met some mighty fine women along the way, too!"

"Why didn't you?"

Storm sighed heavily then. "Too many commitments, and that's all I can say." He looked out at the towering Pines then and nodded. "I have seen some mighty pretty country across Arkansas back there, Bill,... but none of it looked as wild as those mountains off yonder, what's that one called?"

"That's th' Winding stair." Said Billy, also looking at it. "And wild ain't th' right word for this country." He looked down at Storm's gun then. "Can I ask you somethin', Morgan?" And when Storm turned back toward him and nodded.

"That's a damn nice lookin' pistol....what's it plated in?"

Storm smiled and pulled the weapon from it's holster. "That, Bill, is pure silver!...I had a gunsmith plate it with some silver, I ran across three years ago. Did a fine job of it, too!"

"That, he did." Nodded Billy. "Well, what brings you this far South, Morgan?"

"It wasn't the mud, I'll tell ya that!...I've been in that God-awful stuff for two days now. But tell me, where would that road there take me?"

"Where you headed?"

"Someplace different,...someplace I've never been."

"Well, that's th' way, it runs about twenty miles South, another one runs east and west from there!...Either way will take you to Texas, you stay on it long enough."

"Never been to Texas,…I hear it's a big place?"

"You won't believe it!…By th' way, we got a Café inside, if you're hungry, our wives are good cooks!"

CHAPTER FIVE

August seventh…Jarvis Cantrell opened his eyes and lay staring up at the dark, web-covered ceiling of the one-time saloon, and remembered the recurring nightmare of the day he had found the remains of his family. They had been laid out side by side in front of his church, and all had been shot between the eyes. The only clue to what had happened, was the mark of their Assassin,…a cross made of small stones had been placed at the feet of his eldest wife. He blinked to rid himself of the mental pictures when he heard the noise, and raised himself up to look around at the sleeping men on the floor before finally spotting the dark figure stoking the embers to life in the fireplace. He swung his legs off the side of the bar to watch his Lieutenant stand and walk through the outstretched men and come toward him.

"Mornin', Jarvis." Greeted Mitch Kelley as he leaned his back against the bar beside him. "You sleep well?"

"I never sleep well, Mitch," He sighed. "Too many memories and bad dreams."

"You never did find them killers, did you?" He grinned when Cantrell cast an angry look at him. "You talk in your sleep, sir." He shrugged then. "I pretty much know what happened to your family."

"You've rode with me now, for how long,…ten years?…Why ain't you said something?"

"None a my business, Jarvis,…don't know why I said anything now."

"Well the answer is no,…I never found them." He whispered dejectedly. " But I do know that an Assassin did it."

36

"Assassin?...Ain't that just another name for killer?"

"It is,...but there's a difference, Mitch. A killer is someone who likes to kill, someone who kills by accident, or just to stay alive....The Assassin is ordered to kill!...The Mormon Church is it's own Government,...a very large organization!...It also has it's own force of Secret Police, hired killers, so to speak. He is given a name, a description, or maybe a drawing of his victim's likeness, then he stalks him, finds him, and murders him!...The Church then denies their existence!" He sighed heavily then. "My family was executed for something I did, Mitch, something a few of the Elders did not like!...It was to send me a message."

"I'm sure sorry, Jarvis. ...But you said a name, too,...Brig Young, or somethin' like that,...did he do it?"

"Brigham Young." He sighed. "No,...it wasn't him! Brigham Young is the head of the Mormon Church, and supposedly the only man who knows the identities of all the Assassins!...And I believed at the time, that he was the only man who could send them to kill."

"He wasn't?"

"No,...it was someone else, someone close to him. I just couldn't find out who, before I ran out of time!"

Mitch chuckled then. "Knowin' you like I do, it's hard to believe you didn't kill 'im anyway?"

"I was closing in on him, son, but not to kill the man, I just wanted his help!...There were possibly more than two dozen Elders on his staff, and at the time, I was still convinced it could be him, so I did the next possible thing!" He looked back at Mitch then.

"I began asking the Elders my questions, one by one, but no one knew a thing,...or if they did, they wouldn't tell me!...But once I thought it all out, I knew it couldn't be Brigham!,...and if it wasn't him, it had to be one of the Elders!" He sighed again. "I still believe Brigham might have told me who was behind it all, but I had already killed several high-ranking Church Officials in my effort to get to him....Anyway, Brigham was arrested by Union Soldiers, for what, I don't know,... probably framed by that same man!...By then the Army was coming after me,...and that was about the time a friend told me that the Society had also sanctioned my execution,...so, I left Utah!" He looked around the large, dark room again and sighed heavily.

"And here I am, Mitch,...stuck in all this luxury!"

"Yes, Sir,...and if you was any happier about it, neither one of us could stand it." He laughed. "But, you said some other names, too....I already know you was a preacher once, and I know about your family,... but you cried in your sleep when you called out those names,...they was th' names of women, Jarvis,...was you married more than once?"

"No,...I had four wives, Mitch, and I loved each one of them dearly." He sighed heavily again. "I had seven children as well!"

"You had four wives,...all at one time?"

"I'm a Mormon, son, it's our way, has been for many, many years."

Mitch looked at the floor and shook his head. "Mormon,...does that mean you ain't American, Jarvis?"

"It means I'm a Mormon, Son....Mormonism is a religion,...we lived in the ways of the bible, we spoke in the ancient dialect. We were God's desciples!" He sighed again, in obvious despair.

"I'm not a Mormon anymore, Mitch, and I don't have a family!"

"I'm real sorry, Sir!...Guess I'm too damn nosey sometimes."

"Nothing wro,..." Cantrell suddenly reached and gripped Mitch's shoulder, and at the same time, pushed himself off the bar-top onto the floor and stared at the arousing group of men. "What's wrong over there?"

Mitch also turned to look, and they watched as one of the men got to his knees to begin shaking the man in the blankets beside him.

"Let's see what's going on, Mitch." Voiced Cantrell then started across the creaking floor, with Mitch on his heels. By now, several men were awake and, either sitting up, or up on knees watching the activity.

"What going on here, Silk?" Queried Cantrell as they got there. "What are you doing?"

"I don't know, Boss,...I think Chance is dead!" He replied huskily, looking up at them. "Least, I can't wake him up!"

"Tell me what happened, Silk,...what woke you up?" He insisted as he squatted beside him.

"Don't know,...I heard 'im cuss in his sleep last night, loud, too,... and he was slappin' at something, and swingin' his arms around. He hit me, so I elbowed 'im, and he got quiet again, that's all I know!... He went back to sleep, and I did, too,...till just now!...He woke me up again a while ago, grabbed my arm real hard,...then he wheezed and went all limp!"

"Okay," Breathed Cantrell. "Move back a little." And when Silk backed away, he moved forward to check the man's breathing, there was none, and when he touched his neck to check for a pulse, he felt the swelling. "I need some light here, Silk,...get me one of those burning sticks." He sat back on his heels to wait, and when Silk returned to hold the light over Chance, he reached and pulled the man's shirt open, revealing the large red, bulbous swelling on the side of his neck, and it had encompassed part of his lower jaw.

"Jesus!" Gasped Silk. "I ain't never seen nothin' like that, Boss!"

"I have," He said, unbuttoning the man's shirt and pulling it open to the waist.

"A spider?" Gasped Silk as he stared wide-eyed at the very large and angry female.

"A Black Widow Spider, to be exact!" Breathed Cantrell. "This Bitch is big enough to kill us all." He stood, and using his booted foot, raked the fast moving spider out onto the hard planking of the floor and stomped it before angrily looking around the darkened interior of the room.

"Where there's one of these things, there's a thousand." He breathed. "See all them cobwebs?...Okay,...I plan on us being here for a while, so I want this room cleared, you hear me,...ceiling and all!...What you can't reach with a stick, use fire, but be careful, we don't want to burn the place down!" He turned to shake his head at Mitch then.

"I hate spiders!" He said. "Now, when they're done in here, son, I want the same thing done in there where the horses are,...Bitches will bite them, too!...And have them bury old Chance there,...somewhere he won't be found!"

*   *   *

"I don't think rocking chairs is a good thing, honey." Smiled Connie as she gave Billy the valise to load. "But you know what?...A couple of strait-chairs might be nice,...if you can tie them so they won't move?"

"I guess we can do that." He grunted, sliding the bag beneath the tarp. "Providin' we don't try to take too much with us."

"We'll worry about that,...when are we leaving?"

"Well,…it's a little too muddy yet,…don't want a bog down somewhere."

"Then why are we loading the wagon?"

"We're not, it's just one bag less, we'll have to load!…Tarp'll keep it dry. Becides,…we still got your chairs to put in. We'll give th' roads a couple more days to dry out first." He jumped down to lean against the end gate then. "Peter said th' Goodland road comes all th' way through now,…crosses th' Wheelock Road somewhere around th' Jack-Fork!…I'm thinkin' we'll go that way this time."

"Anything to keep from going through that awful Wheelock,… that place scares me!"

"Makes me a little nervous, too!…okay,…it's gettin' late, and I got a throw some hay to th' horses."

"We have to start supper, too." She sighed, and wiped sweat from her face with the tail of her apron. "Won't be long!" She said then started back down to the trading post.

He watched her go as he pulled the bandana from his neck to wipe his own face, and as he retied it, watched her until she cautiously worked her way around to the front of the store and out of sight. Sighing, he wondered briefly when they had stopped having their meals at home, and started eating in the diner? Convenience, he guessed, and sighing again, took the Durham sack and brown papers from his shirt and absently rolled and lit his smoke, taking the relaxant deep into his lungs as he looked up the grade at the two barns, and at the same time wishing he was still at the farm. He missed working the land, gathering his crops, and he even missed the Café.

He shook his head then and grinned. He never dreamed that would ever happen, not after all the times he had asked her to sell the place. But he did miss it,…he missed the infrequent visits of Doc, when he would come in for coffee, or a quick meal. He even missed the people he knew,…and watching the street-traffic from his table at the window. He blew smoke upward and sighed once again. Doing nothing every day was the most tiring thing he'd ever done. He blew smoke skyward again as he stared past the wagon at the rocky slope where Loughmiller had hidden to watch them, remembering the fear and excitement he had felt while chasing the madman, but then shuddered when he thought of how close he had come to dying.

He shook the thoughts away and was looking back toward the barn, when he became aware of the tingling in his neck,…and instantly alerted, slowly dropped the spent butt and exhaled the smoke as he remained still to listen, his right hand very slowly going down to remove the tie-down loop from the Colt pistol while at the same time, searching the areas past the cabin, and in the direction of the prairie for the source of his concern….But then, he shuddered inwardly when he realized that the concern had to be from somewhere behind him.

So intent, was his thoughts on this, that when the twig snapped behind him, he whirled, the pistol appearing in his hand like magic, hammer back and ready to deliver it's stroke of death.

"Billy, wait!" Yelled Rodney as he threw up both hands in a defensive gesture.

Catching himself, Billy quickly lowered the gun and eased it off-cock before holstering the weapon,…and at the same time, releasing his breath in a gush of pent-up energy as he wilted back against the wagon's tail-gate to catch his breath.

"God damn it!" Blurted Rodney as he came forward. "You just scared the shit out of me!"

"Sorry, Rod!" He breathed. "I was deep in thought, man."

"You must have been!…Man, it just ain't natural how fast you are,… what was you thinking about anyway?"

"Mostly about th' farm,…and about Loughmiller!…I was lookin' out there where you caught 'im hidin' that day." He grinned sheepishly then, and reached to roll another smoke as Rodney came on to lean against the wagon beside him.

"I think about that some, too!" He admitted. "And it still scares me!"…What about the farm?" He reached a thin cigar from his shirt and lit it. "You miss it, don't you?"

Billy nodded. "Anyway, th' hair on my neck stood up, and when I heard that twig break?" He shrugged then. "Maybe I ought a stop wearin' a gun altogether,…I'm getting' too jumpy!"

"Oh, no, my friend,…those reflexes of yours saved our bacon a time or two, and I can live with that!…You're the best there is, Billy, but if you quit wearing that gun, you're dead,…or I am, and I sort of like myself too much to die!…Besides,…you have too much to live for, my friend!"

41

"Thanks, Rod,…but sometimes I worry about myself,…you know what I'm tryin' to say?"

"More than you know, old son….And I'll tell you something else I know….If you were losing control, you would not have made the effort not to fight Morgan Storm!...Now, that's a man that worried me some,…he was too calm and collected, and he wasn't the usual braggart type!"

"I think he was relieved, Rod. I don't think he liked killin' any more than I do!...I also think he's very good at it."

"That makes two of us!...Now,…You ain't having second thoughts about this place now, are you,…not at this late date? Just remember, we didn't have much of a choice in the matter!"

"Oh we had a choice, Rod, a couple of 'em. This is just th' one we had to make. Choices, yes,…options, no!...I don't regret it, Rod, I just miss workin' th' farm!...I like bein' rich, too, okay?"

"Now that's what I'm saying!" He grinned, pulling smoke from the cigar and exhaling before reaching up to wipe his forehead. "Rain made it hot, didn't it?"

"A little too humid, too!" Nodded Billy.

"Oh,…I was coming to tell you that Lisa don't like the idea of rockers in the wagon, said she'd rather have a strait-back."

"Well, they think alike, anyway."

"You knew?"

"Connie just said th' same thing."

"Imagine that!" He laughed. "Well, I'll go get 'em, better to do it now, than when it's time to go."

"I'll hay th' horses, then I'll help you."

*   *   *

"You gals out-did yourselves on that venison tonight," Smiled Rodney as he dipped the ladle into the mashed potatoes. "What's different about it?"

"Fried it in honey." Replied Connie. "It was a little too salty."

"It was for a fact!" Commented Billy as he reached for the makings. "But, while we're on th' subject,…I was expectin' corn on th' cob tonight, what happened?"

"No corn," Sighed Melissa. "We forgot to bring it in last night, and this morning it was gone."

"A whole bushel?"

"All of it." Sighed Connie, getting up to get the coffee. "Got to be Raccoons, or maybe opossums, there was shucks and corn-kernels strewn everywhere around the basket." She poured their coffee as she spoke.

"I don't recall seein' many coons around here," Returned Billy and shook his head. "You see any tracks?" He licked the smoke and lit it.

"Of course not, what do we know about tracks?" She replaced the pot on the stove and sat down again. "Our furry friend left a few, though,...and whatever that thing is, it seems to be making it's home around here,...and it's beginning to get a little creepy!"

"Well that's where th' corn went,...it weren't no coon!" Nodded Billy. "What it didn't eat, it likely toted away."

"How come we can't see that Sasquatch, daddy?" Asked Willy. "I sure wish I could!"

"Yeahhh," Voiced Christopher. "I wish I could see it, too,...I'd beat it up for taking our corn!"

"Hush now, both of you, you'll scare Cindy!"

"Is it a munster, mommie?" She whimpered.

"No, honey," Soothed Melissa. "It's not a monster,...besides, it can't get in the house. It's only an animal looking for food, now eat yours, or it might get it!"

"It is sort a funny, though." Said Rodney as he reached for, and lit his cigar.

"What is?"

"That thing is here almost every night, but the horses never seem to be afraid of it, I've never heard a peep out of 'em,...wonder why that is?"

"He's not a threat to 'em, I guess."

"Do you think it has a family?" Queried Melissa. "Maybe that's why it took the corn."

"As long as corn is all it takes, I wouldn't worry too much!" Said Billy. "Just hope it don't start breakin' in, lookin' for it!"

"It wouldn't hurt to know for sure what it is?" Sighed Rodney. "If it was any part of a human being, it wouldn't live like that!...Therefore, it's got a be an animal...I still wouldn't believe it, if I hadn't seen it!"

"Somebody, someday, will get to th' bottom of it." Sighed Billy. "They might be surprised too!"

"Why do you say that?"

"Don't know,...but maybe we didn't evolve as much as we think we did?"

"A throw-back?"

Billy shrugged. "All I know is that if it gets too personal, we might wind up havin' to hunt it down!...You'd think that after all this time the Police would a seen it around here!...Nobody sees anything, it just comes and goes as it pleases."

"Hunting it down might be a chore, too," Added Rodney. "It lives in these hills, you know. Hell, we thought Loughmiller was hard to catch!...Nobody knows what damage something that big could do, probably strong as ten men, and twice as mean when riled!...I don't want to know what it is,...or where it came from!"

"I'm on your side, Rod,...some things are better left alone!"

"Amen to that!"

"Excuse me, please?" Came a voice from the open doorway, causing them all to look up in surprise.

"Come on in, Jonas," Grinned Rodney. "You startled us, man."

"Yes, do come in, Jonas." Added Connie, getting up to come for the plates and utensils he carried. "Would you like some more?"

"No, Ma'am, Mistress Upshur, it was plenty." He smiled and gave her the dishes. "I come to tell Marshal Taylor, that a man is here to see him."

"To see me,...who is it, Jonas?"

"He is here." Jonas moved aside then to allow the man to enter.

"Well, Bass Reeves!" Blurted Rodney, getting up. "Come in, man, good to see you!...Here," He pulled out a chair. "Sit down here, have some supper."

"I wouldn't want to put you folks out none." He grinned then as he removed his coat and hat and sat down.

"You wouldn't be!" Said Connie, quickly setting him a plate and utensils. "Help yourself, there's plenty. I'll get you some coffee."

"Well, I am some hungry!"

"Just help yourself, Bass." Laughed Rodney as he sat down again. "And while you're at it, say hello to my best friend, and partner, Billy Upshur!"

"Yes, sir," He grinned. "I thought so….I'm Bass Reeves." He nodded, quickly shaking Billy's hand. "I think I know you already, th' Marshal speaks of you all th' time!...I'm real glad to know you."

"I've heard a lot about you, too!"

"That's Billy's wife, Connie," Continued Rodney. "His three kids, Willy, Chris, and Angela….And these are my two angels, my wife, Lisa, and my special angel, Cindy."

"I'm pleased to meet you all. "He grinned. "And thank you for th' hospitality."

"Our pleasure, Bass, now eat up, man."

They waited while the Marshal finished his meal, and when he was finally done, he pushed his plate away and grinned up at Connie. "That was mighty good, Ma'am,…best venison I ever ett,…I'm much obliged!"

"You are quite welcome."

"Marshal," He sighed, looking around the kitchen area. "You got a good set-up heah,…real good, even better'n you described it!"

"Thank's,…we like it….Now what brings you out and about?"

"Been trackin' a couple old boys….Three of 'em botched a robbery over in Ada. I was on patrol down that way when it happened,… anyway, Sheriff Gillman shot one of 'em 'fore they could get away with th' money, so here I am….I followed their trail all th' way here,…lost it a couple a times in all that rain, but picked it up again. You ain't seen nobody like that, I guess?"

"They got names?" Queried Billy.

"Don't know 'em, if they do,…other man died. You seen 'em?"

"Couple a greenhorns tried to rob us, a day or so back,…Buster Cates, and Norvell Smallwood,…could be them."

"You got 'em?"

"In jail." Said Rodney. "I ain't got no warrants on 'em, so you're welcome to 'em, if they're th' ones."

"Thank ye kindly,…I'll need to ask 'em a couple questions."

"Whenever you're ready." Voiced Rodney. "Finish your coffee, they ain't going nowhere....How's your arm these days?"

"What's left of it ain't too bad, slug took a chunk a meat out of it, and it gives me fits in rainy weather, and 'specially in winter time,... but I'll live with it."

"And the family?"

"Good, they're good,...I ain't home enough, is all."

"Neither is Rodney!" Exclaimed Melissa. "And I hate it!"

"Yessum,...mine does, too!...Might's well see them prisoners now, Marshal, if you're ready?"

*   *   *

"You sure you want to do this, Bass?" Queried Rodney as the Lighthorsemen ushered out the five prisoners. "It feels like I'm forcing this on you, man."

"Course, I'm sure, Marshal,...you folks done my job fer me, here, least I can do is your'en!...besides,...I done had that Sheriff wire old Judge Parker, I'd be bringin' 'em in, make me look bad, I didn't!"

"Well, I want to thank you,...and here's my reports for the Judge!" He gave Bass the paperwork and watched him put it away in his saddlebags. "You got a long trip ahead of ya with five prisoners,...I could send a couple of Policemen with you?"

"That's all right, Marshal, I can handle these old boys. Besides, I'll be goin' home fer a couple a days, first, then on to Fort Smith....Won't be any trouble, once I hogtie 'em!" He walked around his horse then to gather up the lead ropes while the prisoners mounted their horses, tied the ropes together in a knot then hooked them over his saddle's horn before coming back around to mount his own horse. Once the Choctaw had finished securing the men's feet beneath their mounts' bellies, he tipped his hat to Billy and Rodney and led the five horses off toward the distant prairie.

"Seems like a good man, Rod." Nodded Billy. "Proud, though, maybe a little too proud."

"Yeah,...he does hate to lose,...I get the feeling he thinks he has to keep proving himself,...like he has to be better than anybody else!... Maybe I'm wrong, I don't know. But you're right, he is a good man, and a damn good Marshal!"

"That makes two of ya." Grinned Billy.

"Thank's, Billy....Well, he saved me a trip, anyway, and that's good news!...I'd rather do just about anything than go to Fort Smith."

*   *   *

"Them's some damn big Catfish, Jarvis!" Laughed Mitch as they watched the men cleaning them. "Got a weigh sixty, seventy pounds each!"

"I have seen bigger ones, son....How did they catch these things?"

"Gator found some good-sized hooks hangin' in one a them pier-sheds, used a rope for a line, I guess!...Anyway, speakin' of Gator,...I guess you're still set on disbandin', ain't ya?"

"Pretty much set on it, yes."

Gator, and some a th' men are grumblin' about bein' here too long. They think the Army's gonna find us....Told me they wanted to leave!"

"If the Army finds us, it will be luck on their part, Mitch. That storm wiped out our trail completely!...We're better off right here till the end of the month."

"Why th' end of th' month?"

"Payday,...Cavalry boys want to be at the Fort, come payday,... especially now that they're getting paid regularly again."

"Good point!...Well, I just thought I'd let you know about Gator,... and if we're gonna stay here for a while, we sure could use us some coffee, salt and sugar....I talked to that old Indian over yonder in that stilt-house yesterday,...he said there's a Tradin' Post over at Shockey's Prairie, South of us a ways. I could be there, and back in a few hours, Jarvis."

Cantrell turned to squint his eyes at the distant shack, sitting almost perilously atop logs jutting out of the water. "What's your feeling about the Indian, Mitch, was it wise to let him know we're here?"

"I think it'll be okay, Jarvis. Him and his wife both are old, and he has bad eyesight. Besides, I told 'em I was passin' through, and needed supplies,...they might not even know we're here,...or even care, for that matter!"

"Then go get the salt, by all means!...While you're there, see if there's any news we need to know about!...And what about money, you got any?...You're to buy the supplies, not take them, Mitch, and I mean that!"

"I got two dollars and thirty-five cents, Jarvis."

Cantrell reached into his pocket and gave Mitch a ten dollar gold piece. "The money you have won't buy enough for a week, son,...we'll need enough for four weeks,...a few potatoes wouldn't hurt."

"Sure thing!...By th' way,...when we doin' this disbanding?"

"The day we leave here!...You got other plans, or going with me?"

"I'm with you, Jarvis, you know that!"

"I'm glad, boy. I just want it to be your decision."

"It is!...I'll go saddle up. Oh,...that old Indian also told me, that road out there goes all th' way across Texas, all th' way South to San Antonio."

"Keep all that to yourself, Mitch, let the men choose their own fate."

"Yes, sir,...well,...I'll be back!" He turned and went back into the saloon, and on through to the horses.

Nodding, Cantrell breathed deeply of the slightly cool, rather stiff wind coming in off the river, and watched the men cut up the fish for another minute before looking up to scan the shanties on the far bank of the wide waterway, and was in time to see the troop of cavalry emerge from the tall trees along the road there.

"Gator!" He called quickly, and getting their attention, he pointed. "Get out of sight!" Moving back into the saloon's doorway, he watched the four men scramble for cover then watched as the mounted soldiers rode down to water's edge, sit for a few minutes to use their field glasses and study the silent, deserted buildings, and then to finally retreat back the way they had come.

Gator and the other men watched them leave before coming back to the fish, and while the three resumed slicing up the meat, he came toward the open doors just as Mitch led his horse out and walked it toward the end of the platform and down to the road, and watched until he mounted and rode away before coming on in to talk with Cantrell.

"Where's Mitch off to, Boss?"

"Going for supplies, he'll be back." He started to turn away then.

"Can we talk, Boss?" Asked Malloy as he stepped in front of him again.

Cantrell studied the man's shaggy features for a moment then nodded. "What's on your mind, Mister Malloy?"

Gator shuffled his feet for a moment, looking first at the lolling men in the large room then back at the river.

"Speak up, man!...You got something to say, spit it out!"

"Yes, sir....Now don't get mad, Boss,...but me and some a th' men been talkin', and,...and we ain't comfortable here.....So, I want a ask ya when we're leavin'?"

"I plan on leaving in two weeks, Gator. So what are you telling me,...you want to leave now, is that it?"

"Well,...yeah, we do, Boss. And we don't mean no disrespect to you, Mister Cantrell, we had it real good with you!"

"Who else is in on this?"

"Me, Dusty, Roach, Emmit, Buck and Gomer, all six of us."

Cantrell studied him for a moment longer then nodded. "Then you have my blessing, go!...Got someplace in mind?"

"Mainly,...we just don't want a go to Mexico, Boss, they ain't no trees there!...And we don't want a take our chances with th' Army neither!...So, we're thinkin' Indian Territory, Right across that river there. Gomer's been here before, durin' th' war. He says they's a town up that road over there called Wheelock, nothin' but a saloon and a few houses. I figure we can hold up there till th' Army stops lookin' for us!"

"The Army will never stop looking for us, Gator, remember that!... But I wish good luck for all of you. Feel free to leave any time you like."

"And you ain't mad?"

"No,...I'm glad you're thinking for yourselves,...shows initiative."

"Thank's Boss, I'll tell 'em!...And you ought a leave now too,... they're gonna find you here, Boss, sure as shootin'."

"I'll take my chances, Gator,...good luck! But it does appear to me, you might have a problem getting across that river, it's wide, and it looks deep to me."

"Yeah," He said turning to look at the opposite shore. "We'll need to look for a place to cross,...anyway, we'll be leavin' come dark, Boss, and thank ye kindly." He abruptly turned and went back across the rickety platform to join the others.

*   *   *

August 10,…Peter Birdsong returned in the afternoon with two Choctaw carpenters, and the wife of one of them, and after sitting down with Billy and Rodney, came up with a working plan for the desired walkway. It was to run from Billy's front steps, down beside Rodney's house, and another from Rodney's front steps to adjoin it before continuing down the slope and alongside the Trading Post, making another turn and on to the store's front steps. A handrail would be in place from both dwellings to the store,…and planking for the project would begin the following morning at sunrise, as there was still enough seasoned, left-over logs to do the entire job.

Late that day found Billy, Rodney, and the carpenters laying out the path the walk would take, and helping with the digging of several holes that would hold the support posts beneath it.

The weather was cooperating, and the ground was drying out quickly under the beating of a South wind. Only a few puffy clouds could be seen in the sky above the towering trees, and it was another very hot day. If not for the perpetual breeze that always seemed to be swirling up the narrow canyon to cool beneath the trees, it would be most uncomfortable.

Sunrise on the Eleventh found Billy on his front porch smoking while he sat in his rocking chair to watch the carpenters splitting logs, and the Choctaw were adept at their work, manipulating the old logs and splitting them into long, thick boards, to be cut to length later,… and already being somewhat cured-out from time on the ground, the boards should be less prone to warp once nailed into place.

Tossing the spent butt into the yard, he heard Connie coming toward the door and got up as she came out onto the porch. "Mornin', Honey?"

"Good morning." She smiled, tiptoeing to kiss him on the mouth and then arm in arm, immediately went down the steps and down the slant to the store, where he opened the door and let her inside,…and in the reflected light from the Marshal's office, went on through the store and into the dining area where he quickly built a fire in the stove, and then lit several wall-mounted lanterns for lighting.

Connie went straight to the pump for coffee water and placed the large pot on the stove, added the coffee grounds, replaced the lid and left it to brew while he placed more wood in the flames.

"Are we still leaving tomorrow, Billy?"

"At daybreak, if we're ready."

"We're ready." She sighed. "But I dread that week in a wagon already."

"Quicker'n a trip to Denver!"

"God, yes!" She gasped. "Now where you going?"

"Out to watch 'em split logs."

"Coffee will be ready soon!"

"I'll be back." He left and went across the room then down into the Marshal's office. "Mornin' Men,…Oh,…didn't know you was here, Robert,…good mornin'."

"Good morning, Mister Upshur." He grinned.

"Is Peter up and about?"

"He is with the men outside."

"Good." He went out to the boardwalk then saw Rodney and Melissa climbing to the porch, and waited when he saw Rodney put Cindy down and walk toward him.

"Top of th' mornin', Billy!" Grinned the Marshal as he came down the steps. "Where you headed?"

"Checkin' on th' work-crew, Peter's already there."

"Let's go, then!" He said, and they started around the side of the building. "Tomorrow's the day, Billy,…don't know about you, but I'll be glad to get away for a while."

"Won't bother me none, neither!...Guess we can load up this afternoon, you takin' a ridin' horse?"

"You think we'll need to,…we can use John's carriage to get around in?"

"I'll take a couple just in case, plenty a grass on your place, we don't need 'em."

Peter waved when he saw them and came forward to meet them. "Mister Upshur, Marshal,…good Morning." He shook their hands then nodded toward the workmen. "They will be ready to build the walk soon."

"I can see that!" Nodded Billy. "I was watchin' 'em earlier."

"And I am sorry, Marshal." Said the Tracker, reaching to take folded paper money from his shirt pocket. "There was much happening yesterday when we arrived, and I forgot that I have your money." He gave Rodney the currency then waited for him to count it.

"Three hundred dollars." He nodded. "You get all of yours?"

"Yes,...and I also have this." He gave Rodney the papers.

"From Judge Parker." He said, and then read it to himself.

"Trouble?" Queried Billy when he finally looked up.

"Maybe." He said, looking at the wire again. "Seems the Army has been hunting a gang of Quantrill, style Missouri Raiders for a long time now,...and three weeks ago the Twelveth Cavalry jumped them near the Texas, Louisiana border, but lost them somewhere on the Texas side of Shreveport Landing!...That's quite a ways from here, ain't it?"

"It is, unless they turned North." Said Billy. "If they was comin' here, they'd have to cross th' Red, though,...and that ain't no easy chore, as wide and fast as it is."

"Could be a Ferry farther East of Jonesboro someplace, seems I heard of one."

"Ferry at Jonesboro may still work, too, we don't know." Added Billy.

"I don't think so."

"That wire say who this bunch is?"

"The Jarvis Cantrell gang."

"Don't recall ever hearin' th' name!"

"Neither have I,...but it sys he's a Mormon Minister, wanted for murder in Utah, and for murder and rape during raids in Missouri and Tennessee during the war, and since! Wanted for pillaging and torching entire towns with a force of at least fifty followers, and all this since the war ended....One bad son of a Bitch!"

"Appears he is!" Nodded Billy. "But if th' Army's after 'im, you can bet regiments everywhere have already been alerted, includin' law enforcement!...He'll be lookin' for a place to hide, that's for sure,...and Indian Territory might just look good to 'im!"

"He couldn't hope to hide out for long up here." Sighed Rodney. "Not with that many men,...Peter's Police would find them."

"This gonna put a hitch in our plans, Rod?"

Rodney shook his head and stared at the ground for a minute before answering. "No!" He said, looking back at them. "Unless you're worried, Peter?"

"I am not worried, my friend,…I will bring in more Light-horsemen to stand watch….If these men do come here, you could not make the difference, my friend."

"Good,…and you're right,…but let me tell you something, Peter. Neither me, or this job requires that you risk your life, or the lives of your police unnecessarily, you remember that, my friend!"

"Do not worry, Marshal,…these men will not come here!"

"With Soldiers watchin' for 'em up here, too,…they might not!" Agreed Billy, reaching to roll and light a Durham. "Besides, they'll find it a mite tough to move around in that tangle of wilderness out there." He exhaled skyward.

"It's your call, Rod,…we both know that if it can happen, it usually will!"

"Yeah, you're right!" Sighed Rodney dejectedly. "Okay, we'll wait an extra day, Billy….This paper has two dates on it, that means part of it came through two weeks ago, and the rest a week ago. This information has to be more than a month old!…That's plenty of time to get up this far, if they were coming. If we don't hear, or see anything in a couple a days, we'll leave as planned."

"That's got my vote." Nodded Billy.

"I, as well, think they will not come." Agreed Peter. "But we will be waiting, just the same."

"There you have it, Rod,…and I'm here to tell ya, that a man would think twice before goin' up against a man with two guns on his hip!" He grinned and slapped the smiling Tracker on the shoulder. "I know I would!"

"And you're not alone!" Grinned Rodney. "But just the same,… Peter, I would not pull all your men in on this, three or four is enough!… The rest, you might want to just go with your gut, you know the Wilderness better than we do!…The Cavalry will no doubt be out in force, too,…so if this bunch is here already, maybe they'll see 'em first!… If any of your men spot them, have them go for the soldiers, we don't want them hurt!

CHAPTER SIX

Paris, Texas was slowly coming alive again, only a few of the shops and stores along the off-streets were still closed, but those around the large square were teaming with activity. The boardwalks were full of shoppers and lookers, even the streets of town were having their share of heavy traffic once more, men on horseback, families in buckboards, or in their bulky farm wagons, and some of these already filling the square its self,…something that had not been seen in the last, almost three years.

Two of the boarded-up hotels were reopening, one on Clarksville Road, just off the square, the other on South Church. The Lamar Hotel, as well as the Peterson had managed somehow to remain open through the hard times. The Schoolhouse on West Graham Road had remained open, but holding classes only a half-day at a time because the children were hard put to bring lunches for a full day of learning, that and the lack of a teacher on most days. But it was now back to full capacity, with a full-time, paid teacher on staff.

All the eating establishments were open again, or opening, except for Connie's Kitchen,…and were all doing a meager business. Freight wagons were moving once again, their straining teams of horses, and cracking whips a welcome sound. Nathan Cohn, Clothiers, had finally opened his second store on Bonham Road, just a door down from Doctor Lovejoy's office, and almost directly across the street from the lower Court Building, and the gun-shop beside it. Only this store catered strictly to a woman's needs, everything from toiletries to the latest fashions in women's under, and outer garments.

Williams and Wortham's sporting and ranch equipment, and Hardware had reopened on Main Street, a block North of the square, and the Brickyard had rehired all it's help again. Paris was once again a growing city, a self-sufficient community with it's bright future once again intact, and prosperity just around the bend.

*   *   *

August 13, 1877,…."Come on in, Marshal!" Smiled Judge Bonner, getting up to come around his desk. "I'm glad you're here,…Councilman Bratcher just sent your payroll over." He shook Jim Stockwell's hand and gestured to a chair in front of his desk. "Sit down, Jim, I'll get it!" He went back around and sat down, opened a drawer and passed the envelope to him.

"Cash money this time?…Why's that, Judge?"

"Saving on paper, maybe, who knows?" Smiled Bonner. "So,…what can I do for you, Marshal,…or is that what you came for?"

Stockwell reached a folded paper from his vest and passed it across the desk.

"Cletus just brought me this, and I was wonderin' if you had heard anything about it?"

"I saw Cletus go up, a while ago." He said as he took the paper. He read the rather extensive wire then frowned slightly. "It's the first I've heard of this, Jim,…did Gose, or John Rucker get one of these?"

"Don't know, I'm on my way to see 'em now….It's got me a little nervous, though, I'll tell ya that!…If a gang like that was to hit Paris, a lot a people would get hurt, and me with one Deputy?" He shrugged.

"I see what you mean." He nodded. "Well, you'd best go talk with the Sheriff, and also John Rucker, Jim,…that will give you ten men, between the three of you!…Tell you what, I'll go sit down with Councilman Bratcher and if need be, I'll ask him to okay the hiring of more deputies. That is, if you think this bunch could actually show up here?…Says here, the Army lost their trail over a week ago,…that's a long time!"

"Yes, sir, I know. Have you ever heard of that Jarvis Cantrell?"

"If memory serves, I think I have….I believe I read about him once in a Chicago newspaper, not long after the war ended!…They were comparing him to Quantrill at the time, if you can imagine that?"

"No, sir, I can't! He sighed. "But that bein' th' case, I think I'll station Glenn somewhere out at th' Jonesboro, Clarksville cut-off for a few days,…maybe have John Gose send a man out Lamar Road….It might give us some warning, at least!"

"Do what you think best, Jim. Let me know if I can help." He glanced out through the large window as he spoke. "But right now, it appears we're about to have visitors." They both got up and went to the window as the soldiers were dismounting at the hitch-rail in front.

"Maybe we're about to find out something." Commented Bonner. "Two of them are coming in."

Stockwell watched from his place at the window while Bonner opened the door to admit the soldiers.

"Come in, Captain," Greeted the Judge, stepping aside to allow them entry. "To what, do we owe the honor, Sir?...I am Judge, J.C. Bonner." He said, shaking the Officer's hand.

"Captain Jonas Ford, Sir,…Twelveth Cavalry, out of Fort Thomas, Kentucky."

"Kentucky?...You are quite a ways from home, Sir,…do come in and sit." He gestured at a couple of chairs along the wall as he spoke.

"Begging your pardon, your Honor,…but I am here to see your local law enforcement, can you point me to his office?"

"No need," He said, gesturing this time toward Stockwell. "This is Marshal Jim Stockwell."

Stockwell came to shake the Captain's hand. "How can I help you?"

"Marshal, I'm here to advise you to be watchful. A large force of men could possibly be heading this way, a ruthless gang of marauders they are, too!...Their leader is a sadistic murderer, by the name of Jarvis Cantrell, and they have terrorized, raped and burned their way across several states both during, and since the Civil War!...You might want to prepare for this possibility."

"Yes, sir, I know, we were just reading the wire from Shreveport Landing."

"Good!...I was not sure you would even get one!...These men are dangerous, Marshal, and Cantrell is a madman!...They will hit you without warning, raping, killing, and burning everything they touch!"

"You'd best sit down for a moment, Captain." Gestured Bonner.

Nodding, the Officer sat down while Bonner poured him a glass of water and brought it to him. "Thank you, Judge," He sighed then drank the cool refreshment. "I do apologize,...it's just that we have been in pursuit of Jarvis Cantrell for more than two months!" He gave Bonner back the glass, and sighed heavily again.

"We almost had him at Shreveport Landing, but we lost him in the Texas swamps somewhere North of there. We found the trail again, but then it rained!" He stood then and straightened his Tunic. "We were not able to find his trail again, or since!" He cleared his throat then.

"We are leaving for home in two days, Marshal, we have bivouacked a mile East of here,...and we need supplies for the return trip....So, my question is this,...is there a place I can purchase those supplies, and will they accept a Government voucher?"

"I can answer that, Sir." Smiled Bonner. "Murphy's Emporium, on Church Street will be able to accommodate your list of supplies, but I'm afraid you'll need to see Horace Bratcher at the Farmer's and Merchant's Bank with the voucher. Money is still in very short supply hereabouts, and I'm sure Murphy would appreciate cash money."

"I understand fully,...can you show me to the bank, Sir?"

"Go back to the square and turn right, you'll find it on the corner of Grand Avenue, and Wall, right behind us."

"You have my thanks, Gentlemen." He shook their hands again. "Sergeant!" They abruptly walked out the door then back out to the boardwalk, mounted and rode back toward the busy square.

"Strange one, ain't he?" Grinned Stockwell.

"I do believe he is somewhat stymied, yes!" Nodded Bonner as they watched through the window. "Well,...if there's nothing else, Marshal,...I have case files to prepare, and you have your job cut out for you!...Keep me informed."

*   *   *

Jarvis Cantrell picked a piece of catfish from the tin with his fingers and ate it as he leaned against the bar to watch the other men eat. Some sat with folded legs on bedrolls atop the old weathered floor, while others sat astride their saddles with their plates, but all were sitting in front of the crackling fireplace,...because the wind blowing in off the river was a cool one.

"Wonder if Gator and th' boys made it across that river?" Queried Mitch idly as he fingered more of the fish into his mouth. "I'm surprised they ain't back yet!"

"If they don't get caught first, they'll make it." Said Cantrell, also reaching for more fish. "They won't be back, son. The Army won't associate six drifters as being a part of us."

"Won't have to,...knowin' Gator, he'll start shootin' the minute he see a soldier,...th' man's a lunatic!"

"If that's his destiny, so be it!"

"Do you feel all right, Jarvis,...you've been actin' different here lately,...not like yourself at all?"

"You noticed that, did you?...Well, I'm just tired, Mitch." He sighed then and looked at his second in command. "Okay,...you're right, son. Truth is,...I think I'm beginning to regret all the things I've done, everything!...I used to cherish life, instead of taking it!...All this time, I have been like a man possessed, crazy with hate, and revenge." He sighed again. "I'm just tired,...tired of it all."

"You'll feel different, we get to Mexico, Sir,...we'll both quit this business, how's that?...Maybe we'll buy us a ranch and raise cattle."

"Maybe so,...there's only a thousand miles in our way."

"Yes, Sir,...and it's still seventeen days till the end of th' month, that's a long time to do nothin' but think, Jarvis, especially about th' things you wish you hadn't done!...It ain't healthy."

"You're right about that!" He nodded, reaching for more fish. "Already been here too long, already done too much thinking, and you know what else, Son,...I believe that if I had taken the time to think, a long time ago, I might not be here." He filled his mouth and chewed the fish.

"The Army is still out there, Mitch." He continued. "And they are still looking for us. But,...by the end of the month, they won't be,...so right now, patience is our only ally."

"Well,...you ain't been wrong yet, Jarvis!...And we will get to Mexico, I can feel it in my bones."

"I wish I could, son,...I surely do!"

"Uh, Jarvis,…I hate to do this right now, but,…can I give you somethin' else to think about?"

"Sure, boy, I've always got room for something to think about, what is it?"

"Our money's about gone, I know I ain't got any!...And with your sudden change of heart, it might not be so easy to come by,…and, well,…we will need money before we get to Mexico."

Cantrell sighed heavily then. "I'll do what's necessary, Mitch, don't worry." He grinned at him at that point. "You worried about me, son?"

"I'm," He stammered. "No, sir,…well, some,…I guess I'm worried about both of us,…I don't know!"

"You should never have joined up with me, Mitch,…you could have been much more, than just a wanted renegade,…might yet, if you'll get away from me!"

"I chose my way, Jarvis, it weren't nothin' to do with you. Hell, you put meaning back in my life, Sir,…and I got no regrets!"

"You will have, if you live long enough!...What you should do, is find yourself a good woman and raise a family, now that's a life, Mitch,… nothing like it in the world."

"Naww,…too hard, Jarvis.….A gun fits my hand better."

"That's youth talking, son. Granted you are good with it, but you do need to realize that a gun shoots both ways. I have noticed that you're a little careless much of the time, when using it!"

"You taught me that, Jarvis." He grinned. "Ten years ago, you told me that if I had something to do, do it, don't think about it!...You said that hesitation would get me killed!...You do remember that, don't you, Sir?"

"I do, yes,…and it was said to keep you alive, not make you careless!... You have come a long way, Mitch, you're fast on the draw, and quite accurate,…but now, I'm going to tell you another fact.….No matter haw fast you become, somewhere, there's someone even faster,…and sooner or later, you'll meet him, everyone does!"

"You ain't met 'im yet, Jarvis, and you're faster than I'll ever be!"

"I will meet him, son, the odds are against me now,…I'm sixty-three years old, and rheumatoid!...My back aches all the time, my tail-bone hurts most of the time, and now, I'm beginning to feel it in my arms and hands….It's just a matter of time!…But, caution played a large part in my longevity!…Think about that, Mitch,…think about it hard."

"Yes, sir, I will." He sighed, once again watching the silent men around the fireplace. "You know, Jarvis,…they never said a word when Gator and them left,…and I'd sure like to know what they think about it, wouldn't you?"

"You're right, son, they didn't, but it could be they're glad they're gone."

"Maybe they don't care?"

"That, too." Sighed Cantrell. "And because of that possibility,…I think it's time I tell them our plans." He grinned and pushed away from the counter, walked across the wide room to maneuver around the men on the floor then once in front of the fireplace, turned to face them and cleared his throat.

"You men have been with me for a long time," He began. "you've been a loyal following." He looked each one of them in the face, the room's darkness not allowing him to see their expressions. "And I thank you for that!…But times are changing now. It's not as easy as it once was!…Anyway,…what I'm trying to say is this….Our day is over, Gentlemen,…we are being hounded by every law enforcement agency in the country, the Pinkertons, as well as the Army!…Six of you have already left, and they were smart to do so, men alone have a better chance of surviving." He paused for a moment then broke his news.

"I am quitting, gentlemen, when we leave this place, we will disband, go our separate way. That is the only way for you to survive, as well as for me!…But I would suggest that you wait here with me until time to go….The end of the month is payday for the Army, they will want to be home to receive it!…At that time, we will all leave here two at a time, and at different times, and I do not want to know the direction you take, or your destination, or your plans for the future. From that moment on, we do not know each other."

"And Gentlemen,…this is not up for discussion. I want you all to survive, I want to survive, and this is the only way! Should you want to leave right now, I won't stop you, you are free to go at your own discretion,…but I would hope you will wait!…Thank you all,…and good luck!" He nodded then, and walked back to the bar.

"What if we don't want a break up, boss?" This, came from a man in front, his raspy voice almost an echo in the large room.

"Then don't!...You can all go together if you want,...just not with me! Now please, no further discussions on the matter, Gentlemen."

"I figured you'd get more of an argument out of 'em." Voiced Mitch, turning to lean his elbows on the bar.

"They know I'm right, son. They have decisions to make on their own now."

"I know,...but they won't quit!...This is the only life they've known for ten years now,...they'd never hold down a job for wages!"

"Every man has a destiny to face, Mitch,...and only he can face it Besidess,...getting right down to it,...we'd all be better off dead!"

"Now, why would you say that?"

"We have wronged a lot of people, son, good, innocent people.... There is just no forgiveness for that!" He sighed heavily then, and shaking his head, looked over at Mitch. "I am sorry, son,...I'm just running off at the mouth. Pay it no attention."

"You ain't plannin' on shootin' youtself, or somethin', are ya?"

Cantrell laughed at that. "I do not have the nerve to end it like that!... Besides,...that's one sin that would never be forgiven!...Don't worry about that!"

"Well, you're startin' to worry me some, now!"

"I'm not trying to, Mitch." He sighed. "I'm just tired,...I'll be all right once we're on our way to Mexico."

*   *   *

"What is it, Corporal?" Queried Captain Ford as he looked up from his paperwork.

"A Town Marshal, from that town up ahead,...he's here, Sir,...he's asking to see you."

"Thank you, Corporal." He got up and bent slightly to walk out of the tent. "That will be all, Corporal." He saluted, and after the soldier left, turned to nod at Stockwell.

"What can I do for you, Marshal?"

"Nothing real important, Captain." He returned, shaking Ford's outstretched hand. "I'd just like to know a little more about this Cantrell bunch,...I don't much like surprises."

"Neither do I, Sir,...what would you like to know?"

"Exactly where did you lose his trail,...and when?"

"Well,...we chased them across the border just North of Shreveport Landing, and gave chase into Texas, but they turned North on us....We chased them for another full day until they," He sighed heavily then. "They went into some of the worst Bog we've ever seen,...seemed to stretch for miles!...That's where we lost them completely,...we tried to follow them, but had to retreat out of there."

"In town, you said you found th' trail again?"

"Yes, we did,...there was a Caddo Indian village near by, they steered us around the swamp,...but by the time we found their trail again, it started to rain,...hard!...We lost them for good then, and had to return to Shreveport. That was two weeks ago, now,...almost three. So,...on my initiative, I decided to push further West a ways in hopes of finding them again,...we didn't!"

"You said you chased them across Arkansas?

"Yes, sir, across southern Kentucky, western Tennessee, and eastern Arkansas....We engaged them six weeks ago in Tennessee, killing ten of his men!" He cleared his throat then. "I lost four good men that day,... kids, all of them!...Anyway, we got close again in Arkansas,...but he outsmarted me again." He sighed then and shook his head as he scanned the semi-empty roadway.

"I have not been this frustrated since the war finally ended....And so now, we're going home! Texas will have to deal with Mister Cantrell,... and he is one wily Son of a Bitch!"

"I guess that about answers my question!" He said woefully.

"Marshal,...if William Clark Quantrill was not dead, I would think we were after him!...That should tell you how bad this Bastard is!"

"I guess it should, Captain, but it don't! All I know about Quantrill is what I read, or heard about from others!"

"Well, a worse bunch of murderers never lived!"

"Thanks,...that's refreshing to know!...The wire said he was of Mormon faith,...is that right?"

"A Mormon Minister, to be exact….He went crazy!...Word from Utah is, he murdered his own family, four wives and seven children,… then went on to kill seven or eight Church Elders before leaving the State. Jarvis Cantrell is a mad killer, Marshal, and that's a complete turnaround from a strict Bible-pusher!"

"I do believe you're right!" Sighed Stockwell. "Well,…I do thank you, Captain."

"May I ask what your plans are, Marshal?"

"You mean besides just closin' up and goin' fishin?" He grinned. "I don't know,…I have a total of ten men lined up, and that includes Sheriff's deputies, and those of the state Militia!...We're all still under-staffed, and will be till th' city can afford th' wages again….I could still get some help from the cowboys at th' local ranches, but that's a toss-up, too."

"I do understand, Sir." Nodded the Captain. "But all I can do is wish you good luck,…and maybe ask you about that connecting road over there,…what's down that way?"

"Not a lot, anymore! There's a small Tradin' Post at Shockey's Prairie, east of th' road, about ten miles out,…and there's Jonesboro on th' banks of Red River, but nobody lives there anymore. Jonesboro was a shipping point for this part of Texas at one time, a River Port,… and it was wide open and wild as hell, too! I used to spend most every weekend there keepin' th' peace….Ain't nothin' but a ghost town now, though,…steamers don't come down th' river much anymore, and if they do, they go on to dock at Fort Towson."

"And no one lives there?"

"There's nothing there to live in, just rotting warehouses, and empty saloons. There is an old Choctaw Indian and his wife livin' up-stream a ways in a stilt-house….But there's nothin' else there."

"Forgive my ignorance, Marshal,…but exactly what is a stilt-house?"

"A house built on posts stickin' out a th' water,…we call 'em stilt-houses."

"I see,…so, you are saying that that road dead ends there at the river?"

"It does now, yes, sir!...Used to be a Ferry there, but I heard it now rests on th' bottom of th' river!...Right down to it, I guess th' railroad's to blame for it all."

"Thank you, Marshal....Now, tell me this,...could that be a place where Cantrell might hold up?"

Stockwell thought for a minute before shaking his head. "Yes, sir, I guess it could be,...but I doubt it, it's too dangerous!...Doctor Lovejoy treated a man early this year, th' man with 'im said they fell through th' rotten flooring. Anyway, if Cantrell's not from around these parts, he wouldn't know it was there,...unless he just lucked out!"

"Well, you are probably right,...he is definitely not from these parts!...Don't know about the rest of them."

"You're welcome to check it out, Captain,...I'd even go with you, if you like?"

"As much as I want to get this bunch, I would sure like to, Marshal.... But we have been ordered home. We leave at daybreak."

"Then good luck, Captain."

"I hope, good luck for you, too, Marshal."

"Have you warned Clarksville, and Blossom Prairie, sir?'

"Yes, we have!...Good day, Marshal." He touched his hat in salute and abruptly reentered his tent.

"Yeah,...good day to you, too!" Said Stockwell in his wake,... and shaking his head, he turned and walked back through the camp, accepted his horse's reins from the Private, mounted and galloped back toward town.

He was more worried now than when he received the wire, and he thought about that as he settled the horse into an easy gait on the rutted and dusty thoroughfare. No, he thought, he wasn't worried,...he was scared to death!...If that bunch came to Paris, ten men would never stop them!...Innocent people would die,...no, they'd be slaughtered! He should have asked the Captain how many men Cantrell had,...at least he would know how much of a chance they had at stopping them?

However, there was still a chance they wouldn't show up at all,... and being on the run just might by-pass a town the size of Paris, anyway. They could, in fact, already be well West of the city. After all, a gang of men could travel a long way in the space of two weeks.

Sighing, he reached up to settle his hat firmly on his head then stared gloomily at the random houses as he passed,…and as he watched kids playing in the yards, Mothers hoeing in their gardens, or hanging clothes to dry, he could almost picture the devastation a gang of renegades might leave behind them, and the effect it would have on a sleeping community. He could already feel the fear as he remembered the stories he had heard about Quantrill raids on places like Lawrence, Kansas during the war years. He did not want something like that happening in Paris. He felt that the residents of Paris, and County should know what might be coming,…but like John Rucker had said, creating a panic without knowing for sure, might be even more dangerous.

Residential houses, with their white-washed picket fences became much more numerous the closer to town, and most of the shops, and small manufacturing businesses were open and doing business as usual. As he saw all this, he wished, fleetingly that Marshal Taylor was here,… and especially Billy Upshur!…The dusty road was becoming busy with traffic now,…and cursing his obvious weakness, angrily reined the horse around a loaded freight wagon, thinking woefully that Marshal Taylor wasn't here, he was! It was his job now, nobody else's!…Sighing heavily, and somewhat dejectedly, he slowed the horse to a walk as he neared the middle of town, and maneuvered the animal through the pedestrians on the square as he headed back toward his office.

CHAPTER SEVEN

August 14,...The room was a din of noise as men were all trying to talk at once, chairs were constantly scraping on the hardwood floor,... and as was always the case, the Council room was filled with tobacco smoke, bearable only because of the open windows. The Councilmen were discussing the news and proposals among themselves, and the pros and cons, as usual, were rampant.

At last, Horace Bratcher called for silence with a couple well-placed raps of his gavel on the round block of hardwood, and once everyone was back in their seats, and the noise level had subsided, he once again looked out at Judge Bonner.

"J.C....coming from you, and the Marshal there, as well as the fact that the Army was here, we have no doubt that the threat is real, or that the wire is legitimate,...and do not take this the wrong way because personally, I believe the both of you. But there are some here that think this sort of thing to be unheard of in the post-war!" He sighed then, and leaned forward to search the faces of the other councilmen before looking back at them.

"I am not of that opinion, however,...because, quite frankly,...I believed the same thing back in sixty-nine!" He clasped his hands together atop the table. "I didn't think my bank would be robbed, or that William Upshur's son would be kidnapped, but it was, and he was!...And I, for one wish William Upshur was still here, especially now,...and that does not intend any disrespect to you, Marshal, believe me. You are an able bodied lawman. But a gunman, you are not!...

Anyway, I am only the chairman here, and not the majority!" He paused then to let what he had said sink in.

"Okay,...the request for additional deputies is granted, Marshal,... for you, also, Sheriff Gose,...but not to exceed two men each. I'm sorry,...the city budget can not over extend it's self at this point!... Now,...as for sounding the public alarm about this possible threat, without knowing for sure it will happen,...well, I have to agree with the Mayor, it would only insure a panic, and in all probability, a needless one!

"We are still in the throes of a Depression here, the people of Paris have been in a panic for nearly four years,...they have been devastated beyond endurance, and right now, they are breathing the air of recovery for the first time. They are relishing the freedom from fear finally!... They're spending, and earning money once again!"

"Oh, stop blowing your hot air, Horace!" Interrupted Bonner. "We all know that, and we are all relieved, too!...But that does not relieve the possibility of a raid on out relieved city. I think you underestimate the people of Paris!...If they are forewarned, they will be forearmed, and ready for it,...and if they are forewarned, we can defend against such an attack!...A hand full of lawmen can not do it alone!"

"I'm sorry, J.C., but the answer is no!...You will have to make do with the extra deputies,...and that is a unanimous decision!"

"All right, Horace," Sighed Bonner. "I won't recommend the Marshal inform the public,...not right now! But, if you are wrong, and we are raided, I've a feeling you'll all pay for this mistake!" He looked at Stockwell and Gose then. "Let's go, Gentlemen." They got up then and started to leave, as did the other people in the room.

"One more thing!" Said Bratcher, again rapping his gavel, and stopping everyone. "I must warn all of you, especially those of you who are just here to observe....We hold these open meetings for your benefit, as it gives you all a say in how our fair city is governed,...but if you want these meetings to remain open, you will not speak of this when you leave here today. A panic at this stage of our recovery would be turmoil!...Thank you all!"

Bonner ushered them out in the midst of recurring noise and frustration. "Well," He sighed, once they were out on the boardwalk. "Gentlemen, I can feel for you at this point,...but I can not legally advise you, because frankly,…I don't know how!…Good luck, just,… just do what you have to do at this point….Good day!" He quickly turned and descended the steps then walked back across the square toward his office.

"That's that, I guess!" Sighed Gose as they watched him, and then stepped aside to make room for several others to go down into the square. "You really think Cantrell's on his way here, Jim,…it does seem a little far-fetched?…And don't get me wrong, they didn't convince me of anything in there, I'm as worried as you are!"

"Hell, I don't know, John." He sighed then, too. "I want a think this bunch is already a hundred miles somewhere away from us,…it's been three weeks since the cavalry lost them!…But, I don't know?…I'll tell ya one thing, though, this ain't doin' my ulcers any good!"

"Well, if it's any consolation, I think they're gone, too!…I also think we can't take the chance, speculation never won a war! If they are hid out around here somewhere,…once they find out that cavalry is gone, they just might hit us!…There's still a military out-post at Greenville, I think,…maybe we should send a wire to them?"

"If they're still there, they already know, and are prob'ly out lookin' for 'em already.…Where could a gang of men, that large, hide, John?… The only place I can think of, would be,…" He looked at Gose with open mouth.

"Jonesboro!" Blurted Gose. "I'd forgotten about that!"

"God damn it, John, I convinced the Army they couldn't be there!" He gasped, becoming quite fidgety as he scanned the busy square. "I thought that, and I believed it, John,…what was I thinking?"

"Maybe you didn't want 'em to be there, Jim….hell, I don't either!… You think that Cavalry is too far away to catch?"

"Yeah, I do. That Captain Ford said they was leavin' at daybreak,… they'd be six or eight hours away by now."

"We could still send a rider?"

"We'd be a man short then,…and we might need every man we've got! We can't take th' men we got, and run off half-cocked to Jonesboro, neither!" He sighed. "If they're there, they'd cut us to pieces."

"Then what do you suggest?"

"Beats hell out a me!...Keep spotters out there, I guess,...then hope they can get here in time to warn us!...I've got Glenn out where that Cavalry camped right now, he's hid in th' trees there."

"Then I'm gonna station another man out on th' Goodland Road." Said Gose. "They could by-pass us on the North, and go to Indian Territory."

"That's hoping for a little much!" Sighed Stockwell. "But that's a good idea,...and I guess we could send a man, or two to Jonesboro, you know, to sneak in and take a look around,...we'd know for sure, that way?"

"If they're caught, we're a man or two short of what we've got!... That's a bad idea!" Gose sighed again as he watched the crowded square. "That Council was wrong, Jim, look out there. Half the men in town are wearin' guns, and they'd use 'em, too, if it came down to it....I think we ought a tell 'em what's going on, all of 'em!...You can't raid a town, if the town's waitin' on you,...not, and get away with it!"

"I'm on your side, John,...but we both know we can't do that, not without th' Mayor's consent, at least!...We'd be out of work when it's over."

"We might be alive, too!" Returned Gose. "Okay, Jim,...this is your call, you're Town Marshal,...give us a working plan, man."

"Yeah, thanks,...okay, I will!...Starting tonight, we'll have four men patrolling th' square on foot, maybe hide themselves in the sunken doorways along the boardwalks. If Cantrell hits us, it'll likely be at night, and it will start right here on the square, that's where th' bank is!...They're on th' run, so they'll try and blow th' safe quick, grab the money and run!...If they do any burning, or killing, it'll be as they're leaving. But I don't think they'll even bother with that!" He looked at Gose then and shrugged. "That's what I'd do!"

"I like it!" Nodded Gose. "It's a good plan. But to do it, we'll need to pull our men in from the outposts."

"You're right. Okay, if you will, John, send one of your deputies out to bring 'em in!...I'm gonna go rehire a couple of my old deputies. I'll see you, and your deputies in front of my office at dusk,...tell Rucker, will ya?"

*   *   *

Sheriff Gose and his five Deputies, as well as John Rucker and his Militia, were all on the long boardwalk of the Lower Courthouse when Stockwell, and his three deputies came out and after greetings had been established, the Marshal cleared his throat.

"Most of you know Clem here, and Rufe,…they'll be stationed on the square tonight, along with two of Sheriff Gose's deputies, one man on each side of the square. Each one of them will be responsible for his, as well as that part of the square across from him. What I mean is, if Rufe here is on the south side of the square, and he is hidden in a sunken doorway there, he'll be able to see the north side of the square, and the four streets coming in. Th' man on the east side will watch the west side, north can watch the south, and so on. That way, every street into the square is covered, and that man will not have to show his self to see it!…You can each decide what side you want, grab you a crate, keg, or somethin' to sit on, and don't make yourself visible."

"I hope I didn't confuse any of you,…but should this bunch ride in, be sure it is them before you open fire. The rest of us will be in our office asleep, all of us!…We'll hear the shot and come running, and men,…if it happens, stay under cover, don't get careless!"

"How'll we know it's them, Boss?"

"Who else will be ridin' into town at night with thirty men?… Besides, they'll go to th' bank, and they'll prob'ly fan out to watch th' square!…You'll know.…Now if you fire on them, that'll be our signal, and gents,…if you do fire that gun, take one of 'em down with that shot, all of ya,…it'll be that many less, we'll have to fight."

"We keep this up, for how long, Marshal?" This came from one of Gose's deputies.

"Nobody knows, Casey,…maybe a week, maybe more. Now listen, all of you,…we don't know that they'll hit us at all,…this is just a precaution! This damn Depression has put us in th' poor-house, the whole town,…but what little we got left, we damn sure want a keep, and most of it's in that bank down there!…Like I said, they might not hit us at all, but it's better safe, than sorry!…Any more questions?" And when they shook their heads.

"Okay,…be on the square by six o'clock,…you'll walk a beat until every store has closed for the night, all, that is, but th' saloons,…we can't force them to close early, because that would be warning th' public!…

And we have been ordered not to do that. We will be doing this every night, till one of us tells you different!...And good luck, all of ya."

*   *   *

August, 15,...Peter Birdsong returned with four of his Light-horsemen, having left on the eleventh again to visit Fort Towson, and they were met at the hitch-rail by Billy and Rodney as they dismounted.

"Anything going on out there, Peter?" Queried Rodney as the policemen filed past them into the office.

"All is quiet, my friend....On my way, I saw thirteen horses at the hitch-rails in Wheelock,...and more horses at three of the houses there, where no one stayed before."

"Yeah, they was empty when I was there, too." Sighed the lawman. "What do you think, could it be them?"

"I do not know,...But I counted nineteen horses in all." Shrugged the tracker.

"Were you seen?"

"No, my friend,...I did not pass on the street as I went to the Fort. But once there, I found Sergeant Neville, and I told him of this. He also knows of this Jarvis Cantrell....He will see about it, I think."

"Then, we should let the Army handle it!" Sighed Rodney, and glanced at Billy. "Don't you?"

"That's not for me to say, Rod." He shrugged. "But Neville's a good man, I'm sure he'll check it out!"

"I have Light-horsemen watching the roads." Continued Peter. "One is watching Wheelock....If this is Mister Cantrell, he does not have so many men, I think....We will be ready if he comes here!"

"Of that, I'm sure!" Nodded Rodney. "But none a this is feeling right to me. Cantrell may, or may not be in Wheelock,...but if he is, I can't let you face 'im alone." He looked up at Billy then.

"I'd like you to take Lisa and Cindy and go on to Paris,...I'll hang out here for a few days. If Cantrell does show up, it's better they're not here anyway."

"I can't argue that one, Rod,...but I don't like the idea of you stayin' here alone, neither, you've never gone up against a bunch like this before, neither one of you!"

"We won't be alone, Billy, we'll be together. Between the both of us, we'll handle it!"

"We'll leave in the mornin'" He nodded.

"I do not think he will come here!" Argued Peter.

"Neither do I!" Said Billy. "But it's th' Marshal's call."

"It's not worth the gamble, Billy. It's my job to keep the peace here, Peter's, too!...So get my wife and baby out a here, okay,...I'll be along in a few days?"

"We leave at daybreak, then....But you're gonna have to tell Lisa,... she might bean me."

"She's gonna bean me, for sure!" He grinned.

*   *   *

Jarvis Cantrell slowly used the rope to pull himself along the rocky bottom of the fast-moving river, and the current was so strong that it forced him to work hand over hand on the rope, as Mitch did the same from shore, to walk his way up out of the water's swirling current.

"Good, Lord, Mitch!" He panted, finally pulling himself onto the rocky embankment to sit for a minute. "Current's faster here, than in the Colorado, I believe, could barely stand up at all out there!"

"Well, are ya clean?" Grinned Mitch.

"Clean as I'm going to get without soap, clothes, too, I think!" He untied the rope from his waist and gave it to Mitch. "Your turn, son!"

"I'm ready!" He grinned, tying the wet rope around his own middle. "I am some rank, too!" He sat down and pulled off his boots, while Cantrell pulled his on and got up to grab the rope.

"Take your time, boy!" He yelled as Mitch tenderly walked the rocky gravel into the swift water, and once the short length of rope was played out, he released it, allowing the thick support post to hold it taut.

Sighing, he sat down on the rocks and shivered in the gusting southern breeze as he studied the opposite shore and wondered how much longer their luck would hold out? Sooner, or later someone was going to spot them, or become suspicious enough to investigate the smoke in the air, he thought, looking back toward the row of warehouses. But so far the wind has taken care of that for them,...and it was strong, for an August!...The only other person that might actually know they were here, or even care that they were here, was the old Choctaw Indian and his wife in, what Mitch called, a stilt house,…and he did not think they presented any danger to them.…But if the Army should talk with them?

It was those in the shacks across the river that worried him the most. The Army patrols could talk to them next time, because at least one, if not all of them knew they were here, and if asked, would surely inform the Army of their presence. He sighed then,…as it was, they were definitely not trying to keep it a secret, openly fishing off the pier, bathing in the river,…hell, they deserved to be seen!…Were they just lucky, or didn't anyone care? Maybe they were like most folks, he thought,…if it was none of their business, ignore it, it would eventually go away! Or maybe they were just waiting until they were asked?

He knew that both scenarios were applied. He also knew the Indian didn't trust the white man, or the Army. But, given that, he also knew it would be questionable they would be safe here for another fifteen days. But he knew the Army well enough to know they would not be much of a hindrance by then,…and they, so far, had been a relentless adversary.

What was he to do in Mexico, he wondered,…if they were lucky enough to get there? Mitch was right, they would need money there like anywhere else, and there was no time to get it legally. He sighed then, it wouldn't be enough anyway, working for a dollar a day, and found, wouldn't buy beans!…They would have no choice, but to steal what they needed and here lately, he was finding himself not wanting to do that any longer. But it appeared he would have no choice now, he had lived with hatred for too long, and to the point that he wondered why,…what purpose did it ultimately serve?

It all has to stop somewhere, he thought sadly,…he couldn't sleep anymore, for seeing the men, women and children he had taken part in killing,…the towns he had burned, and for what?…For this, he thought, looking around him again. He had nothing to show for his union with the Devil, nothing but regret,…and sadness,…and it was too late to return to God,…and that's what he now wanted!…It was all too late!

He was jerked from his thoughts then when Mitch yelled at him, and he got to his feet to help pull him from the water.

"Man alive!" Gasped Mitch as he scaled the incline. "I wouldn't want a jump in there with my pecker hangin' out, Jarvis!" He laughed, pulling himself onto the shore enough to sit down. "I must a been nudged a dozen times by some big-ass fish, man!...I even touched one of 'em, sucker had to be five feet long!" He untied the rope and then tugged on his boots. "Shit it's cold, Jarvis, I'm freezing my ass off,...let's get in front a that fire, man!"

"Sounds good to me, son." He laughed. "I'm a mite too old for this sort a thing!...liable to catch my death of pneumonia!"

"Come on Jarvis!" He laughed, getting to his feet to slide his gun belt over his arm onto his shoulder. "You're too damn crusty to die,... hell, you have been wet, in a cold wind a hundred times!"

Cantrell looped his own belted weapon over his shoulder and together, they climbed back up to the sagging platform and walked briskly back to the old saloon at the far end of the row of warehouses and went inside.

"What happened to you?" Laughed Silk as they hurriedly walked across the creaking floor toward them. "You fall in th' river?"

"Jumped in!" Said Cantrell with a noticeable chatter as they made their way in front of the fire. "Something the rest of you need to do, by the way!...You stink to high heaven!" He sat down on the floor beside Mitch and worked his boots off then both got up and stripped down to their unions, draping pants and shirts over the saddles on the floor to dry.

"Well?" queried Cantrell as he backed up to the fire's heat and stared at them. "How about it, Gents, just walk down there and jump in, the rope is already there!"

"Rope?" Questioned Morgan White from his seat on the floor. "What's that for?"

"You want a drown, don't use it!" Laughed Mitch. "But, you'll never swim out without it!"

"Go two at a time." Added Cantrell. "Tie the rope around your waist and walk out into the current,...the man on shore can help you in, and out when you're done,...and keep your eyes open!...Now, go on, if you're going....Silk, you and Morgan go first,...and do not take your clothes off, they smell as bad as you do!"

"Yeah!" Laughed Mitch again. "Keep your pecker in your pants, too,…them big-ass cats might take it for a worm!"

"Kiss my ass, Mitch," Growled Silk, and then looked across at Morgan as he got to his feet. "Come on, Morg!...My ass is chafed anyway, don't know about your'en."

Morgan White got to his feet. "We stay in this dump much longer, I'm gonna be chapped all over!" He huffed, and then followed Silk across the groaning floor."

"Say, Boss,…you really gonna break us up,…or was you funnin'?"

"That I am, Dutch!" Sighed Cantrell. "In fifteen days, you'll be on your own, all of you….Times are changing, boys,…too many lawmen after us now."

"I ain't been a cowhand in so long, I forgot how."

"Once you've done it, you don't forget, Milton,…it's the same with all of us, it'll come back to you….But, I'm not telling you to punch cows for a living,…keep doing what you're used to, if you want. I'm just saying, it won't be with me!...I am done, boys, I'm tired of it all!"

"They're gonna hang us anyway, Boss,…a few of us got our mugs on wanted posters already!"

"We all have our burdens to carry, Curley."

"Come on, Curley, think about it!" Sighed Mitch. "How's th' law gonna know who you are?...One or two men on horseback don't draw much suspicion,…you'll be just another out of work drifter, in a country full of 'em….They won't hang you for that,…'specially if you don't give 'em your real names?"

"Won't have to tell 'em who I am!" Argued Curley. "With a face like mine, it'll be easy!...Appears to me, our best bet would be to stay together!...Like you always said, Boss,…there's safety in numbers."

"That was true, once, Curley." Sighed Cantrell. "But, not anymore, they'll be looking for twenty men, not two riding alone!...Besides, it's not up for discussion!"

"Well, it ought a be, Boss, that's all I can say!...This just don't seem right!"

"As long as you don't mention my name, you'll be okay, Curley!"

"You and me can ride together, Curley!" Said Billy Jack suddenly. "I got friends in New Mexico."

"Sounds like a plan to me." Nodded Cantrell. "You and Billy Jack will do okay."

"Where you goin', Boss, you don't mind me askin'?"

"Me and Mitch are going to Mexico as planned, Curley,…and so can the rest of you, if you want,…just not with us. Once we disband, I never want to see you again, any of you!…I will not be the cause of your demise!…I have watched enough of you die, as it is."

"We can't go far without money!"

"You're right about that, Windy,…but that will be up to you as well."

"Well, what about that loot, we buried in Arkansas, Boss,…we can't just leave it there for somebody else to find?"

"Yeah,…that's right!" Voiced Billy Jack excitedly. "It belongs to us, let's go get it!…What do you say, men?"

"Billy Jack," Sighed Cantrell. "I do not want to know what you do, once we disband!…If you want to go back for that money, you have my blessing,…but I will not!"

"You mean, we can have it all?"

"You can have every dollar of it, Boomer!…As for me, the risk is too great,…it will be risky enough just to get to Mexico."

"And you might not even find it!" Broke in Mitch. "It was dark when we buried it."

"We'll find it," Voiced Billy Jack. "I memorized ever rock and tree in that clearin'!"

"And you made a map, Boss, I remember!" Added Dutch.

"Yes I did, and you are welcome to it, Dutch. I'll get it for you directly."

"You're okay, Boss, thanks!"

"That may be, Dutch," He sighed. "And I thank you. But you'd best remember something, all of you!…We buried that gold under duress,… that Cavalry would have caught us for sure, otherwise,…and they may have already found it!…In fact, I'm pretty sure they did."

"Well, I'm gonna go see!" Voiced Billy Jack. "The rest of you with me?" That was followed by a unanimous vote of approval.

"Then I wish you all good luck!" Nodded Cantrell. "But I still suggest you wait here until the end of the month."

"That was a shit-pot full a gold, Jarvis." Said Mitch as they both turned to face the fireplace. "You sure you want a give up that map?"

"You having second thoughts about Mexico, Son?"

"No, sir, nothin' like that!...But a share of that could set us up real good down there."

"Yes it could!...But we both knew that money would be found when we buried it, Mitch!...And we knew we couldn't go back for it,... these men knew it, too!...Chances are, there'll be men waiting there, expecting us to come back for it!...Uh-uh,...a good tracker will know we stopped in that clearing, and he will also find the stash,...already has! Isn't that why we buried it, Son,...to gain the time to get away?"

"I can't argue with logic like that!" Sighed Mitch. "But it is a shame."

"That, it is, now forget about it, son."

"Already have!...You really think th' Army'll quit lookin' for us at th' end of th' month,...close as they was, I can't see 'em givin' up like that?"

"I'm betting everything on it, Mitch." He grinned at the younger man then. "Not only that,...but, by the end of the month, everyone else will believe we are long gone from this part of the country. They will stop looking for us, altogether!"

CHAPTER EIGHT

August 16,...After the hoopla, of blowing out the candle atop the whipped icing on Willy's birthday cake, the night before, they were up well before dawn. Billy and Rodney helped the women and children into the wagon and passed the supplies to Willy over the tailgate. When they were done, and the girls had placed kids and supplies comfortably for travel, he motioned the Marshal aside.

"What's your plan here, Rod,...I know you got one?"

Sighing, Rodney looked up at the twinkling, early morning sky. "Peter and me are going to Wheelock, Billy." He looked back at him then. "If Cantrell is there, I want to know it!...Besides, if he is, it's better to fight him there, than here, anyway,...but don't tell Lisa, she's already upset enough!"

"Why not let th' Army handle Wheelock, Neville's an able man?"

"I hope he has already, and if he has,...or Cantrell's not there, I'll come on to Paris from there!...At any rate, I want a talk to the Commandant at th' Fort for the latest news about it, maybe Neville, too!...Anyway, that's my plan....We're gonna ride along with you to th' Wheelock Road." He turned then to watch the dark shapes of saddled horses coming out of the darkness, and the slim figure leading them.

"What did you tell Lisa?"

"That we're goin' on patrol,...she knows we're going with you that far."

"Good." He went to meet Peter then, taking the Roan's reins from him and coming back to secure the mare's reins to the tailgate on the wagon.

"I guess we're ready, Rod." He went and immediately climbed up to the tall seat, slapped the lines against the mules' backs,...and with a creaking lurch, the wagon twisted and swayed on the uneven grade until they were on the road and at that point, Rodney and his Deputy galloped their horses around the wagon to take the lead before slowing to a walk on the well-packed new surface. Willy chose that moment to crawl over the seat beside him, and they settled down for their long, hot ride to Paris.

"Everything okay in th' wagon, Birthday Boy?"

"Everybody's asleep."

"That's where you ought a be!"

"I ain't sleepy!"

"Them rifles where th' young'uns can't get to 'em?"

"They're under the seat, Daddy, mama covered 'em up!...I thought Uncle Rodney, and Uncle Peter were staying here, daddy, where they goin'?"

"They're just ridin' with us a ways, they'll be goin' back,...you sure you don't want to crawl back there and go to sleep?"

"Uh-uh,...I want a watch the sky!"

"In that case, think you can keep these jug-heads in th' road while I roll a smoke?"

"I know I can!"

Grinning, he passed him the reins and reached Durham sack and papers from his shirt, rolled and licked the thin cigarette in the light from the moon before turning, and leaning partially into the dark of the wagon to hide the flare of the match,...and then lit up before turning around again.

"What did you do that for, Daddy?...Never mind, I know,...some outlaw could a seen it, right?"

"Don't want a make 'em a target, do we?"

"No, Sir!...But they can't outdraw you anyway, can they, daddy?"

"I sure hope not,...you still watchin' th' stars?"

"A little, I'm afraid to look up, these dumb mules might go off the road."

"Want me to take 'em?"

"Uh-uh, I want a drive for a while,...can I?"

"Go ahead, but keep 'em at a walk."

"I will."

Grinning, he propped a foot up on the headboard and relaxed against the seat-back as he studied the dark outline of his oldest son's face, and at the same time remembering the stormy night at the café, when Rodney and Connie told him he had a son. He had almost broke down and cried on the spot, too surprised and happy to contain himself. He had thought he would never see her again, before that night, and to think he had almost decided not to come home at all, for fear his reputation would disappoint Doc and Mattie too much. But he had, and his life had changed afterward, in fact, he thought, if not for the tragedy with Ben Lang, and the fact that Lang had ordered his folks killed, his life would have been perfect. It was anyway, he knew, because he was never happier, or more proud of his family than he was right now as he watched his son drive the wagon.

He had really grown up strong, he thought, despite the turmoil in his young life,…and his youngest was going to be just like him, he thought, tall and strong! Christopher would be some darker of skin, though, probably due to his Spanish heritage, whereas Willy had taken his complexion from him. And Angel, he smiled widely then,… she would be an olive-skinned beauty, just like her mother. Yes, he thought, the happiness he was feeling now, more than made up for the unhappiness he used to feel at being a gunfighter with an unwanted reputation! Because he had realized something when Willy was taken from them,…sometimes a man has to kill to protect his own, and he was just blessed with the ability to do it. He had slowly become thankful for that as well,…even the men he had killed had deserved to die, because they were trying to kill him, or somebody he loved. That didn't make it right, he knew, but it eased a hurting conscience.

He held his hat over his face to cover the cigarette and drew smoke into his lungs before mashing out the butt on the seat between them, and blowing the smoke skyward, he donned the hat to watch the brilliant display of light atop the Winding-stair Mountain as the sun began to come up,…and the treetops appeared a dazzling shade of lime and aqua greens from where they were on the road. He watched the mule's bobbing heads for a minute, then the backs of Rodney and Peter a few yards ahead of them, noticing how small Peter actually looked on the back of the big, black horse, and though, Rodney's horse was smaller in stature, him and the tracker appeared the same height when looking at them. He shook his head and grinned. They were the two best people in the world, he thought, and damn good lawmen, both of them!

He thought then of their ordeal with catching Maxwell Loughmiller, and how the tracker had suffered with his disappointment of not being able to track him. But then again, Loughmiller had led them all on a damn good chase! He smiled then, and for the next hour, settled down on the hard, wooden seat and thought of his family trip to Denver the first time, and between that, and keeping a watchful eye on Willy's driving, he was able to relive every gut-wrenching hour of that misadventure.

He was still quite deep in thought as they crossed the bridge and entered the waving grass of the prairie, and he absently looked out over the wide stretch of battlefield, and remembered the night of the battle with Treasure hunters. More like a massacre, he thought sadly, thinking the men had no idea why they were dying. That was a dark spot on his memory, something he was not proud of,…but at the time, knew that it was necessary to save a way of life. But the downside of it was that it didn't save a way of life at all, because White Buffalo left anyway!

He had often asked himself since then, if he would have done what they did, had he known they were going to leave? He still had no answer for that one, he thought, then sighed and turned his attention back to the road ahead of them. They were just coming into the outer fringes of the wilderness, and it was quite light on the road now, with the sun showing it's self over the towering pines atop the hills,…and it's heat was already being felt by the time they entered the cool shade of the trees spreading over the road. He was so busy relaxing, that when the sudden, shrill whooping screams shattered the stillness, he was almost thrown from the wagon's tall seat when the team suddenly brayed in fear, rearing and jerking the wagon toward the trees alongside the road.

Billy caught a fleeting glimpse of Rodney and Peter as he fought to right himself enough to grab the reins from Willy and stop the terrified mules. Getting their mounts under control, the lawmen rode back to the wagon with drawn guns as Billy urged the team back out of the ditch and onto the road again.

"Billy!" Screamed Connie, as her head and shoulders suddenly appeared over the seatback, only to be pushed aside to make room for Melissa beside her. "What in God's name was that?"

He stopped the animals and set the parking break before answering. "I think that was probably our furry friend!" He sighed, looking back toward the trees.

"It was the Shampe!" Grinned Peter and put away his pistol.

"Rodney, are you all right?" Gasped Melissa.

"Aside from almost wetting my pants, yeah!" He groaned, also holstering his gun. "Otherwise, I'm just, happy as a lark!...Old Sasquatch came calling, that's all!"

"Well, we could have done without it!" Breathed Connie as she stared at the dark beneath the trees.

"You okay, Billy?" Grinned Rodney. "You look like you just seen a ghost, you and Willy both."

"That thing unnerved me real good that time, Rod, my mind was on everything else, but that!" He put his arm around Willy then. "You okay?"

"Yeah, I'm okay, daddy!...That wasn't near as scary as that big Rex thing was!"

"He's right about that!" Nodded Rodney. "I'd about forgot that!"

"Well, I remember it!" Gasped Connie. "And they both scared me to death!"

"God, me, too!" Breathed Melissa as she looked into the wagon. "Didn't bother the babies, though, they're still sound asleep!"

"Well, it's gone now." Grinned Billy. "Lead off, fellas." He waited until they were once again a dozen yards ahead before clucking the mules into motion. "You gals roll up that tarp if you get hot, let some air in back there."

"Do you think the Sasquatch will come back, Daddy?" Queried Willy as he peered at the trees. "I sure wish I could see 'im."

"Beats me, son....But I got a feelin', if a man got too close to that thing, he could get hurt!"

"You think it's the same one that comes to see us?"

"Could be, I guess,...unless there's more than one of 'em."

"I'll bet there's a whole bunch of 'em, a whole town maybe!"

"I don't think I'd go that far,…three or four, maybe,…at least around here."

"I still wish I could see 'im!…I bet it wouldn't hurt me, neither!"

"I'd just as soon not take th' chance, son….But you might see it someday, who knows. Right now, though,…you ought a put your hat on, if you're gonna stay up here."

*   *   *

It was late in the day by the time they made it to the Wheelock road, and at the women's request decided to camp for the night and so, urged the team across the road and up the small embankment, pulling the wagon into a grouping of Pines and stopped. Willy climbed down to help Peter prepare a spot for the fire, and to gather up some wood, while Billy and Rodney helped the women down and brought in the supplies.

The small fire was crackling by the time they were ready to cook, and the men and children sat around the blaze on blankets to talk while the meal was prepared.

"You know,…this really ain't too bad!" Sighed Rodney, lying back against his saddle. "I like camping in the open like this."

"Me, too, Uncle Rodney." Grinned Willy.

"Me, too!" Voiced the other three almost in unison, causing all of them to chuckle.

"Do you think that Shampe followed us, Uncle Peter?" Blurted Willy.

"Who can know, Little Wolf," He grinned, and then waved his arm above his head in a circle. "We are his guests here,…all of this is his home, and we must respect that!"

"Gosh!"

"Well, as long as he don't scream again!" Smiled Connie then continued to slice potatoes into the large skillet of melted lard to fry. "That was so unnerving!"

"I'm not comfortable just thinking it might be out there somewhere!" Added Melissa.

"I do not think the Shampe will harm us." Encouraged Peter. "I have never heard of such a happening."

"Yeah,…but it might throw rocks at us!" Insisted Rodney with a grin.

"Maybe, yes, my friend,...but only if he is afraid, or angry. A brother once told me a rock came out of the trees and almost hit him,...but when he looked, no one was there, only the smell."

Shaking his head, Billy rolled and lit a Durham before blowing smoke upward. "Well, I don't think our furry friend will bother us, if we don't bother him, folks,...so let's us just enjoy ourselves."

"If it wasn't mad at us already, why did it scream at us this morning?"

"Hard to say, Lisa, maybe it was sleepin' there somewhere, and we woke it up!...If it was mad at us, it would a thrown rocks at us."

"Okay," She sighed. "I'll drop the subject. But if that monster hurts me tonight, guess who I'm coming after?" She laughed then and looked at Connie. "He thinks he's fast on the draw!"

"There is no wrath like a woman scorned, sweetheart!" Said Connie with a grin. "You'd best remember that,...all of you!"

"Yeah, so there!" Laughed Melissa. "Consider me scorned!...So you all better be careful."

"You have my personal apology, Madam." Grinned Billy.

"That's better!" She pouted. "Now, you get to eat!"

*   *   *

It was close to dawn when he opened his eyes, and sitting up in his blankets, spotted someone reviving last night's fire,...and putting on the eyeglasses, he recognized the slender tracker and threw the blankets off.

"Good morning, my friend!" Smiled Peter as he squatted to pour water and grounds into the large coffeepot. "Did you sleep well?"

"Good,...you?" He got to his feet, and yawning mightily, retrieved gun and holster and buckled it on. "Don't have to ask, Rod, there." He grinned, tying the holster to his leg and then, still grinning, bent to pick up a dried pinecone and lobbed it at him.

"What th?" Gasped Rodney as he quickly sat up in his blankets. "What is it?"

"Time to rise and shine, Marshal!" He grinned. "Tryin' to sleep your life away?"

"Appears I am!" He yawned and quickly threw the blankets off, and as he did, Billy drew and fired, the gun seeming to appear out of nowhere, and as the large Rattler's striking head exploded from it's body, he weakly sank to his knees in the dead pine needles while the sudden explosion echoed and re-echoed throughout the tree-covered hills,... and then he released the air from his aching lungs.

Rodney had vacated the blankets the instant Billy fired, having seen the deadly serpent in the same instant, and his face was chalky white as he mutely stared down at the wriggling mass of headless death. Both Connie, and Melissa, still screaming, quickly climbed over the wagon's tall sideboards and jumped to the padding of needles, both running toward them in their stocking feet,...and both closely followed by Willy.

"Are you all right, my friend?" Soothed Peter as he squatted beside Billy.

His answer was drowned out, by Connie's screaming as she dropped to her knees beside him. "Billy, what's wrong?" She gasped loudly. "What happened?" She threw her arms around him and began to cry. "Are you hurt, oh, my God!"

"I'm okay," He said loudly. "Just a little weak!" He held her away from him and straightened, and then raising his arm, allowed Peter to help him to his feet.

"What happened, Billy?" Urged Connnie, still hugging his arm against her.

"That is what happened, Mistress Upshur." Said Peter calmly as he pointed at Rodney's blankets.

"Oh, My God!" She gasped, looking quickly at Rodney.

"Rodney!" Screamed Melissa, just realizing it was him that was almost hurt,...and running to his side, wrapped her arms around him and cried.

Billy realized he still held the pistol, and holstered it as Rodney, still quite ashen-faced, guided Melissa over to stand in front of him, his shaking hand extended to grip Billy's with such force that he grimaced in pain.

"Easy, Rod." He grinned. "You okay, man?"

Rodney looked down at himself as he released Billy's hand. "Aside from peeing all over myself, I'm just happy to be alive!...And you know what else,...I ain't a damn bit ashamed of it!...You saved my ass again, old friend, and you did it before I could even blink! Thanks, Billy, you don't know how much."

"Yes, thank you, Billy." Sobbed Melissa, coming on to hug him. "We love you!"

"Come on you two, don't embarrass me, okay?...I'm just lucky I seen th' thing!"

"Lucky, my ass!" Grinned Rodney sheepishly, then glanced at Peter. "Was that what you would call luck, my friend?"

"No, I would not!...I did not see the snake because I was watching Mister Upshur....I was watching his hand, and could not follow it! There is magic in his hand, Marshal, of this, I am sure."

"Do not call it luck, Billy." Sighed Rodney. "Because we all know better! You are the best there is, my friend, and don't ever forget that!... How did you ever see that thing in time, anyway?...All I saw was its head exploding!"

"I don't know, Rod, I thought I saw the blanket move when I threw that pinecone,…you threw off th' blankets before I could warn you. Everything else was pure reflex, so let's just drop it, okay, people?...I'm just lucky, that's all!"

"Yeah, well, thanks anyway,…Lucky." He grinned then. "I'm gonna go change my pants,…HEY!" He yelled, running toward the wagon in time to catch Cindy before she fell over the sideboards.

"God, I forgot about the babies!" Gasped Connie, as Christopher and Angela came on to hug her and Billy. "I'm so sorry, angels, did you hurt yourselves?'

"Heck no, mama, I'm six years old!" Sniffed Christopher as he clung to Billy.

"I've got a splinter, mama!" Sobbed Angela. "Can you get it out, it hurts?"

"We'll get it out later, baby."

"This is one big Rattle Snake, Daddy!" Laughed Willy as he held the body of the large Diamondback above his head, allowing the headless end of it to drag the ground at his feet.

"William!" Shrieked Connie. "Put that thing down this instant!"

"It's dead, mama."

"I don't care, put it down!" She glared at him until he tossed it aside.

"The coffee is ready, my friend." Smiled Peter.

"And I need it!"

"Okay," Sighed Connie. "While you have your coffee, I'll break out the venison and cold biscuits for breakfast. "She and Melissa led Cindy and Angela back toward the wagon.

"Okay, boys." He grinned. "If you're gonna have coffee with me, you better go pee before you go in your pants, too. Go on now, and watch for snakes."

*   *   *

The cold meal, and hot coffee was a meager offering on a chilly mountain morning, but was quite adequate to begin another day's long journey. Billy placed his tin on the ground beside him to roll and light his morning smoke, when he saw Peter stiffen and cock his head to listen,… then suddenly get to his feet.

"Many horses are coming, my friends,…more than ten, I think."

Both Billy, and Rodney got to their feet, and all three walked to the tree-lined embankment overlooking the road, and after stopping long enough to tell the women and kids to move back to the wagon, they squatted down behind the trees there and waited for a glimpse of the riders. Five minutes later, Billy grinned and got to his feet, quickly recognizing Sergeant Neville.

All three of them moved out of the trees to stand on the embankment, and when the Sergeant saw them, he raised his arm to stop the patrol.

"HOOOOO!" Yelled the soldier behind Neville, stopping the troop, while Neville studied them for a minute before dismounting and coming to look up at them.

"Good to see you, Sergeant." Grinned Billy. "Come on up and have a cup."

Nodding, Neville turned to the soldier behind him. "Have the men dismount, Corporal, and then join me." He offered his hand up for Billy to help him up the embankment, where he adjusted his jacket and eyed all three of them.

"Marshal Taylor!" He grinned, reaching to shake Rodney's hand. "Shoulder healed nicely, I see."

"Yes, sir, it did,…nice to see you, Sergeant."

"And Marshal Birdsong." He said and shook Peter's hand before turning back to Billy. "And you are,...Upshur,...is that right?" He grinned, shaking Billy's hand as well.

"Bill Upshur, Sergeant." Grinned Billy. "Come on into camp."

Peter gave the Corporal a hand up the embankment, and all four walked back into the trees together.

"Hello Sergeant." Smiled Connie as she gave him his hot tin cup. "Do sit, won't you?...Just pick yourself a blanket."

"Thank you,...Missus Upshur, Right?" And when she nodded, he smiled at Melissa. "Missus Taylor." He shook her hand before turning to appraise the four children. "You folks going somewhere?...Seems like every time I see you, you're either coming, or going."

"Goin' to Paris for a few days." Said Billy with a grin. "What brings you out this way, Sergeant?"

"Jarvis Cantrell!" He stated, his eyes going to the discarded length of dead Diamondback. "I see you had a guest for breakfast,...we wondered where that shot came from?"

"Damn thing was in my bed this morning!" Said Rodney as he gave the Corporal his coffee. "Uninvited, I might add!"

"No doubt,...they do grow big up here!" He sipped his coffee before looking across at Peter. "Marshal, we checked out Wheelock yesterday, and you were right, there was a bunch of hard-cases there, but none that matched Cantrell's description, all too young. The men there said they never heard of him!...They also told me that six men had left there a couple a days earlier, and they didn't know them neither." He took another swallow of coffee then.

"That's not to say they didn't know them, or Cantrell, you understand,...or that Cantrell was not there someplace hiding from us. I will say this,...if they're here, they didn't cross at Jonesboro, ferry's on the bottom of the river!...I did, however bivouac a dozen men at the Jonesboro, Fort Towson cut-off, and two dozen on patrol farther east. We have also received word that soldiers from Fort McCullough are watching the Goodland crossroads down by Red River."

"Thank you, Sergeant!" Nodded Peter. "I also have men watching Wheelock."

"No thanks necessary, Marshal,...and I think we may have seen your man on our way here."

"If Cantrell ain't up here somewhere." Queried Rodney. "Where do you think he might be?"

"My opinion, Marshal?...What I think don't really count, Sir! But if it did, I'd remind you that the wire we got was two weeks old when we got it, and is now close to a month old. My opinion would be, that Cantrell and his bunch are somewhere in the middle of Texas by now, and on their way to Mexico!...If what I thought counted, mind you."

"We understand fully, Sergeant." Returned Rodney. "And I think you are right!"

"Anyway," Continued Neville. "I'm gonna bivouac eight men right here for a few days just in case,...and you had best keep your eyes open. You got people watching your holdings?"

"We have it covered." Nodded Rodney.

"Good,...then by your leave, we'll hunt for a place to camp."

"Why not right here," Voiced Billy, "We're leavin' anyway, and it's snake free!"

"But, I would still beat the bushes some." Replied Rodney. "Snakes that size, usually come in pairs!"

"I have found that to be a fact!...Well," He sighed. "This will do just fine, I think." He turned to the Corporal then.

"We'll camp the men on this spot, Corporal, make the preparations!"

While they talked, the women, and Willy packed and stowed the supplies back in the wagon, and Willy tied the Roan back in place,... and a short twenty minutes later, Neville watched as Rodney tied his horse to the tailgate with Billy's mare and came back to join them.

"Peter," Grinned Rodney. "If you need to, you can wire me in care of the Marshal's office in Paris. Is there anything else you need before we go?"

"No, my friend, all will be well at the mountain, do not worry."

"Thanks, Peter." They shook hands then watched as he mounted the black and reined him down the embankment and back up the new road at a gallop. "Well, Sergeant," He said, reaching to shake his hand again. "Till we meet again?"

"That's just liable to happen!" Grinned Neville, as he shook both their hands.

"I'm glad you're goin' with us, Rod." Said Billy as they walked to the wagon and climbed up on the seat….Once seated, he picked up the lines and turned for a look into the wagon. "Everybody in and ready?"

"We're ready, honey." Said Connie as she rolled up the sides of the tarp. "Let's go."

He clucked the mules into motion and eased the wagon down into the rutted road again, turned to wave at the Sergeant then continued east toward the Jack Fork,…and after fifteen minutes of nothing but the sound of wind through the towering pines on either side of them, he peered at Rodney.

"What's wrong, Rod?"

"What,…oh, nothing!…I guess I'm still wondering if I shouldn't have stayed here for a few days?"

"No,…you shouldn't!" Voiced Melissa from inside the wagon.

He grinned then. "maybe I'm still shook up over that snake!"

"He was a monster, all right."

"Yeah,…ya know, that makes three snakes you've killed,…and all of 'em were trying to kill me!…What if you ain't around next time?"

"Might not be a next time!…You think that sulfur might really work?"

"Neville swore by it, I don't know!…We don't even know if your idea works,…whoever heard of layin' a rope around the camp?…Some say it does, though. All I do know, is that it was too damn close for comfort!…By th' way,…you ain't gonna tell anybody about me soiling my pants, are you?"

"I wouldn't do that, Rod." He laid the reins across the wagon's headboard then, and rolled a smoke. "Besides,…you ain't th' only one ever done that!" He licked his cigarette and lit it then picked up the reins again, urging the mules to a faster walk along the worn and rutted thoroughfare.

It was mid-afternoon by the time he reined the mules left onto the new part of the Goodland Road, and it was hot,…if not for a thirty mile an hour southerly wind, it would be unbearably hot!

*   *   *

"I would give twenty dollars in gold for a steak, Jarvis!" Blurted Mitch as he chewed the fish and swallowed it. "If I had it, I would!...Anyway,...I might never eat a fish again, after this."

"Come now, son," Grinned Cantrell. "Fish is good for you, food for the soul!"

"That may be,...but happiness is a good steak,...and maybe some fried taters and gravy?"

"Right now, we're good to have this,...and it's free for the catching!"

"You're right about that!" He grinned, filling his mouth again. "Just think, though,...if we didn't have salt?"

"There ya go!" Smiled Cantrell, also filling his mouth with the flaky meat. "Besides,...you do seem to be the only one complaining." He said, nodding toward the dark figures of the men in front of the old fireplace. "They are happy to have it!"

"But, Jarvis,...they don't know any better!"

Cantrell laughed then. "You could be right, boy." He suddenly jerked his head toward the door and raised his hand. "Listen!" He whispered quickly, and the both of them strained eyes and ears at the darkened doorway.

"I don't hear anything. "Whispered Mitch, as he placed his tin on the bar.

"I did,...there, hear that?"

"Yeah,...somebody's out there!" Mitch quickly snapped his fingers, getting the men's attention, then raised his hand up for silence as he continued to listen. The footsteps became audible on the groaning platform outside, and pulling his pistol, he quickly moved the thirty feet to the door and flattened himself against the wall beside it.

The eleven men all drew their weapons and got to their feet, but on a gesture from Cantrell, remained still to wait. All eyes were on the saloon's closed door as the flickering orange light of the fire eerily outlined their faces and clothing against the darkness of the large room.

The seconds continued to tick by, for what seemed like minutes before the door slowly began to open,...and then slowly, daylight silhouetted the man as he stepped inside. But he had no sooner entered before Mitch stuck a gun in his side and gingerly pried the pistol from his grip.

"Get on over there by th' bar!" Ordered Mitch, and prodded the man forward until they stood facing Cantrell.

Cantrell stared at the man's unshaven face in the dim light, and as recognition slowly took over, he stared at him in disbelief! "What's your name, friend?" He asked, still not sure who he was.

"You know who I am, Reverend!...It's been a while."

"Don't be a Dick-head, man!" Snapped Mitch, jamming the gun's barrel hard into his ribs again, and bringing a grunt of pain from him. "Tell th' man your name!"

"It's okay, Mitch!" Said Cantrell in an anger strained voice. "His name is Gabriel McAllister!...I thought I knew him as a friend, once,... now, I don't know who he is!...Have Curley bring his horse in!"

"Bring his horse in, Curley!" Said Mitch loudly. "Take a look around, he might not be alone."

"There's no one else, Mitch!' Sighed Cantrell. "They always work alone."

"They,...who's they?...What am I missin' here, Jarvis?"

"He is a Mormon assassin, Son!" He peered harder at the man's dark features, and in the dim, flickering, light, McAllister's eyes seemed to mirror the unfeeling coldness in him.

"I have often thought you were not who you pretended to be, Gabriel,...and now that I know for sure, I have to admit you played your part well!...Never the less, I'm very disappointed in you, because, God forbid,...I liked you!" He sighed heavily then, and leaned back against the bar.

"It's been fourteen years since an Assassin murdered my family, Gabriel!...Would you be that cowardly man?"

"I would not have done that!"

"Well, I thank you for that, at least....Do you know who did?"

"No!" He returned in a dead voice.

Cantrell sighed heavily then shook his head. "Then, as a friend, once,...will you tell me who sent you to murder me?" And when McAllister didn't answer, Mitch jabbed him with the gun again.

"He asked you a question, Jackass,...who was it?"

"Never mind, Mitch,...they live by a code of silence, he won't tell me....How long have you been hunting me, Gabriel?"

"Almost five years, Reverend,...and I did not want the job."

"I understand....How did you find me?"

"When the soldiers stopped looking for you at the swamp, I knew you had not gone far."

"That was seventeen days ago,...what took you so long?" And when he got no answer, he looked toward the other men. "One of you get some rope and tie this man's hands!" He looked back at McAllister while this was being done. "Sorry, Gabriel," He sighed. "You leave me no choice!...It is not something I want to do." Silk finished tying his hands behind his back, just as Curley came in with his horse and led the animal across the floor.

"Put it with the other horses!" Ordered Mitch, and nodding, Curley led the animal past them toward the back room. "What do we do with Mister McAllister, Jarvis?"

"Just a minute, Mitch....How many of you are hunting me, Gabriel?"

"I wouldn't know that, or even who they are, Reverend."

"Then tell me why a man of your obvious training, and experience walked into a trap like this,...can you tell me that?...You walked in here like a Greenhorn!"

"I didn't believe you were here,...I was only checking the buildings when I heard movement in here."

"Do you believe this shit, Jarvis?...He's lyin' out his ass to us!"

"No, Mitch, he is not!...They may not talk at all about what they know,...but when they do, they don't lie,...unless it will aid them in their objective."

"That's hard to chew, Sir!" Argued Mitch. "I'm sorry, but nobody hunts a man for five years,...think about it, Jarvis,...five years?"

"I've learned a little about the Church Assassins." Sighed Cantrell again. "They will not return home until the job is done. They never stop,...and they don't usually fail."

"Well,...Mister McAllister just did! How do you know 'im, anyway?"

"He was a member of my congregation for ten years, joined the Church as a young man!...Gabriel here has supped at my table on numerous occasions, even played games with my children afterward,...

94

and seeing him here now, makes me ashamed of my Mormon heritage!... It truly does."

"Then let me kill 'im, Sir,...and beggin' your pardon, Jarvis,...but this is one evil, sorry son of a Bitch!...He's worse than anything we ever done!"

"Another will take my place, Reverend." Exclaimed McAllister. "You are marked for death."

"I have no doubt of that, Gabriel,...we are all marked for death.... If I let you live, will you quit and go home?"

"I will face certain death, either way, Reverend. The answer is, no."

"We can't let 'im live, Jarvis!" Insisted Mitch.

Cantrell placed his hand on McAllister's shoulder. "You leave me no choice, Gabriel." He sighed then and nodded at Mitch. "No guns, son....Curley, you and Silk go with him, you, too, Billy Jack,...and don't be seen!" He looked back at his assassin then and smiled sadly. "I'm sorry, Gabriel."

*   *   *

August 18,..."Come in, Marshal!" Urged Judge Bonner. "What's on your mind today?"

"I don't think I have a mind anymore, Judge!...After all my rantin' and ravin', nothin's happening!...I'm beginnin' to feel like an idiot for even askin' you to call that meetin' with the Council!"

"In the first place, Jim,...calling that meeting, I believe was my idea, and I would not feel that way about it, because you were right!... Even if nothing happens, you went on record for doing your job,...and the Councilmen know that!...Besides, if nothing comes of it, it's a good thing,...if it does, they will know to follow your judgment next time.... It's politics, Marshal, learn it well, and you'll go a long way!"

"I don't know anything about politics, Judge,...I'm worried! I've had men watching the square every night for three nights now, and aside from the usual saloon drunks, and brawls, it's business as usual at th' jail!...I don't know, Judge, maybe they're right, I've got no proof we're gonna be hit by Cantrell, or anybody else!...Maybe I ought a call off th' weather-watch!"

"Give it another few days, Jim. If that wire was not legitimate, that Cavalry patrol would not have come here!...Cantrell may be long gone from these parts,...but if he is not, the possibility of a raid is relevant.... Besides, the City Council is your boss, they expect you to be wrong sometimes, and right most times!...It's politics, pure and simple."

"I'll do it your way, Judge." He sighed. "I just feel a little helpless, that's all."

"My boy, that's part of being a lawman,...trust me, this will work out in your favor."

"I hope so, Judge....Well," He sighed, getting to his feet. "I'd better go check th' streets. Thanks, Judge." He turned and went to the door, nodded back at Bonner, and left.

*   *   *

After another night in the open, they were up at daybreak and once again on the newly-finished portion of the Goodland Road, and at mid-day were approaching the long span of bridge across the Kiamichi River.

"Ain't hard to tell Peter didn't build this one!" Commented Rodney as the wagon went up the slight grade and onto the planking.

"Army-built!" Nodded Billy as he slapped the lines on the mules' backs. "Road, too, likely."

"I never realized there could be so many people living around here, a road is a lot a help to 'em, I guess."

"It does sort a divide th' wilderness, don't it, even if we ain't seen th' sun much since yesterday."

"Trees are thick, that's for sure."

"They're not that bad,...in fact, they're no thicker now than when we came through here th' first time."

"When did we come through here?"

"When we came to find your big bird!"

"Oh, yeah,...but that wasn't right here, Billy, we didn't cross this river."

"That's true, we was a mile or so east of here, but the trees were just as thick! But, I guess it is some different, that was three years ago,...and this place can change overnight."

"I believe that!"

They were almost across the long bridge, and Billy was scanning the trees ahead of them as they approached the slight descent to exit off, and tightening his grip on the lines as they made the road again, he quickly hauled back on the reins. "Whoaaa, mules!"

"What's wrong?" Queried Rodney.

"That!" He said, nodding his head at the six men as they rode out of the trees onto the road in front of them.

"Son of a Bitch!" Breathed Rodney.

"Billy, what is it?" Asked Connie, raising up for a look over the seatback.

"Listen to me, honey," He said in a low voice. "You and Lisa grab a rifle and lever a cartridge in!"

"Why?"

"Just do it!...And when I tell you to, lay th' barrel across th' seatback between us here, and aim it at th' chest of one a these men, both of ya pick a target, and if I tell you to shoot, shoot that man, you understand?...Lisa, aim yours out th' side a th' wagon, but don't shoot unless I say so!...Tell Willy to keep th' kids down."

The six men stopped their horses in front of the mules, and each of them had a pistol trained in his and Rodney's general direction. Billy stood up in the wagon-bed, as did Rodney, and each had already removed the loops from their weapons.

"Howdy, folks!" Grinned the heavily bearded man on the lead horse.

"What do you want?" Returned Billy, his eyes on those of the man, because he knew the eyes would tell him when to draw and fire.

"And before you talk too much, Mister," Said Rodney. "Know that I am a Federal United States Marshal,…so you might want a put them shooters away!"

"That don't mean spit to us, Marshal!" He grinned at them, showing very yellowed, rotting and broken teeth. "We been runnin' over law-dogs, like you for ten years!...You ain't nothin'!"

"What do you want?" Repeated Billy.

"Them guns, first off!" He grinned. "Then ever'thin' else you got!" He laughed then, as did the other five men.

"Now, honey." He said in a low voice,…then in a louder voice. "You want these, too?" He smiled as the outlaw's eyes fell on the menacing barrel of the Winchester.

"You raise that pistol any higher, this rifle here will blow your head off!…man next to you as well!…You might want a look at th' side of th' wagon."

The man stared at the rifle's barrel for a minute longer, then sneered and raised his pistol.

Billy drew and fired, his slug tumbling the man back over the rump of his rearing horse. He shot two more of them as they tried to control their mounts, and fire their guns at the same time, the multiple explosions shattering the stillness.

Rodney had drawn as Billy shot the second man, killing two more of the, would be highwaymen, and at that moment, the sixth man yelled shrilly and threw up his hands.

"I quit, I quit!" He screamed, throwing down his gun. "I quit!"

"Get off that horse, you shit-head!" Growled Billy, and as the man quickly obeyed. "Watch 'im, Rod." He holstered his pistol and climbed down, having to move Melissa's rifle barrel aside as he did.

"You can put it away now, Lisa." He said. "You did good!" Once on the ground, he walked to confront and look the frightened man in the eyes, what he was able to see of them,…shaggy, almost shoulder length hair protruded in matted, filthy strands from beneath his soiled hat and his, just as shaggy beard tended to cover his mouth and lower face completely.

"You're one filthy son of a Bitch!…You know that,…look at yourself!… Who th' hell are you, anyway,…our wives and kids are in that wagon?… What's your name?"

"Ga,…Gomer." He gasped. "Name's Gomer Price!"

"Who th' hell, was he?" He ordered, nodding at the first man he shot.

"Gator Malloy,…Th,…that other one is, Sidney Roach, and, and Dusty Savage over yonder. Them other two are Emmit Sands, and Buck,…don't know his last name."

"Where'd you come from?" Asked Rodney as he walked up beside them.

"Pa,…place called Wheelock,…we,…we needed money, 'at's all!"

"Where'd you come from before that!" Demanded Billy. "Speak up, Gomer!"

"I,...N,...North,...I don't know, man!" He sobbed.

"You're lyin'! Growled Billy. "You'd better damn well tell us where you came from, Gomer,...and make it quick!" And when the man opened his mouth to speak, they were startled by the ear-splitting explosion, both of them ducking habitually as Gomer grunted loudly. His body was lifted slightly then pitched into the tall grass alongside the road.

Billy had caught a fleeting glimpse of the man called Gator as he ducked, saw the pistol in his hand as it was re-cocked,...and in the same awkward movement, as he was ducking, drew and fired again, and then sighing heavily, he straightened and holstered the gun again and looked at the ashen-faced Marshal. "You okay, Rod?"

"Yeah," He nodded. "I was not prepared for that!...Guess he didn't want old Gomer to talk."

"Where was that question headed, anyway?"

"I was about to ask him where Cantrell was?"

"Well he's here somewhere, there was six of 'em, and Neville said that six men left Wheelock, a few days ago, add it up....Then again, he may not be here,...these six were on their own,...they had no idea how to do a hold-up,...too used to taking orders!...And you heard that one, they'd been running over lawmen for ten years! They was bragging, when they should a been shooting!"

"Hey,...that's damn good, Rod!"

"Bout time, don't you think?"

"Billy!" Shrieked Connie hysterically. "Rodney, get up here!"

"What's wrong, Honey?"

"It's Lisa,...she's bleeding, and I can't wake her up!"

"Oh, God, No!" Shouted Rodney and rushed headlong for the wagon. He wasted no time in scrambling up to, and over the wagon's seat, and Billy was right behind him.

Rodney dropped to his knees and lifted Lisa in his arms. "Lisa?" He shouted. "Lisa, Honey, talk to me?" He saw the blood on her head then and quickly brushed her soaked hair aside to see the bloody crease in her scalp. "Thank, God!" He moaned. "Lisa,...come on, Baby, wake up!" She groaned then, and opened her eyes, only to see him crying as he hugged her.

"You're hurting my head, Rodney!" She moaned, pushing him away.. "What happened, why are you crying?"

"You got shot, baby." He sniffed. "I'm just scared." He smiled up at Billy, and then Connie and nodded. "Bullet creased her head, she's okay!"

"Thank, God!" Groaned Connie then looked back at Willy's pale face as he still held the younger ones tight against the floor of the wagon,...and all three were fighting him, and crying their eyes out.

"You can let them up now, honey!...I'm so proud of you."

All three rushed to cling to them, while Rodney wrapped Cindy in his arms and laid her down next to Melissa. He looked back up at Billy then. "I was never so scared in my life, Billy." He said shakily. "I could see my whole life going to hell!"

"I know, Rod,...scared me, too!...Now, get her some water, make her comfortable, man, we'll camp here for th' night!" He nodded at Connie then. "You help 'im, okay?" He smiled warmly at her then nodded at Willy.

"Come on, son,...let's catch up them loose horses." And together, they climbed back down to the ground again.

"You okay, son?" He asked, running his hand over Willy's head.

"I was scared, Daddy, that's all. There was so many of 'em!"

"I know,...now go on, catch up them horses, and don't spook 'em,... they're still jittery as hell." He walked to the bodies and one by one, removed their gun belts and retrieved the handguns, then looped the belts together and tossed them up into the floor of the wagon and then sighing, returned to squat beside one of the bodies to search it and before he was done, he had removed wallets, knives and everything of any value, and placed everything in a small pile at the road's edge.

"I got 'em all, Daddy." Breathed Willy as he led the animals in beside the mules. "Want me to to get the rifles?"

"Tie th' horses to th' wagon first." He stood then and unfolded a piece of paper he had found in Gomer's pocket. Rod was right, he thought as he read the poster. He grunted to his feet then and walked to the wagon.

"Hey, Rod!" He said, knocking on the sideboard, and when Rodney looked out.

"Lisa okay?"

"Yeah, she's fine, thanks."

"Well, you'll want a read this!" He gave him the poster then went to search the horses while Willy climbed up the tall wheel enough to deposit the rifles over the side and beneath the seat.

"Rifles are under the seat, Daddy, all six of 'em!"

"Thanks, Son,...now get a cloth bag, or somethin' from mama and put them things yonder in it."

He took several boxes of different caliber ammunition from the six saddlebags, and not much else, and these he passed up to Connie in the wagon then sighing, began searching the roadside for a place to set up camp, seeing it deep under the trees, and off the road about twenty yards.

"All done, Daddy!"

"Good,...now, climb up there on th' seat, and put th' bag under it. Tell mama, and Rod, I'm gonna lead th' team off th' road, and to hold on!" He made sure the horses were secured to the wagon then went to grab the mules' bridle straps, turned them, and then led them off the road, having to cross a shallow man-made ditch that caused the wagon to lurch and sway awkwardly as it was pulled up and into the tall grass, and then finally into the trees.

Once the wagon was positioned, he instructed Willy to clear a wide area for the fire,...and to watch for snakes, then loosed one of the captured horses and went back to the road for the bodies.

CHAPTER NINE

Willy had the fire going in time to help Billy drag the last carcass off the road and into the grass then together, unsaddled the captured horses, loosened the cinches on the other two and staked them all out to graze, after first letting them drink from a wooden bucket they carried for the occasion. Watering the mules, they unhooked them from the wagon, and leaving them fully harnessed, staked them out as well.

Melissa slept most of the afternoon with her aching head, but they all knew she needed it and of course, Rodney stayed in the wagon to watch her, while Connie, having nothing else to do, spent the afternoon watching the younger children,...and preparing for the evening meal.

Willy, at the request of his father, brought cleaning kit, and the captured handguns from the wagon then sat on the old log they had brought up near the fire, and watched him clean his own pistol first, and then the others.

"You can put 'em back now, son." He sighed then, and watched as Willy complied. "We'll do th' rifles later!" He called after him. He rolled and lit his Durham before moving off the log to pour more coffee into his cup, and at the same time, thinking that it was too hot to be drinking coffee,...but somehow, hot coffee helped keep him cooler, and smoke from the fire helped keep away the gnats and flies,...and especially the large, black, and very aggressive mosquitoes! Moving back to the log, his eyes flicked to the six dead men in the grass, a dozen yards downwind of the camp, and as he sipped the hot liquid, sat down and wondered why six of Cantrell's men had been alone in the wilderness.

Had Cantrell really disbanded?...'If he was smart, he did' he thought, and then shook his head as he silently hoped they were not all somewhere in the Kiamichi, because if they were, the killing might be be only just beginning. Rodney was right, he thought grimly. Those six had no idea how to pull off a robbery on their own, having always had twenty or thirty men to back them up....Only an amateur would do what they did! Maybe they were just trying to prove their toughness, their independence,...their ability to work alone and on their own,... without Cantrell? Whatever it was, they were all pretty dumb to sit their horses without pointing even one pistol directly at them!...What were they thinking, he wondered,...that their very presence would be enough to make us give up?...That was stupid! He thought this drearily as he recalled how that wild shot had almost killed Melissa.

They were too used to being told how and what to do! He sighed and took another swallow of coffee. This Cantrell must be one strict son of a Bitch!...Sighing again, he watched Connie and Angela as they peeled potatoes for a minute then peered off toward the road. Where would Cantrell hide, if he was up here, he wondered?...How many men had left him?...That was the question!...He sighed again and drew more smoke into his lungs as Willy came back to sit down.

"Daddy,...can I ask you something?"

"How else are you gonna find out somethin', if you don't ask?" He grinned and reached out to ruffle the hair on his head. "Shoot!"

"Can I have one of them rifles,...I'm old enough?"

"Eleven is not quite old enough to be carryin' a gun, son." He grinned then and laid his arm across the boy's shoulders. "Besides,... you got a l;earn how to shoot first,...and I'll teach you when I think it's time."

"It's time now, Daddy,...I can already shoot, real good, too! Uncle Peter taught me!...can I have one, Daddy, please,...one I can call my own?"

"Why is it, you never told me about that?"

"I don't know,...I thought you might get mad!...Are ya?"

"I guess not,...Uncle Peter's a good teacher. But there's a whole lot more to shootin' than just knowin' how to shoot!...And it takes a while to learn all that." He sighed and mashed out the stub beneath a boot-heel.

"Tell ya what, Son,...you pick out one a them rifles, th' one you like best, and I'll check it out for ya. If it's a good gun, you can keep it."

"Gosh, thanks, Daddy!"

"Providing you do not load it!...When I'm ready to let you practice, we'll load it and shoot together."

"What about Uncle Peter, can I load it when he's with me?"

"As long as I know he's with you. You don't follow my rules, you'll lose th' gun, is that clear?"

"Yes, Sir!...Can I pick one now?"

"No, said Connie quickly. "There's plenty of time for that!"

"Awww, mama!"

"She's right, now get your cup and pour us some coffee,...and here comes Uncle Rodney, pour him one." He watched Rodney climb down from the wagon then reach up to help Cindy down,...and at that moment, Chris and Angela came from the fire, Christopher to sit on the log by him, and Angela to fairly leap onto his lap.

"Whoaaa, sweetheart,...you keep growin' you'll be too heavy for your old daddy."

"I know!" She laughed. "I'm almost all growed up!"

"Me, too!" Yelled Christopher.

"You both are!" He grinned, pulling Chris against him in a hug.

"How is she, Rod?" He asked as Rodney accepted the coffee and sat down.

"Sleeping off a headache, but she's okay, thank God!...That was close, Billy."

"Yeah, it was. I shouldn't have used either of 'em as a decoy, like that."

"And pray tell me, why not?" Said Connie, looking up from her potato slicing. "We're a family,...and it takes all of us to survive sometimes!...Lisa will tell you the same thing, too!"

"That's a fact!" Nodded Rodney as he took Cindy onto his lap. "Don't blame yourself for that,...we're all in this together....I just don't like being that scared."

*   *   *

Mitch came out onto the massive platform to find Cantrell sitting against the front of the building, his legs stretched out in front of him.

"I wondered where you was, Jarvis?" He grinned, sitting down beside him. "Want a talk about it?"

"Talk about what, Son?"

"Whatever's botherin' you?...You been actin' different ever since we killed that Assassin fella!"

Cantrell sighed. "You're right,...it does bother me, Mitch!...Seeing that man,...a man who had laughed with me, laughed, talked and played with my family!...He was a friend,...at least, I always thought he was. But,...how could a friend betray a trust like that,...if he was a friend?...Mitch,...it put me in a murderous rage again!"

"I understand, Sir,...but you know he would a tried again if you had let 'im go,...he said so his self."

"Oh, I know that!...But, you know, I don't believe he really wanted to kill me, Mitch,...He was doing what he was trained to do, follow orders,...and he knew that if he failed, he would be marked for death himself!

"You think more of 'em will come after you now?"

"Someone is already coming." He sighed. "And he could be closer than we think!...Gabriel has been hunting me for five years,...and when he didn't return after the first three, or so, the man who sent him likely believed he was dead!...It's just a matter of time, Mitch,...they won't quit!"

"We'll just have to stop them, too, Jarvis!...Besides, old Gabriel didn't appear to be all that smart, he walked right into a trap!"

"He didn't know we were here, Mitch, he wouldn't lie about that. In fact, he likely thought we were not here at all,...he was just searching the buildings....As good as these Assassins are at what they do,...they are still human,...Gabriel McAllister made a mistake, that's all."

"It's scary that nobody knows who these men are, Jarvis."

"The Assassins don't even know who the Assassins are, son."

"That's what's crazy about it all." He sighed. "Them Elder fellas must really be pissed!"

"I executed several of the top leaders,...and I made no bones about it!"

"That would do it, I guess!...How th' hell do they choose a man to be an Assassin,...do they hire gunmen and train 'em, or what?"

Cantrell grinned then. "That's a conversation I used to have with Gabriel from time to time,...and at the time, I thought he was only guessing at the answers he gave, like everyone else did!...But now I know it for the truth. The Assassin is chosen at the age of six years, they are taken from their families, by whatever means they use,... and raised in a classroom!...They see no one else, talk to no one else, except their instructor, one of the Elders!...All they do is listen and learn, all day, every day, sun up, sundown,...and by the time they are old enough, they are ghosts, and able to kill in more ways than you can imagine,...and they can get away without leaving a trace....That is the Mormon Assassin, Mitch, and God only knows how many there are. Silent killers all of them,...and the shame of it is,...they believe they are doing God's work, because they are taught to believe the Elder is next to God himself."

"Gabriel obviously didn't think that way, Jarvis,...he was,...almost apologetic."

"Yes,...he did seem that way,...but that would not have stopped him, son. Anyway, they can obviously be whatever they choose to be, because until yesterday, I never suspected Gabriel to be anything other than a friend, and devout parishioner and now,...now, I am ashamed to have ever been a Mormon, Mitch!...Mormonism is not what God intended it to be. I am the direct result of that!...They are killers, and so am I, I do not, however believe that the Church is corrupt,...only the few that are in control. Those few are the Devil's true disciples!...But in the end, they won't win, God will see to that,...they will be found out and destroyed, I believe that....We will all be destroyed someday!" He sighed. "Mormon religion is a beautiful thing, Mitch!"

"That's not th' way you just described it, Jarvis."

"I described the dark side of it, every power has one,...even the United States Government."

"You tellin' me they have Assassins, too?"

"That I am, every soldier is an Assassin,...they follow orders."

"I think I was better off not knowin' all a that, Jarvis,...I truly do!"

"Well,...now you know what's bothering me."

"Well, I'll say it again, then,…we'll handle whatever comes along."

"I'm not worried about living, son, I'm too old for that!…I'm worried about dying without the love of God!…I don't know how to get there from here?"

*   *   *

They were having their evening meal early, as Melissa, her head wrapped in a clean bandage had decided to join them again,…and though Rodney was still worried, he had agreed to let her up and about, and they were all sitting atop the log eating, while Willy and the other children sat on blankets spread on the ground.

It was still quite hot, and humid under the trees, but the fire's smoke was doing the job of keeping the pests away, however there were still many pesky mosquitoes that were being randomly swatted. Billy cleaned his plate and placed it on the ground before reaching for tobacco and papers, and as he tapped tobacco into the brown paper, Rodney was reaching for a cigar.

"What say we bury them bodies, Rod?" He licked the smoke and struck a match to it, then to Rodney's cigar as the Marshal peered across at the carcases. "That, or we could turn 'em over to th' Army, they're supposed to be camped at th' river."

"I couldn't stand the smell for that long, Billy, they're already getting ripe!…What are we, anyway, two days from the river?"

"At th' rate we're goin', yeah."

"We'll bury 'em,…take the horses to the ranch."

"Works for me. I'm damn glad you decided to come with us, Rod,… they'd a been a bit much on my own!"

"So am I,…but I'm still worried about Cantrell.…Was these six all the men he had, and if not,…just how many more am I gonna have to hunt down?"

"He likely had twenty, thirty men with 'im,…maybe more. But, if he disbanded, they could be anywhere!"

"And so could he." Nodded Rodney.

"Well, you're not going back, are you," Gasped Melissa. "Not now?"

"No, baby, I'm not going back,…don't over-excite yourself!"

107

"I expect he'll keep a few men around 'im," Continued Billy. "He'll want some kind a protection."

"I'd like to protect him!" Blurted Melissa. "With a rifle bullet."

"You're not alone, Lisa!" Smiled Connie.

"Me, too!" Added Willy.

Yeah!" Chimed the echoing trio.

After the laughter subsided, Rodney looked back at Billy. "Where would you be, if you were him?...You've had some experience with this sort of thing, we both have,...but I mean, before Loughmiller....You hunted men for two years....Where would you hide?"

"That's an easy one!" He chuckled. "I'd be half way to Mexico by now!...It'll never be safe for 'im here anymore!...I'm willin' to bet there's a thousand a them posters floatin' around with his picture on 'em!"

Rodney nodded. "Mexico makes sense to me, too,...but these six men don't, unless he did send 'em packing?"

"Dumb as they was, that wouldn't surprise me!...I don't know, Rod, maybe they didn't want a go to Mexico."

"Well, they should have!" Blurted Connie.

"Daddy,...I hear horses coming!" Said Willy urgently, causing Billy, and Rodney to get to their feet.

"I hear 'em, son."

"Cavalry." Nodded Rodney as they caught a glimpse of them through the trees.

"Hoooo!" Came the loud voice then, and they knew they had stopped.

"I'll handle it." Said the Marshal, and quickly walked off around the wagon.

"You all stay put." Said Billy and went after him.

Several of the soldiers had dismounted, and were squatting in the road talking when they walked out of the trees,...and when the officer saw them, he got to his feet to watch their approach.

"That's close enough, Gentlemen!" Warned the officer, stopping them just off the road. "Can I ask your names, and what you're doing here?"

"I'm Federal Marshal, Rodney Taylor,...this is my friend, and partner, Billy Upshur....And I believe we can help you, sir."

"In that case, Marshal. I am Major Wilkes, out of Fort McCullogh!... What has happened here, there is what appears to be blood on the road?"

"It is blood, Major....Six Jarvis Cantrell men tried to rob us a few hours ago, my wife was wounded."

"I'm sorry to hear that, Marshal, is she hurt bad?"

"Creased her skull, she'll be all right."

"Good,...now, did you say they were Cantrell's men?"

"Yes, sir, I did,...this poster was in one of their pockets." He gave him the poster, and while he looked at it, turned to cast a look at Billy's expressionless face.

"Where are they now?" Queried the Major as he put the paper away.

Rodney turned and gestured back toward camp. "Laid out in the grass back there."

"Show me!"

Nodding, they both walked ahead of them back to the bodies, and then stood aside while the Major examined the corpses,...and after a couple of minutes, Wilkes stood up and came back to join them.

"I guess they could be Cantrell men," He nodded. "But then again, they could just be outlaws, there's just no way of knowing!...How did you manage all six of them, Marshal, weren't they armed?"

"They were armed, yes, sir!...And we only managed five of 'em,... one was killed by one of his own!...I was questioning the one called Gomer, and one man wasn't quite dead." He shrugged. "Guess he didn't want him to tell me where Cantrell was."

Wilkes nodded. "I'll have to take your word for that, Marshal, my having no way to identify them as such."

Billy motioned for Willy as they talked and sent him for the bag of personals he'd taken from the bodies,...and when he returned, he took the bag and offered it to Wilkes. "Here ya go, Major."

"What's this?" He quizzed, taking the bag from him.

"It's what was in their pockets."

"Thank you, Mister,...Bill Upshur, is that right?"

"That's right." He said tightly, suddenly agitated at Wilkes' attitude.

109

"Billy's my business Partner, and best friend!" Said Rodney again. "We own a Trading Post about thirty miles, or so north of here in the mountains."

Wilkes nodded then turned toward the Medic as he approached. "What's your verdict, Doctor?"

"Lead poisoning, Mister Wilkes,…all deceased!"

"Very good,…now, if you will, the Marshal's wife was injured by a stray bullet, would you take a look, please?"

"Of course, where is she?"

"I'll show you!" Voiced Willy, and led the Medic back toward camp.

"What do we do, now, Major," Asked Rodney when they were gone. "We were just going to bury them when you showed up?"

"My men will do that, Marshal!...With the report you're about to write, and the information I already have on the hold-up attempt, it will be sufficient to satisfy the Colonel!" He turned away then. "Corporal!" And when the soldier turned toward him and saluted.

"Get a pad and pencil, the Marshal has a report to write,…and get a burial detail in here on the double!"

"Yes, Sir!"

You men seem to be a force to reckon with!" Said Wilkes as he looked back at the bodies. "Taking down even five armed men is a remarkable feat,…I commend you for it!"

Thank you, Major,…but it's my job!" Nodded Rodney. "And nothing to brag about when you take a man's life!"

"That is a fact, Sir!...But this country needs lawmen like yourself and I, for one, am glad you're here."

"Pad and pencil, Sir!" Said the Corporal as he came back.

"Thank you, Corporal,…give it to the Marshal, please." Rodney took the material and both him, and Billy walked back to camp as the Major went to supervise the burials.

Billy grabbed their cups and went to pour the coffee while Rodney sat down and began writing, and coming back, sat down beside him to add his two cents worth and together, spent the next twenty or so minutes recording the events of the day,…and as he finished the two page report, he had Billy witness it and as Major Wilkes walked into camp, he also signed it.

"That should do it, Marshal." He said, looking over the papers. "I like your precise neatness, Sir,…very detailed, right down to the victims' names….I thank you!"

"No, sir, thank you!" He grinned. "I was not looking forward to digging six graves,…and thank your Doctor for me, too."

"My pleasure,…Where you folks heading anyway,…you're a long way from your store?"

"Our families live in Paris, Major,…we're just going for a visit!"

"Well, good luck to you, both of you." He shook both their hands, nodded at the women then walked away to watch as the last two outlaws were laid to rest. Once they were properly covered, he said words over the graves then all went to their horses, mounted and rode on across the Kiamichi River Bridge.

"Straight, and to th' point, that one." Commented Billy as they left. "I ain't sure I like 'im, neither!"

"Career soldier in the making!" Grinned Rodney.

*   *   *

August 19,…They were up at daybreak, and after coffee, more biscuits and last night's cold, leftover potatoes and venison, Billy lowered the wagon's tailgate and laid it down flat,…tying it there with rope before stacking the six saddles and gear on it. Rodney and Willy tightened Billy's Roan, and his horse's cinch-straps and led all eight horses back to the wagon.

"Should a just saddled all of 'em, Billy," Commented Rodney as they approached. "Saddles take up a lot a room."

"Too many saddled horses behind a wagon create questions, Rod. Two is okay. "He took the reins from him and secured their two to the tailgate, then he picked up two coils of the captured ropes and gave one to Rodney.

"Make a halter at each end of it, Rod, and put 'em on them two there,…tie 'em to my saddle horn." He took his rope and did the same to two more of them, looping that one over Rodney's saddle horn, and the last two horses behind those.

"That might turn a few heads at that!" Agreed the Marshal. "Will,… you keep an eye out back here, okay,…one gets loose, yell out!"

"I will, Uncle Rodney." They set about repacking the wagon then and at last, were towing the caravan out onto the road again.

"What are we, Billy,…three days away from the mountain?"

"Working on number four, Rod,…we still got two, maybe three days to go,…bar no trouble!" He slapped the mules' backs with the lines, urging them to a faster walk along the dusty trail. "Seems trouble is all there is, anymore." He sighed then. "You'd think people would stop and think a little,…life's too short, as it is."

"Amen to that!…But if things ever do change, it won't be in our lifetime!…When ya get right down to it, men today ain't much different than those cavemen we saw."

"You're right." He grinned. "If them apes could a talked, there wouldn't be any at all!"

"I don't know, Billy," He sighed. "I guess life is what you make of it, because I don't believe man will ever change."

"You're likely right there, too!…But, thinkin' about all that,…wonder what kind a damage that meteor made all them millions a years ago,… you know that fallin' rock we saw?"

"I forgot all about that meteor!…Damn if I know." He shrugged. "Who knows, maybe that's what killed off all them dinosaurs?… I'm just damn glad that arch worked, because as long as that tunnel was open, we were still there!"

"Yeah,…and I think about all that sometimes, hell,…I even think about that light in th' sky!…And as much as I don't believe in such things, it's damn hard not to!"

"Well, don't tell anybody, Billy, but I think about it, too.…And I'll tell ya something else,…it took some kind a powerful sons of Bitches to build all that,…and I, personally, never want to meet 'em!"

"Especially if they're an unfriendly lot!" Laughed Billy.

"Which reminds me, Billy,…did Connie ever hear from that Professor of antiquity,…you know, about them strange marks on that arch?"

"I don't believe she did, no.…He probably thought she was just another nut, or somethin'!"

"No doubt, he did!" Nodded Rodney. "Education does sometimes breed ignorance, and that Professor would be an example of it!…Think you'll ever want a go back down there?"

"For what, Rod,…I ain't lost a thing down there!…Even if we wanted to, not one a them arch tunnels stayed open long enough to get all th' way through 'em! I wouldn't want a be in one when it closed up!" He shook his head then. "It's best we leave well enough alone."

"Ahhh, well,…it was just a thought!" They both laughed then, and changed the subject.

*   *   *

They began passing more and more of the run-down shanties as the hot day wore on, some quite close to the road, but most nestled snugly against red clay bluffs, or hidden in dense thickets of Pine and Scrub-oak,,…and all with half naked children in the yards playing,…but all were watching the odd-looking caravan of wagon and horses go by. They had met only one wagon on the new road thus far, but that all changed when, by mid-afternoon they were suddenly on the old existing Goodland Road, and the transformation was easy to spot by the thick, tall grass and weeds growing in the lane's middle, as well as the tall, waving reed-like grass along both sides. But if not for the deep, dry ruts in the trail, it would still have been an easy ride in the wagon.

They began meeting whole families of Choctaw in rickety wagons, forcing them to drive off the side to allow them to pass. Several men and boys, all riding bone-weary mules, and all carrying water-jugs and hoes as they came from the fields,…and each and every one seemed to be accompanied by a mangy, flea infested hound that, when not stopping to scratch, were barking shrilly and nipping at the feet of the trailing horses. But the insects were the most annoying as flies, gnats, and large Mosquitoes seemed to be swarming the closer they came to the river. The only reprieve they had from being totally overcome by the pests was the persistent south wind, that still gusted to almost thirty miles an hour at times.

They had not talked, but briefly for several hours now, and as the afternoon wore on, those in the wagon had fallen asleep to relieve the monotony. Neither Billy, or the Marshal had tried to smoke in the face of the wind, not wanting to chance a grass fire from an accidental ember, as they both knew what the results would be. But finally, they were both relieved to see the camped soldiers ahead of them.

"What say, we stop here for the night, Billy, I'm bushed?"

"You don't have to ask me twice,…better wake th' folks."

Fifteen minutes later they were being flagged down, by soldiers wielding rifles, but just before getting to them, Billy reined the mules off the road and in behind the one large tent some twenty yards away, which was a temporary barracks they had set up for sleeping. The four Noncoms followed them off the road, still calling for them to halt, and were silently waiting as they climbed down from the tall seat.

Rodney jumped the last foot or so to the ground where he stretched his stiff muscles before confronting the armed guards, and was smiling broadly when they approached.

"Sir, you are supposed to stop when ordered!…I need to ask your business here, and you are lucky you weren't fired on!"

"Yeah," He grinned. "Sorry about that, Private!…I'm Federal Marshal Rodney Taylor." He placed a thumb under his vest and held out the badge until he was sure they had all seen it. "Now, who are you?" He shrugged then, the question pending and half-grinned as the Private finally realized it as such.

"Sorry, sir,…Private Jeffery Stokes!…We are just following orders, Sir!"

"And doing it well, Jeff." He grinned. "We've been in that hot wagon for four days, is it okay if we camp here for the night?"

"Well,…we have no orders to the contrary, sir, so I guess so.…Who is with you?"

"This, here is my partner, Billy Upshur." He turned as Billy walked up, and after greetings were exchanged. "Our family's are with us, Private, we're on our way to Paris."

"Very well then, but be advised we have no means by which to accommodate you."

"We're very able to do for ourselves, Jeff,…we won't be any trouble." He sighed then and looked back at the road. "Have you had any suspicious travelers through in the past few days?"

The Private grinned. "Most everyone looks suspicious, Marshal. We have had a few rough looking men ride through, but they seemed to all check out.…All heading East toward Fort Towson."

"How about six men together, all filthy and shaggy?"

"No, sir,…nothing like that,…at least not riding together!"

Rodney nodded. "We had a run in with six men yesterday, and we believe them to be part of Jarvis Cantrell's bunch."

"Cantrell?" Gasped the Private. "That's who we're looking for! If they came this way, we missed them, Marshal,...but I don't think so, we haven't had that many come through at one time,...and we questioned them that did!"

"I believe you, Jeff!...Will Major Wilkes be coming back tonight?"

"Do you know the Major?"

"We met him yesterday." He nodded.

"The Major will have our hides if we did let them through!" Breathed the Private worriedly. "But I'm sure we didn't miss them, not six of them!"

"I'm sure you didn't, Jeff,...these men have been dodging Army patrols for years, and they're good at it!...Now, when will the Major be back?"

"Oh,...later tonight, Marshal. Since they opened the new road, he's been taking the patrol out!...He usually makes a wide circle, returning by way of the McAllister Road,...the Atoka cut-off comes in about fifty yards south of here."

"Thank you, Jeff." He nodded. "If you will, explain that we're here."

"Yes, Sir,...have a good night, sir."

"They had to have come in this way, Billy." Sighed Rodney as the soldiers left. "It's the only way across, this side a Jonesboro,...and they couldn't cross there!"

"Could a slipped by at night,...or come across one or two at a time, it's what I'd a done."

"That has to be what happened."

"If they ain't all up here, it means th' rest are roughin' it, and already headed west somewhere."

"That's my guess, too,...but they could still cross into the Nations at some point,...there's Colbert's Ferry up in Grayson County, Texas. Pretty wide open territory up that way."

"Army's likely watchin' for 'em up there, too." Sighed Billy. "Well, I'm tired, let's stake out them horses, Rod."

Nodding, Rodney turned to look at the wagon. "Better help th' gals down first, they're liable to break a leg."

"Don't just stand there!" Voiced Connie from atop the large wheel. "We could use a little help here!"

"We're on our way!" Grinned Billy.

*　　　*　　　*

August, 20,…."What do you think, Jarvis?" Queried Mitch as they watched the soldiers dismount.

"Don't know yet,…they're going down to water's edge. Got a civilian with them there,…yeah,…that's a Surveyor, Mitch, must be the Army Corp of Engineers!...About that bridge, I guess."

"Well, I hope they don't come snoopin' up here." Voiced Mitch nervously. "Be hell to pay if they do!"

"I'm more worried about that old Indian and his wife….If they go and talk with them, they just might tell them we're here."

"I shouldn't a went and talked with 'em the other day, damn it!... They find us, it's my fault."

"We haven't exactly been trying to hide here, son,…openly fishing, bathing,…they've all seen us. Be patient, we haven't been seen yet!... You've been out back there, is there a way to escape, if we need it?"

"Given time, yes, sir!...We'll need to climb a bluff, but it ain't that bad."

"Then we'll have the time, there's not but a dozen men down there, counting that Surveyor….Just be patient, there's not enough men there to build a bridge."

"I ain't got a problem with bein' patient, Jarvis, it's th' men, I'm worried about!...Bein' here so long is gettin' th' best of 'em."

"I'm feeling the pressure myself, son. But if we leave now, we'll have to run again, and I can feel that, too!...No, somehow we have to hold out for another ten days, at least….I have always believed that good things come to those that wait!"

"Explain that to th' men, why don't ya?"

"I'll talk with them again, once these soldiers leave."

"Well, that might be a while, look across th' river there." Four more soldiers, and a civilian were dismounting at the road's continuance, and they watched until they saw the civilian produce a long pole and come to water's edge where he placed the pole on the ground and held it upright.

"Part of the crew!" Sighed Cantrell, and watched as the man on this side began looking through his instruments to periodically wave an arm at the man across the way.

"It won't be long now, Mitch!...Let's us just settle down and watch, come on, relax, and they both eased themselves down on the rough planking in the dark of the doorway to wait.

The soldiers were there until almost noon, and aside from an occasional look from a few of them, none ventured up to explore the remains of Jonesboro.

"You think we're okay now?" Sighed Mitch, as he watched them mount up and leave.

"Yeah, we're okay now." He grunted to his feet, as did Mitch and moved back into the room's darkness.

"Relax, boys!" Said Mitch, watching them all make their way back to sit down on their saddles again. "They're gone." They continued on across the floor to once again stop and face the twelve men.

"What was that all about, Boss?" Queried Morgan White as they made themselves comfortable again.

"That was just a surveying crew, most likely men hired by the Army Engineers, you all seen that sign down there!...There's nothing to worry about."

"Well, if you'll pardon me sayin' so, Boss,...but that's cuttin' it a little close for my comfort!"

"Mine, too, Mister Cantrell," Voiced Silk Murphy. "If we're gonna break up anyhow, whats to keep us from leavin' now,...we could a done had our hands on that loot we hid?"

"Yes, sir," Broke in Dutch Henry. "If Gator and th' others made it, we can, too!"

"Wouldn't surprise me if Gator and them weren't already there!" Added Billy Jack.

"Gentlemen," Sighed Cantrell. "In all the years we've been together, how many times have I been wrong in my decision making?"

"That would be never!" Answered Mitch quickly. "And you men know it."

"That ain't what we're sayin', Mitch!" Argued Curley.

"Okay, boys!" Broke in Cantrell with authority. "I will say this again!...The whole southern part of this country has been alerted about us,…it is crawling with cavalry patrols,…and all of them looking for us!…Law enforcement is looking for us, not to exclude Bounty Hunters, or the Pinkertons….And that being said,…I think you men might cope with the law, or even a bounty hunter,…but you can't win if the Army catches you!" He gave them a moment for that to sink in.

"Gator, and the others were foolish to leave, and if they are not caught by now, it will surprise me."

"Knowing old Gator, they're dead alreay." Commented Mitch. "And you all know I'm right!"

"Maybe," Said Cantrell. "Maybe not!…Now, I'm tellin' you men what I told Gator,…if you want to leave now, I won't stop you!…But think of this,…you have got it in mind to go back for that money, all eleven of you, and that's what will get you caught,…and I'll tell you why. Because once you leave here, not one of you will trust the other enough to split up and go back separately,…you'll be too afraid one of you will get there first and take it all!…That is what will get you caught!"

"You will be caught, Gentlemen, and most likely killed!…But you would be right, too,…someone will beat you there, and they will take it all,…and I believe they already have!…The Army has Indian Scouts tracking for them, and I am here to tell you, that those scouts have already found that loot,…and they did so, not an hour after we buried it!…And do you know why, I know this?…Because I had you bury it there to buy us time to get away!"

"Now, once again,…if you want to go, you have my blessing,…but you will come closer to getting there if you'll wait another ten days…. That is what Mitch and I are going to do!…Besides, we're all broke now, and I had hoped we'd stay together long enough to pull one more job before we disband."

They were all silent for a time after that, each of them obviously torn between their desire to return to Arkansas, and to stay and be part of one last raid with Cantrell,…and after looking at each other for a time, they all either shrugged, or nodded their approval.

"We'll hang with you long enough to pull that job, Boss." Nodded White. "We owe you a lot more'n that!"

"I appreciate that a lot, men, thank you!" With that, both him and Mitch walked around them back to the bar where he leaned against the top on his elbows.

"You didn't tell me you planned another job, Jarvis, when did that happen?"

"Three minutes ago." He sighed then turned around to lean his back against the long counter.

"What have you got in mind," Urged Mitch. "A stage?"

"I don't know yet!...I just know you're right, we will need money to get to Mexico. I'm thinking we can maybe rob us a bank, disband, and be on our separate ways before the Army can retaliate!" He shrugged then. "But I still believe that eleven men will get themselves caught,... and if they do, one of them will give us away."

"Well,...like you said, Jarvis. "A man has to face his own destiny."

"That he does, Mitch." He sighed. "That he does....But I would like to postpone mine for a while."

*   *   *

"Come in, Marshal." Smiled Judge Bonner. "Have a seat."

"I'll just be a minute, Judge." Sighed Stockwell as he came on to sit down. "I have decided to call off the all night crime watch, it's been six days since that wire came in....I think Cantrell's half way across Texas by now, anyway."

"Well," Sighed Bonner. "It does appear logical that if that bunch was still in northeast Texas, they would have already shown themselves."

"I still plan to keep a man on night duty, to rattle doors and such,... and then hope I'm right!"

"Then do it, Jim, it's your call!...I'll inform the Council this afternoon,...I have a meeting with Bratcher."

"Thanks, Judge." He got up as he spoke, nodded at Bonner and left the office. He pulled his pocket watch and checked the time before walking on to the double, glass-inserted doors and out onto the boardwalk. He closed the door and stood there to watch the street's activity then wondered again if he was right?...He had come to the conclusion a long while back, that he did not have what it takes to be a City Marshal,...and he knew why,...he was afraid! Not of doing what his job required, but that he would be wrong when he did it! He was disappointed in himself, mostly with his decision-making. Why did he make a decision, and afterward be afraid it was the wrong one?

Stepping to the edge of the boardwalk, he rolled and lit a brown-paper cigarette, taking the nerve suppressant into his lungs as he thought of Jarvis Cantrell, and the wire from Shreveport. Captain Ford, and Company had come all that way without finding any sign of Cantrell, and knowing the country between Paris, and there, he was wondering why a gang of killers would even go that way, it was all marshland? It would be more likely for them to continue south, or go west toward the town of Dallas.

'They can't be coming here', he thought. If they were going to take the time to raid another town, especially with the Army on their heels, they would have already,...maybe Clarksville, it was smaller in size, and would offer less resistance!...They are nowhere near Paris, he thought, blowing smoke skyward. There was just no place forty or fifty men could hold up, and remain undetected for a month....Unless?...He shuddered inside at the thought. Could they actually be in Jonesboro?... Those warehouses could hide a hundred men, and no one ever went there any more,...except for the Choctaw,...maybe!...But even they were too superstitious to explore those empty buildings, too many evil spirits,...too many killings there in its day.

If they were not already gone, they must be in Jonesboro, he thought,...it was the only place in a hundred miles where that many men could hide and possibly hope to be undetected for a month.... Maybe he should send a man to check it out, if they were not there, he would certainly feel a lot better?...If they were there, the man he sent would surely be killed,...and he could not bring himself to send a man into harm's way like that! None of his deputies had the know-how to do something like that without being seen, not even him!...Besides, he thought grimly, If Cantrell was there, it would take a troop of soldiers, or a large Posse to flush them out,...and he had neither.

No, he thought then,...all he could do is wait and when something happens, act on it! It didn't make sense that a gang of wanted men would hide out for this long, anyway, or could hide out for this long without being seen....Using that logic, he sighed, almost sure that nothing was going to happen. But then again,...if it did, it would surely happen here, Paris was the wealthiest town around, and that was not saying much, because everyone was still broke! It did not make sense, not after all this time,...and sighing again, he turned and walked down the boardwalk to the square then around the corner on his way to see Sheriff Gose.

*   *   *

Just before dusk, Rodney reined the team off the Goodland Road and stopped the wagon under a large Cottonwood, some thirty yards away.

Billy climbed down on his side of the wagon and helped Willy down, and the three of them began tromping down the tall grass in a large circle to prepare for camp. Willy began pulling up grass in the center of the area to clear a spot of bare ground for the fire, as Billy and the Marshal helped the women and kids down,...and while they stretched aching muscles and tended to private matters, him and the lawman staked out the horses and team before bringing in the supplies for the night's meal.

Willy and Christopher brought in wood for the fire, and Billy stooped to strike a match to a tuft of dry grass and placed it under the twigs. Rodney had retrieved the last coils of rope from the confiscated saddles and together, they laid a circle of hemp around the campsite.

"You really believe this old wives' tale, Billy?"

"I've learned to believe a little bit of just about everything!...Besides, ain't it you that said every legend is based on truth?"

"Yeah," He grinned. "I guess it was. Anyway, I hope this one is, I'm sick of snakes!"

"We're in Texas now, they don't grow that big."

"Maybe not, my friend, but they're just as damn deadly!"

"William," Voiced Connie. "Get the large skillet, and the pot from the wagon, honey."

"That will is gonna grow to be a good man, Billy,...tall and strong!"

"Yeah," Agreed Billy, reaching for the makings. "I'm proud as hell of 'im,...and a little worried."

"Worried, about what?"

"His interest in guns!...Peter's been teaching him to shoot."

"I wouldn't worry about that, old son, Peter's a good teacher."

"I know,...but he thinks of me as a hero, or somethin'. I think he might have his sights set on bein' a gunman, like me,...and I ain't a

121

good role-model for a growin' boy!...I got a teach 'im th' difference, Rod, and it's gonna be hard!"

"I agree," He sighed. "Okay, then we'll both teach him the right way,...we can talk with Peter about it, too. I'm sure he never gave it a thought,...he's afflicted with a bit of hero-worship his self, you know?"

"I have noticed that!" Grinned Billy. "Anyway, night before last, he asked me for one a them rifles we took,...and I gave it to him!"

"Why?"

"I couldn't say no,...said he wanted a rifle he could call his own.....I did tell 'im he couldn't load it, though."

"It'll work out, Billy,...Will's got a good head on his shoulders! He reached a cigar from his shirt and lit it. "You know somethin', Billy,...we better be careful out here, as dry as it is. Look at the cracks in th' ground there, must be a while since it rained down here. One good spark, and this timber would go up in ashes for twenty miles."

"I think of that every time we make camp, Rod,...but it's calm enough here."

Rodney nodded. "When do ya think we'll get to the ranch?"

"Tomorrow afternoon sometime, I guess."

"Good,...you all can stay there with us while we're here."

"One night, maybe," Sighed Billy. "I ain't gonna intrude on your in-laws that way,...we'll stay with Doc and Mama while we're here. We'll leave th' wagon there, though, we got plenty a ridin' horses now."

"Why, you can use the carriage, it's a two-seater?"

"We'll see."

Rodney was silent for a minute then. "Not to change the subject, Billy,...but I just had a thought!...What if Cantrell didn't disband at all, what if those six just ran off on their own?"

"Anything's possible, Rod, what you thinkin'?"

"It's just a thought, but what if he should raid Paris, wouldn't that be a kick in the ass?"

"More like a disaster,...but I don't really think he's here, Rod,...at least not now!...It's been too long, no place to hide."

"Oh, I can think of a place to hide, and chances are, no one would look there!"

"That would be Jonesboro, right?"

"Exactly,…nobody much goes there anymore,…it's a ghost town!"

"And who told you all that, Rod, it's only been a couple a years?"

"Sergeant Neville, last time I went to the Fort. Only thing still there is a couple a them stilt houses, the Choctaw fishermen live in….He said the whole place looked like it was about to fall in."

"If that's th' case, I'm sure Jim's already thought of it, don't you?"

"Yeah, I know he has, but he might not have the man-power to check it out!…Last wire I got from 'im, he was down to just one deputy, and Gose only had two!…Said the town didn't have the money for salaries, and it wasn't all due to the Depression, either!" He chuckled then.

"He said the Council allowed the purchase of a Steam Pumper earlier this year, convinced Bratcher the fire Department needed it!"

"Might need it, too, hot as this summer's been!"

"I can see where it might pay off, it's supposed to shoot water three stories high!"

"Might beat a bucket-brigade, at that!" Sighed Billy. "But getting' back to Cantrell, Rod….I don't think Paris has to worry about him, or Jonesboro. If he's got half a brain, he's half way to Mexico by now!"

"I'll give that a big, Amen!" Laughed Rodney. "And knowing Jimbo, he would, too,…I know he's been worried stiff about all this!… Remember when I got that wire about Loughmiller?…He was on pins and needles."

"Stockwell's a good man,…but get down to it, he might not have what it takes to be a lawman!"

"I've had that thought a time or two." He nodded…."Ahhh, well,… it's up to him now!…Heads up, Billy,…here comes Willy with his rifle!" And they watched as Willy proudly carried the rifle toward them.

"William!" Said Connie loudly as she looked up from peeling the potatoes. "You put that gun right back in the wagon, young man!"

"It ain't loaded, Mama, and it's mine, Daddy gave it to me!"

She glanced darkly at Billy. "I know he did, but now's not the time to play with it!" She looked back at Billy with a scowl, and that was as if to say, you have lost your mind!

"It'll be okay, honey!" He nodded. "I told 'im to choose one."

"This is the one I want, daddy." He grinned, holding up the gun. "I unloaded it like you said!"

Rodney took the rifle from him and checked the action before giving it to Billy. "A damn good choice, appears brand new!...Probably got it in one a those towns they raided."

"It does look pretty good!" Nodded Billy. "Got a be fairly new, it's th' first one I seen." He checked the barrel for a serial number then. "Eighteen seventy-four, Winchester. Good choice, son." He sighed then. "Pretty dirty, though....First thing you need to do, is clean it, dirty guns misfire."

"They can blow up in your face, too!" Added Rodney.

"We'll clean it after supper." Said Billy, giving it back to the boy. "Put it away for now."

Willy took the rifle and showed them the stock. "I carved my name on it already." He grinned then, and took it back to the wagon.

"Billy Upshur!" Scolded Connie. "He's too young for a gun, and you know it!"

"It'll be okay, honey,...we'll teach 'im to use it."

"Oh, oh!" Grinned Rodney. "Here comes your second in command."

"Can I have a rifle, too, Daddy,...Willy's got one?"

*   *   *

August, 21,...By late afternoon, Billy reined the mules off the road onto the narrow, overgrown lane on the last mile and a quarter leg of their journey, and as the familiar two-storied structure came into sight through the thick blanket of trees, Melissa was already holding Cindy as the girl stood on the seat between Billy and the Marshal with excited expectation.

"Now that I see it again." Exclaimed Rodney. "I miss this place, too!"

"I do, too." Sighed Melissa. "But it's still too big."

"I can't see Grammy, Mama!"

"We're not there yet, baby,...they don't know we're coming."

"It's a surprise, honey." Grinned Rodney.

"Like Christmas, daddy?"

"Something, like that."

They were out of the trees now, and turning into the large front yard of the old ranch house, and it was not until they were almost to the front porch's tall steps, that the door opened and Mister and Mrs. Gabbett rushed across the porch and down into the yard. Billy stopped the wagon, and Rodney climbed down to hug Mrs. Gabbett then shook John Gabbett's hand before reaching up to take Cindy as Lisa lowered her down,…and once she was in her Grammy's arms, he helped Melissa down.

While the two women cried and hugged, Rodney, and John Gabbett walked around the team where Mister Gabbett vigorously shook Billy's hand and greeted Connie and the kids. As Connie and the two youngest went around to join Lisa, and her Mother, the three men, and Willy freed the eight horses, and then him and Mister Gabbett led them off toward the barn, while Billy and the lawman led the wagon and team in their wake.

The women were already in the kitchen when they entered the door into the spacious sitting room, and as the three of them eased themselves into the cushioned armchairs, Gabbett went to the liquor cabinet for a bottle and glasses.

Both Billy, and Rodney quickly stood and removed their gun-belts before sitting down again to receive the drink.

"Here's to better times!" Toasted Gabbett.

"Here, here!" Voiced Rodney as they drank the fiery liquid.

"More, Gentlemen?"

"No, thanks!" Grinned Billy, and placed the glass on the low table between them. "You sure got th' place lookin' good, John."

"It took a while." He smiled then nodded at Rodney. "Thank you for bringing Lisa home, both of you."

"Well, it has been a while." Shrugged Rodney. "And Billy needed to check on Doc and Mattie anyway, so, here we are."

"Any trouble on the way?"

"Six outlaws tried to rob us, Mister Gabbett!" Blurted Willy with an excited smile.

"Good Lord,…what happened,…is that why Lisa's head is bandaged?…I was about to ask about that!"

"She was grazed by a wild shot, John,…she's fine."

"Thank God for that!…Times don't seem to be getting any better, do they?"

"No, Sir, they don't!"

"Tell me,…how in this world did you ever take on six men like that?"

"Daddy outdrew 'em!...Uncle Rodney, too!" Exclaimed Willy.

"That's enough, son!" Billy smiled at Gabbett then. "We was lucky, Mister Gabbett."

"From what I have heard about you, son, I doubt that!...Thank you for being there."

"How are things in town, John, back to normal yet?"

"Rodney,…by the looks of things, I'd say we're getting there. People are going back to work now, stores are reopening, crops being sold again,…makes a man proud to see it!....But then again, we don't get back to town much, just to buy a few supplies now and then."

Rodney leaned forward and looked toward the kitchen, before turning to Willy. "Will,…what I'm about to say here, you should not repeat, to anybody, okay?"

"I won't, Uncle Rodney."

Nodding, he leaned forward. "While the gals are in the kitchen, we have something to tell you….Billy, and myself have close to three hundred pounds of gold out there in the barn!...And both, Lisa and myself have decided that half of it should belong to you!"

"What?" He gasped. "Gold,…where,…I've been all over that barn!...I haven't seen any gold."

"It's under the floor!...Remember, I told you about the mine?"

"Yes, but,…I don't know, son?...You've already, as much as given us your ranch, why are you doing this?"

"Just sharing the wealth, John,…besides, you can help out Sabrina, and her family."

"Then, I am humbled, Rodney."

"There are some stipulations that go with it, John!...Number one, you can't tell anyone you have it, and number two,…you can never sell but a small amount of it at any given time,…and you can figure out why?...Me and Billy are gonna tell Mister Bratcher that you, and Doc Bailey may be coming in to sell gold from time to time, but,…only a few ounces at a time!...Now, here's the thing to remember….If asked, Billy and me are prospecting the land we bought, and we are bringing what little we find to you and Doc,…okay?"

"Absolutely!" He smiled. "This,…is mind-boggling, to say the least!…Thank you, son."

"It's our pleasure, John."

"Is it okay if I tell Myrna?"

"Sure,…but I don't think you should tell anyone else, not even Sabrina."

"I understand.…Now, how long will you be staying, Son, we have a lot to catch up on?"

"I wouldn't worry about that, you'll be ready for us to go by then!"

"I doubt that, Marshal!" He chuckled. "But the reason I ask, is that Sabrina and Benny are coming in a week or so, and they'll be excited to see you."

"Oh, boy!" Exclaimed Willy. "I can't wait to see Benny."

"Well, I don't know, John." Grinned Rodney. "We planned on a couple weeks, maybe three."

"Make it three!…Now, William, what about you all,…we have the room?"

"Thanks, John,…but we'll be goin' on to Doc's sometime tomorrow."

"Come to dinner, you men!" Sang out Myrna Gabbett.

*   *   *

August, 22,…They arrived at Doc's house late that afternoon, and after Willy dismounted and came to catch Angela as he lowered her from the saddle, Billy dismounted to help Christopher and Connie down. Willie took the reins of all three horses and led them around the fenced yard toward the barn in back.

"My Lord, Son!" Exclaimed Doc when he opened the door, and he quickly shook Billy's hand and hugged him.

"Hi, Grandpa!" Chorused Chris and Angela as they wrapped themselves around the old man.

"My, my!" He sniffed, hugging them tightly. "How these young'uns have grown,…and look at you, Daughter!" He laughed, reaching to pull her into a hug as well. "As beautiful as ever!"

"Thank you, Doc." She laughed. "I love you, too!"

"Go on in the house, Mattie's in the kitchen, honey,…you, too, kiddos." He grinned widely at Billy then. "It's damn good to see you, Son." He sniffed. "But, we're missing one here,…where's my other Grandson?"

"He's tendin' th' horses, Doc."

"Well, come on in, boy, the Old Darlin's fixing supper right now, and the coffee's hot!" They both grinned then when they heard the shrill shriek, and continued on across the sitting room and down the hall to the kitchen.

Once Willy came in and received hugs from the old couple, he sat down with his cup of coffee while the younger ones had their milk. "I couldn't lift the gold off the saddle, daddy, you'll have to do it."

"Gold?" Queried Doc. "What gold, son?"

"Your gold, Doc." He grinned. "I'll bring it in later."

"Now, don't you go bringing us any gold, William,…you should keep that for yourselves. Besides, we still have most of the money you left here four years ago."

"I know, Doc!…But if you want, or need anything, we want you to be able to get it!…We want you to have it."

Doc cleared his throat and sighed. "How much gold are you talkin' about?"

"A hundred and forty-one pounds." And when the old man's eyes widened. "We weighed it all out this mornin', and crushed it into dust and small nuggets….Got it all in twelve ounce bags!"

"Where am I gonna keep all that, son?…My word, look at Mattie and me, we're both in th' winter of life here!…Gold is for th' young, me, and my old Darlin' will never live to spend the money we have."

"Then, you can keep it for me, okay?…If you like, I'll take half of it to Ross when we go to th' farm, how's that?"

"Then, I'll keep th' rest for you!" He nodded. "And yes, you do that, Ross needs it worse than we ever will,…and if you find somebody else that needs it, you can take the rest!…A hundred and forty pounds of gold,…boggles the imagination, don't it?"

"All right, you two watch your elbows!" Boomed Mattie as she set the table with plates and hardware, and Connie came in behind her placing the food on the table.

They said grace, and the meal was eaten in silence. When they were done, Billy and Willy left to see to the animals and to bring in their belongings and satchel of gold, before once again sitting at the table over coffee and conversation.

CHAPTER TEN

Billy, Willy and Doc Bailey spent most of the next two days of summer's sweltering heat repairing things around the Bailey home. The roof was in need of help, as were some of the outside siding boards. Some of the planking on the barn's roof and sides had wood to be replaced as well,… but it was hot, and the twenty to thirty mile an hour wind, that seemed to never let up, made it even hotter, and seemed to want to blister the skin on their faces as they worked, forcing them to take frequent water breaks. But today being Tuesday, they knocked off at mid-morning to clean up, as Billy was to meet Rodney in town to call on the bank.

*   *   *

It was much the same in downtown Paris, Hot! Women along the boardwalks were constantly fanning themselves with their paper fans, while the men wiped faces and necks with sweat-stained bandanas, and fanned themselves with their hats. The streets were at times deserted, save a few lone horsemen, or a buckboard or two as families were leaving town for home. The shade provided by the many trees in town, and the covered boardwalks were the only reprive from an already record-breaking summer,…and it left some folks short-tempered, and others just obnoxious. But through it all, business continued to flourish in the Cotton Center, and according to the newspaper in town, much better than some of the larger cities and towns in other states. But the South was seeing the light at the end of the tunnel,…the Recession was fast coming to a close.

Because it was so hot, Rodney, Melissa, and Cindy were content to stay at the ranch with the in-laws. Sabrina and young Benny arrived a week ahead of time on the Southern Pacific, and Rodney accompanied his father in law to the Depot to pick them up,…and although he had thought of calling on Jim Stockwell while in town, had decided to put it off and return to the ranch. He did, however plan to see him when he met with Billy on Tuesday.,…and of course, Melissa was in heaven at home with her entire family once again,…and although the action he was used to at the mountain, was not present here, Rodney did manage to cope with his anxiety for Lisa's sake, and getting along well with the Gabbetts helped as well.

*   *   *

Aside from the steamy heat, and being mostly cooped up inside the dark saloon, there was surprisingly less bickering, arguing, or fighting among the men than Cantrell thought there would be. Surprised, because he knew what a hot summer could do to a man in captivity,…and that was exactly where they were! They were feeling trapped, and a bit helpless with nothing to do, but wait. The muggy heat was at times, almost unbearable inside the abandoned structure, however, the nights were still quite chilly from being so close to the fast-moving water of the Red River,…but the large fireplace made those bearable for them.

They continued to catch, and eat the large Catfish, and a few Gar from time to time,…and by now, all of them were used to bathing almost daily in the river's swift current, and that served multiple purposes for them. They could bathe, clean their clothing, and cool themselves all at the same time. Well, as clean as one can be with no soap,…but they were still careful about it, only venturing out two at a time to bathe, and only in the waning heat of late afternoon.

Cantrell was becoming more restless, himself as the days dragged by. He knew the odds were continuing to stack up against them, the longer they stayed, and that's why he had been placing a sentry along the road in for the past week. He had, in fact, almost decided to leave a couple of times and take their chances,…but each time, he would think about the sleepless, relentless days and nights during the all out pursuit across Arkansas. At the time he ordered it, he'd had a bad feeling about burning that small community in Kentucky, but had relented to the wishes of his men, who at the time had been more than thirty strong. He had discovered, almost too late that they were being followed by the Army, and had barely escaped a deadly ambush just North of Memphis, Tennessee. He lost ten men in the ambush, but managed to make it to the Arkansas Wilderness.

However, the Army patrol did not break off the pursuit, instead they came after them and never let up. That was when he had decided to leave a more noticeable trail, and to bury the valuables where they could be found in hopes of delaying the chase long enough to escape fully,…and it had worked for a time, until they were almost caught napping again in Louisiana.

He thought of all this when he would become impatient, and of the men he had lost,…and that alone is what kept him on his schedule! The troops that were after him had not been home in more than two months, and they had not been paid, nor seen their families in that time. That knowledge is why he believed they would surely give up the chase now, and leave. Especially since he had managed to finally elude them,…and now he was reasonably sure, that in another few days they could leave without Army intervention, at least for a week or so. He was also reasonably sure that local law enforcement would think them already gone elsewhere, leaving them free to hit some small nearby bank, disband, and be on their separate ways before anyone knew who they were after,…and by then, there would be no more Cantrell's Raiders, only a couple of out of work cowboys on horseback trying to cross Texas.

*   *   *

August, 28,…Judge Bonner looked up when he heard the knock, and smiled broadly when he saw who it was through the glass in the door. Getting up, he came around the large, oaken desk and hurried to admit them.

"Mornin', Judge." Grinned Rodney.

"I wouldn't have thought of you two for fifty dollars, Marshal!" Still smiling, he held out his pudgy hand to grip Rodney's. "And you, too, William,…how in the world are you?" He shook Billy's hand as he spoke then stepped aside. "Come on in, men, what do you know, and where have you been for so long?...Have a seat!"

"We just have a minute, Judge." Nodded Rodney. "And where we've been, we don't get that much news, so we don't know all that much!"

"What news we do get is slow in coming." Added Billy.

"I understand,…how's the family?"

"Very good, Judge,…never happier."

"Well, it is damn good to see you both!…Have you seen Jim yet?"

"No, sir, that's who we came to see, and thought we'd say hello to you first,…he in his office?"

"I believe so,…I haven't seen him leave!…You going to be in town long?"

"Don't know yet," Grinned Billy. "We've been here for a week already, checkin' on th' folks."

"How is Doc Bailey, and his wife, William, I haven't seen them in,…God, Son, it's been so long, I can't remember?"

"It was a bit too dangerous for 'em to be out much, sir, what with all th' robbin' and muggin' goin' on th' last couple a years. They ain't as young as they used to be."

"Tell me about it!…Say hello for me." He looked back at Rodney then. "Does this visit have anything to do with this Jarvis Cantrell bunch, Marshal?"

Rodney shook his head. "Not really, sir. We planned the trip before we got the wire about 'im. But it did worry me some, especially when six of his men tried to hold us up on the way in."

"Cantrell's men?" And when Rodney nodded. "Well, that don't make sense,…unless they've disbanded and scattered!…If they have, they're likely long gone from these parts!"

"We think so, too." Nodded Billy.

"What about these six men, you bring them in?"

"We buried them, Judge." Returned Billy. "And, no, they didn't talk."

"Too bad." Sighed Bonner. "Jim has been walking on tacks for two weeks now.…I have never seen a man so worried, or confused."

"Jim's that way, Judge." Sighed Rodney. "But when it comes down to it, he'll take care of business!"

"I am sure of that!…But,…I would like him to be a bit more like you, though,…but, he is a good alternative!…So, what about you, Marshal, things going your way up there in the Nations?"

"Pretty much, yes, sir....Billy and me also own us a Trading Post, and it's doing very well, too,...and now,...begging your pardon, Judge. But, we'd best go see Jim, we got a lot to do today."

"Of course,...it's a breath of fresh air seeing you two, drop back by before you leave town, hell, we haven't seen you men since the picnic out there!...Come to think about it, William,...that's the last time I've seen Doc, to talk to him! Please say hello for me?"

"Yes, Sir, I sure will!" They both got up and went to the door, and with a wave back at Bonner, they left and quickly climbed the three flights of stairs and walked into Rodney's old office, and at the same time, startled a dozing Jim Stockwell, who had been leaning back in the old wrap-around arm-chair with his feet propped on the roll-top.

"What th' hell?" He gasped, but then grinned widely at them and got to his feet.

"I thought that was me sitting there for a minute, Jim." Grinned Rodney, and came on to shake his hand. "I used to sleep there, ya know?...How are ya, Jimbo?"

"Okay, I guess, Marshal, pull up a chair!" He took Billy's hand then and shook it. "Good to see you, Mister Upshur, come on, have a seat!" And once they were seated, he sat down again.

"What brings you to Paris, Marshal?"

"A visit." Nodded Rodney. "And it's good to see the town getting on its feet again....Now, what about you,...things okay for ya?"

"Most times!...But you know me and my hang-ups....Been havin' some stomach trouble lately, and accordin' to Doc Lovejoy, I got a couple a ulcers."

"Hate to hear it. The wife and kids okay?"

"They're good," He smiled. "We're all good,...kids are with th' wife's folks over in Greenville for a week."

"What's the latest on this Cantrell thing, Jim,...we heard you was worried some?"

"You been talkin' with Judge Bonner!" He sighed.

"Saw 'im on the way up." Nodded Rodney. "Any more news?"

Stockwell shook his head. "Nothin' since we got that wire, Marshal,... and I didn't really get worried too much, till that Army Captain came in and told us he'd been chasin' that bunch all the way across Tennessee and Arkansas, before losin' 'em somewhere here in north Texas!...And with only a dozen men between me, Gose, and John Rucker!"

"Don't feel bad, Jim,...that would a worried me, too!"

"Personally,...I don't believe they're in North Texas anymore!" He continued. "But, if they are,...and as smart as Cantrell seems to be, I think I know where he'd be?"

"Jonesboro." Nodded Rodney. "Did you check it out?"

"Marshal, there ain't a man among us with th' gumption, or smarts enough to go up there without bein' spotted, including me!...And all twelve of us wouldn't be enough to flush 'em out a there, anyway." He sighed then. "I missed my chance to get th' Army to go look!...I told that Captain Ford about Jonesboro, but I also told him I didn't think they'd be there!"

"What did he say?"

"Not a thing,...said they'd been ordered home."

"Well,...Don't beat yourself up over it, you had no way of knowing."

"True, but if I had insisted, I know they'd have checked it out!"

"No use to dwell on it, Jim,...we all make bad decisions."

"Well, I don't recall you makin' any, Marshal!"

"That's because I didn't tell you about 'em!...Anyway, if I didn't," He grinned, reaching to place a hand on Billy's shoulder. "It's because I had the best there is to help me."

"Yes, sir,...and if I could handle a gun like him, or even you, for that matter, I wouldn't worry so much!"

"Oh, yes you would. Being a lawman is a mind thing, what I mean is,...you use your mind first, then your gun,...and you have got the mind for it! What you lack is confidence in your decision-making. Work on that first, Jim,...and then the gun."

"Yeah, well,...I'm tryin', Marshal, thanks for the encouragement."

"You're welcome. Now,...if it'll make you feel better, I'll ride to Jonesboro with you to check it out?"

"We both will." Nodded Billy. "Wouldn't take a day."

"Oh, no." Sighed Jim. "I really don't think they're there,...not anymore. It's been too long!"

"Neither do we!" Said Billy. "They're likely on their way to Mexico by now."

"That's what I think, too." He nodded.

"Well, Jim." Sighed Rodney. "We have to go see Horace Bratcher before we leave, so we'll be going." They both got up and shook Stockwell's hand. "We'll be here for another few days, if you need me, I'm at the ranch."

They went back down the stairs, waved through the glass at Bonner then went out to pause on the boardwalk.

"Whose idea was it to leave our horses at the Livery?" Sighed Rodney, taking his hat off to fan his face with it. "I don't remember it ever being this hot, Billy,...or ever going this long without rain!...John said it rained the last time in June. I'll bet it's a hundred in the shade here!"

"Want a go get th' horses, Rod?"

"No, I'll live!" He said, settling the hat on his head again. "Let's go." They walked down the boardwalk to the square and was about to go down the steps, when Rodney stopped him again.

"Look across the square there, Billy. Am I blind, or does that bank building look empty?" They both stared at what they knew to be Horace Bratcher's bank, or what used to be his bank,...the building's windows were boarded up, as was the glass-paneled front door. "I thought Ross said he changed the name of it, he said nothing about him moving the bank,...but, where to?"

Billy sighed as he stared at the building, then caught a man coming out of the corner hardware, and stopped him. "We're lookin' for th' Farmer's and Merchant's Bank, friend, can you help us?" The man pointed down the boardwalk then walked away. "Yeah,...thanks!" He muttered then turning to Rodney.

"It's at the end of th' block here, Rod, come on."

"Okay, I see it now, corner of Grand." And grinning, they stayed on the boardwalk and walked the length of the block, stepped into the street and crossed it, having to stop a couple of times for a freight wagon,...but at last were stepping up to a covered walkway again.... After sidestepping a few shoppers, they crossed to the bank's double doors and went inside.

"Fancy place!" Commented Billy as he followed Rodney to a Teller's window.

"Sure looks expensive." He breathed, and then nodded at the Teller.

"Marshal Rodney Taylor, we need to see Horace Bratcher!"

"Yes, sir." Nodded the balding man, and gestured with a nod at a glass-inserted door. "That door right over there, Marshal."

"As I live and breathe!" Smiled Horace Bratcher, quickly getting to his feet to greet them. "My two favorite people,...how are you, Marshal Taylor?" He shook Rodney's hand then turned to Billy. "William Upshur!" He shook Billy's hand vigorously." We miss you in Paris, son,...we were all sorry to see you move away."

"Thanks, Horace,...when did you move th' bank?"

"Well," He said, going back to sit down again. "Sit down, boys, sit down!" And when they did. "As you may know, I almost lost my bank in Seventy-four!" He sighed then. "Made some really bad investments, I did....Anyway, I was desperate,...I mean, I was about to lose everything I had, including everyone else's money!...Anyway, I proposed an idea to a couple of lending firms, who were going under themselves, and they agreed to pool their assets with mine. Sort of like selling shares in my business....It helped, too, but not enough to really do what I needed,... so I proposed my ideas to Farmer's and Merchant's Insurance group, and they bought it!"

"Then,...after a year of success, and them being a major shareholder, they insisted I move the entire bank into their building and of course, I had to change the name....My old building has been up for sale ever since, and hopefully, it'll sell now the economy is turning around and that, Gentlemen,...is my story! Now,...what can I do for you?...And William, I do hope you're not closing your account today, withdrawing five thousand dollars at this time would hurt a little."

"I'm not here to do that." Grinned Billy.

"No, Sir," Began Rodney. "But we do need to arrange something with you. As you might have heard, Billy and me bought some land from the Choctaw Indians, quite a large piece of land up near the Arkansas border. Anyway, what time I'm not working, we do a little prospecting on our land,...and, it's paying off some....Not real big, but we're finding dust!...Well, what we do find, we are bringing here and leaving with John Gabbett, and Doc Bailey,...and we wanted to tell you that they may be coming in to exchange it for money from time to time!...We want to be sure you can handle it for them,...sort of quietly?... We wouldn't want folks thinking they had gold laying around."

"Is it the same quality as that you sold me in seventy-one?"

"Yes, sir, it is." Nodded Billy. "We bought that land."

"Then I will be most happy to accommodate them,…I will handle it personally.…And don't worry, I know what gold does to some folks, I'll keep it discreet!"

"We do thank you." Nodded Billy.

"Nonsense, I'm glad to do it, what else could I do for the man that saved the bank's money, so many years ago?…It's my pleasure."

"In that case," Smiled Rodney. "We'll leave you to business."

"It's good to see you both." He got up to shake their hands then to show them out, escorting them to the front door, to once again say goodbye.

"Well, that was easy." Smiled Rodney as the door was closed.

"A lot easier than walking back to th' Livery!" Laughed Billy. "Why didn't we just ride into town?"

"Why, you want a tire th' horses out out?…Not on your life, my friend,…this heat's a killer!"

"Tell it like it is, Rod." He laughed. "We are plumb stupid!"

"I want you to remember, you said that,…not me!"

*   *   *

August, 29,…"Doc,…you sure you and Mama won't ride out there with us?"

"Son, we would love to go,…but it's just too blamed hot!...You all go ahead and enjoy your visit."

"Well, I'll take care of your rig, Doc."

"Don't worry about that, son."

"See ya tonight then,…everybody in?" And when they all said yes, he clucked the team into motion west along the Bonham Road, and four miles later was turning north on the familiar road to the farm.

It took every bit of two hours to cover the eight miles, but they were turning down the Pecan, and Cottonwood shrouded lane to finally rein the horses into the large frontyard of the rambling farmhouse.

"Hi, Jeremy!...Hi, Jesse!" Yelled Willy as he jumped to the ground in a run, and was closely followed by Christopher and Angela.

"Hi, Willy!" They yelled back, and ran headlong to meet him, and once the jumping and greetings subsided, all five of them broke into a run toward the corrals.

"Guess we're home." Smiled Connie then saw Reba and waved. "Hey, Reba!"

Billy got to the ground and helped her out as Reba came toward them.

"My Lord, what a surprise!" She exclaimed, quickly hugging Connie first, and then Billy. "I'm so glad to see you all, and Ross will be, too!"

"Where is Ross?" Queried Billy, still taking in the vista of tall pecan trees and fields of crops.

"He took fresh water to the hands, over in the North fields, they're weeding cotton today. Come on inside, I'm making lunch, and he never misses a meal!"

*   *   *

"I want a thank you again for th' great time we had at the mountain." Said Ross as he pushed his plate back. "We'll never forget it, especially that treasure in the burial room,...now, that's what I call wealth!"

"Yes," Said Reba with a mocking tone. "He brings up the subject at least twice a day!" She laughed then. "But it was beautiful,...and that gorgeous hidden valley, my, my!"

"We love being there." Smiled Connie. "But I have to admit, we miss being here, too!...Our house seems so lonesome out there."

"I know,...we try not to even look at it." Sighed Reba. "Ross even suggested we put a lighted lamp in the window at night."

"Why don't you just move in it?" Smiled Billy. "It's vacant."

"Move in it,...are you serious, Boss?...That wouldn't be proper."

"Why not, it's empty, and I'm tellin' ya to?...Besides, this place is too small, you got two growin' boys to think about!"

"That's a wonderful idea!" Added Connie.

"Course, you'd have to move your well-pump into th' kitchen, maybe do a little repair, but you can handle that. Besides,...you can let your top hand move his family in here."

"Smiling, Ross looked up at Reba. "What do you think?"

"I think, yes, of course!...Thank you, Billy, Connie!"

"And that's not all." Said Billy, getting up from the table to retrieve the satchel by the door. "You won't have to move a thing, you can buy all new furnishings,...leave this stuff here for th' hand." He took a pouch of the gold from the bag and laid it on the table as he spoke.

"Is,...is that what I think it is, Boss?" Breathed Ross, reaching to heft the pound of dust.

"Almost seventy pounds of it, Ross,...and it's yours to spend as you see fit!...Farm equipment, furniture, wagons, whatever,...and you don't have to account for it!"

"My, God, Boss!" Stammered Ross, and was still hefting the heavy pouch.

"You can send the boys to College now." Smiled Connie,...and then rushed to hug Reba while she cried.

"I have to warn you, too, Ross." Said Billy. "You know what gold does to some men. You can't let anybody know you have it,...cause they'll find some way to try to take it from you!...You can't sell, or trade too much of it at a time, that'll raise questions,...and I suggest you not trade any of it in Paris!...Go to Bonham, Greenville, Dennison, maybe... you can find anything you need there....I sure wouldn't want anything bad to happen over this."

"Don't worry, Boss!" Choked Ross. "I know how to handle it."

"I know you do, I'm just remindin' you of th' sort a men that's out there."

"We've had that experience, too!" Sniffed Reba.

"Then it's settled!" Nodded Billy, taking the pouch and replacing it in the satchel."It's yours now, hide it well!" He grinned when Ross leaned to peer into the satchel. "That's seventy twelve-ounce bags there, Ross, seventy Troy-Pounds of gold."

"I don't know what to say, Boss?"

"Don't say anything, just pour me some more coffee and change th' subject!...Besides, I want a hear about this year's crops, everything."

*   *   *

Cantrell looked each man in the face as he walked through them, and finally stopping to stand in front of the old hearth. "We leave here day after tomorrow, Gentlemen."

"It's about time, boss!" Called out Morgan White.

"Yes, it is, Morg….Now, when we leave, we'll go two at a time through the back door there, get on that road and ride south!...Mitch says there's a town due southeast of us, and a larger one to the southwest. Tomorrow we'll decide which one to hit,…we'll ride into town just like we leave here, two at a time to mingle with the town-folk!...Once we're all there, we'll take the bank,…and this time, Gentlemen,…we do it quickly, and quietly,…and with no killing!...I want that understood!... Once we have the money, we scatter,…we go our separate ways as soon as we split the loot!...Any questions?" He waited for a moment, and when no one said anything.

"Good,…now you've got till then to think about what I just said,… no killing!...You do, I'll throw the money back, and we leave empty handed!" Nodding, he made his way back to the dark bar to lean his back against it and study the men as they talked among themselves, and they were just barely visible in the darkness.

"You think it'll go that smooth, Jarvis?"

"The bank?...Sure it will, Mitch,…and believe me, I wouldn't say that if Gator Malloy was still with us.….That Gentleman has instigated more than one senseless killing!"

"Well, I've been half expectin' 'em to come crawlin' back!...You could put all six a their heads together, and they wouldn't know how to survive out there."

"They won't be back, son." He sighed. "I fear the worst for them already."

"I'd say you're prob'ly right,…Gator's a lunatic!...Which one a them towns we gonna hit, anyway,…be more money in th' bigger one?"

"Don't be too sure, Mitch,…this Depression has left the country pretty much broke!...We'll just have to take our chances with what's there.….And as far as the bigger town goes, there's more lawmen there,… and civilians to get hurt!"

"And a better chance for one of us to be shot!" Sighed Mitch..

"Exactly!...Anyway, I'm leaning toward the smaller town."

"It's hard to believe we been here this long without bein' found!... It ain't natural."

"I agree." Nodded Cantrell. "But, I think it proves my point, too. The Army is surely gone by now, except for the area Forts here abouts,…by the time we leave here, those soldier boys will have been paid and already drunk somewhere. Even local law enforcement will have forgotten all about us."

"They likely think we're half way to Mexico by now," Chuckled Mitch. "And I wish we was."

"We'd be caught, or dead already, son. The entire state of Texas would have been out looking for us….This is the only way, believe me!"

"Oh, I do believe you, Jarvis,…I've just always had a problem with patience."

"I have noticed that!" He grinned to himself, and looked around the darkened room. "This is a good place to hide, Mitch!...In our whole time together, we've never had it so good. It's dry, we have fire, fresh fish to eat,…we've had more rest than we've ever had,…I sort of hate to leave it!"

"Well, I feel trapped here, Jarvis….I don't know, I just feel safer in the open, at least I can see what's comin' up on us."

"You're young yet, one day you'll learn to appreciate what I'm saying,…and when you do, you'll know I was right!"

"I already know you're right, Sir!"

"Where's your folks, Mitch, I've never heard you speak of them?"

"Ain't got none, Jarvis,…And I'd like to leave it like that!...Besides, you're my kin now!"

"And that makes me proud, too!...You have become like a son to me, Mitch,…and you're not much older than my eldest would be,…if he had lived."

"Thanks, Jarvis."

"No, no, …thank you, son." He cleared his throat then. "Now, tomorrow,…I would like for you and the men to shave, Mitch,…we look like wooley Mammoths, all of us!...I'd like us all to look like ordinary cowboys when we leave here!"

"You gonna shave off your beard,…I never seen you without it?"

"Neither has the law!...If we're not recognized, we might make it to Mexico with our hides on."

"Sounds good to me,…oh, oh, here comes Morg, I think."

"We're goin' fishin now, Boss!" Said Morg, as him and another man passed them and walked toward the door.

"Keep your eyes open, men!" Returned Cantrell then glanced at Mitch. "Put Sam and Dutch on look-out tonight, Mitch,...and I think a man should be on guard while they're fishing."

"You got it Jarvis,...and I'll have one get th' fire going, too."

*   *   *

"When you planning on leaving, kids?" Queried Doc as he chewed.

"Not before Monday," Said Connie quickly. "I'd like to go to Church on Sunday,...all of us!"

"Looks like we're leavin' Monday, Doc." Grinned Billy then spooned more potatoes onto his plate. "Good potatoes, Mama,...and you don't know how good this steak is, after eatin' venison for so long!"

"Why, thank you, William." She smiled. "My, my," She sniffed, suddenly becoming emotional.

"What is it, Mama Bailey?" Asked Connie, quickly reaching to touch the older moman's beefy arm.

"Nothing, honey." She sniffed again, then dabbed at her eyes with the table linen. "Sixteen years ago, there was a frail, frightened little boy sitting in William's very chair there,...he had a bandage wrapped around his eyes,...and he was eating chocolate cake, and drinking his coffee! Walter was sitting right where he is now." She wiped at her eyes again then blew her nose.

"I'm so sorry,...you'll have to forgive a sentimental old woman!"

"Thanks, Mama." Grinned Billy. "I love you, too!"

"Come on now, old Darlin' dry up over there!" Chuckled Doc, as he was also blinking away the dampness in his eyes. "See, you've got your Daughter in law sniffling."

Connie laughed and blew her nose as well, and then got up to retrieve the coffeepot.

"Well," Boomed Mattie. "It just so happens, that I baked William a Chocolate cake today,...and when all of you have cleaned your plates, I'll serve it."

"Yeaaaa" Echoed the children, causing Mattie to smile even wider.

"I thought that might get a rise!...You and your darling wife have such beautiful children, William."

"We think so, too, Mama, thanks."

Doc cleared his throat then. "How did the town look to you, son?"

"Pretty much th' same,...but different than when we was here last. We was surprised th' bank moved!"

"Horace Bratcher was a Godsend for the folks in town, son. The bank almost went bust, but he found a way to survive, and help the town at the same time!...You just got a hand it to a man like him."

"Amen, Doc....By th' way, he's all set to take th' gold if you need to cash in some."

"I won't need to, but it's good to know,...oh, I almost forgot, son.... As you know, during th' Depression, we have pretty much been shut in here, so I spent a lot a time reading my medical books. Anyway,...last year, I wrote a letter to a Physician friend of mine in New Orleans....I didn't think I'd ever hear back from him, what with th' country in such sad shape, but I did!"

"I got a lengthy letter from him a month ago,...and he and I both now have a theory as to why you are so adept with that pistol of yours!... He said, that by you being hit with that rifle-butt in the frontal lobe, it was highly probable that it affected that part of your brain that controls your motor skills, in fact,...he said it probably is what sets you apart from other men, in that respect!" He sighed then. "Course, it is just a theory, Medical Science don't know all that much about it yet!... Anyway, I wanted you to know."

"Well, it's beyond me, Doc." He grinned.

"Something else, too!...Don't you think it's about time you paid a visit to your parent's graves, son,...maybe talk with them a little?... Because, whether you believe it or not, they will hear you."

"Doc." Sighed Billy, blinking away a sudden influx of tears. "It is time,...but I can't, not yet....Right now, I can't even think about 'em without wantin' to cry like a baby,...and if I went there, I would!...I just can't bring myself to do it!...At least, not yet."

"I think we understand, son, but think about it, will you, these children need to know their true Grandparents."

"I will, Doc,...I'll think about it!" He pushed his plate away and drank some of the hot coffee to clear the sudden lump in his throat.

"All right!" Said Mattie gleefully. "Chocolate cake time!" She and Connie got up, and while she sliced the large, fluffy cake, Connie got clean saucers down,…and with the atmosphere suddenly changed, the conversational mood turned to happier topics.

*   *   *

August, 30,…Billy got out of the carriage and tied the reins to the hitching post before helping Connie out and together, stood for a minute to look the deserted building over.

"My, God, Billy, it's so devastating to see our Café like this, especially after all the wonderful times we had running it!…And look, somebody broke out the glass in the door."

"With all that was goin' on this past few years, I'm surprised they all ain't broke!" He took her arm and they climbed the steps, and when he pushed open the door, she almost cried. The dining area was in total ruin, paper littered the floor, and it was not hard to see that it came from the walls. There was only four tables still intact, and the rest lay in broken disarray across the room,…and there were no chairs to be seen. The old pot-bellied stove was gone, and the stovepipes had been knocked from the ceiling and now lay in pieces on the floor.

"This is so heartbreaking, Billy." She sighed, and then went on into the kitchen. Pots, pans and skillets were on the floor, and most of the dishes were broken and scattered atop those, along with the silverware. Only the old cookstove remained with it's stovepipe still in place and it appeared, by the debris in the oven, and on the floor, that they had found the chair's remains.

"Someone's been living here, Billy!"

"Hobos, most likely."

"The only thing they didn't destroy was the counter-top and stools."

"Doc said it's been vacant since it was robbed."

"I know,…guess Alice didn't want it anymore after that!"

"What about your Mexican friend, you offer it to her?"

"Marguerita?…She said she'd like to have it, last I talked with her,…I guess she didn't have the money to run it."

"Well, we can put a for sale sign on it, what do you think?"

"I suppose so,…but it'll have to be cleaned up first!"

"Maybe Marguerita can help with that, we can pay her to clean it up."

"That's an idea,...we'll go by her house on the way back."

"We can list it at th' Land Office, too....But it still might take a while, ya know?"

"I know,...at least we can pay the taxes up on it, it isn't like we're not used to waiting!...Anyway, I can't seem to give it away, so waiting won't matter none."

*   *   *

"Come in, Jim." Nodded Sheriff Gose as Stockwell entered. "Pour yourself some coffee."

Thanks." Nodded the Marshal then grabbed a tin cup from a table by the stove, and poured it full with the strong liquid.

"What's new, Jim?" He asked as Stockwell sat down.

"Not a whole lot, John." He sighed. "I sent wires to Clarksville, and Texarkana,...they ain't seen hide nor hair of anybody resembling a Cantrell man. So,...I think we can finally write that scare off our list for good!...Anyway, like I said before, the only place a gang that size could hide out is in Jonesboro, and they wouldn't a stayed this long, if they had."

"I agree,...this thing had you shook up pretty bad, didn't it?...I mean, you looked real worried at that Council meeting."

"I was,...but hell, I am every time a new experience comes along,... in my Genes, I guess."

"Don't feel bad, my friend. I was nervous as hell myself, when I read that wire."

"I just couldn't think of a worse disaster,...and when th' Council wouldn't let me warn anybody,...I couldn't tell ya how I felt, man."

"One thing came from it, Jim,...I've got depuries workin the County again." Grinned Gose. "And you got two more men than you had, at least we accompolished that!"

"True,...well, I want a thank you for your cooperation, John."

"Hey, man, this town is both our responsibility, you don't need to thank me! Anyhow, Wilkins said he he saw Marshal Taylor in town, Bill Upshur, too,...anything to that?"

"They're here, came by th' office Tuesday. They're visiting their folks."

"Be good men to have around, if Cantrell did come to town!... Marshal Taylor sure can handle his self." Sighed Gose. "I sure thought Gus Thornton would kill him that night!"

"He is plenty fast, John,...but have you ever seen Bill Upshur shoot?"

"Can't say I have, no. Is he faster?"

"I never saw 'im shoot neither, but th' Marshal says there ain't nobody faster, anywhere!...And that's funny, too!" He said seriously. "If he's that fast, why ain't nobody ever heard of 'im,...I mean, he's got a have a reputation, look at Longley, or Wes Hardin, they're all famous men!"

"They're also wanted men." Grinned Gose. "And I ain't never seen a poster on Bill Upshur."

"Could a been a lot a reasons for that, John....The biggest bein', he might not a used his real name back when....Now don't get me wrong here, John. Bill Upshur's a good friend a mine, and I don't care about any reputation he might a had!...But what is curious, is that when I try to start a conversation about 'im with folks I know,...folks I know, knows him,...nobody will talk about 'im!...Well, other than to say he's a fine man, and hell, I already knew that!"

"Then, why not leave it at that?"

"I can't,...I'm too damn curious!...Listen to this!...You weren't here at th' time, but back in sixty-nine, Bratcher's bank was robbed, and Billy's son was kidnapped!...We didn't have jurisdiction in Indian Territory, and that's exactly where those men went. Well, Bill Upshur went after 'em all by his lonesome, brought his son back, too,...and the bank's money!"

"Seems I did hear about that." Nodded Gose. "And you're right, because it was Horace Bratcher that told me about it,...and after he did, he dropped the subject. I didn't think much about that at the time,... still don't, I guess."

"Bill Upshur's a real fine man, I know that much!" Sighed Stockwell after taking a swallow of his coffee. "Pulled me out a th' street when Thornton's man shot me,...and nobody else even offered."

"I remember that." Nodded Gose. "I agree with you, too, I don't know a better man!...But you know what I have learned, Jim?...There's some things you're better off, no knowing!"

147

"Well said, John." He grinned then drained his cup and got to his feet. "Just wanted to tell you about sendin' them wires,…guess we can breathe easier now,…see ya later."

"Later, Jim, and thanks."

*   *   *

"What do you say, John," Urged Rodney as they stood at the corral to watch the horses. "If you don't want 'em, I'll take 'em back with me?"

"Well,…sure, I guess. Four horses shouldn't be a problem, never know when I might need them!"

"Six horses, John,…Connie and Willy's riding two of them."

"Six is okay, too, I'll buy enough hay for the winter, they'll be fine!" He shrugged then, and turned to lean his back against the corral. "I'm not much of a rancher, son….And no part of a horseman, as you probably know! I never even had a carriage, or a horse until we moved out here, now I'm going to have eight of them."

"Then I'll take 'em back with me, John, don't worry about it."

"Oh, no, son, I'm looking forward to taking care of them,…it's high time, too, I'm a rancher now!…Did you know, it took me all day long to learn to harness my team to the carriage the first time. McGleason was there, but I wouldn't let him help me,…wanted to do it myself!…I've got a good supply of oats, and Barley, that I feed the team at night,… so I've gotten quite used to taking care of them."

"Okay, John, as long as you're sure, and they'll survive just fine on grass and hay, you won't need to worry about any grain."

"That's good to know, and I accept!"

"Good,…then I'll write out a note of authority, in case the brands are questioned. If someone accidentally lays claim to one of 'em, just give it to him!…But just for the hell of it, make him show you some proof of ownership! But I doubt that'll happen, they're not much to look at."

"They'll be fine, my boy….Now, you still planning to leave tomorrow?"

"If Billy gets back tonight, yes, sir." He shrugged. "If not, we'll leave when he does get here."

"Well, let's hope he waits a few more days, we are really enjoying your visit." He sighed then. "It gets a little hard sometimes, not having to go downstairs and open the store every morning,...I've been a Merchant for forty years, you know."

"Yeah, I know. I know what you mean, too!...I've only been here a few days, and I feel like I'm shirking my duties as a lawman by being here."

"How do you like chasing bad men in the wilderness?"

"There's nothing like it. It's dangerous work, and it scares me sometimes,...but I like it!"

"Well, you are a capable young man, Rodney,...and I don't think I ever told you that!...Never told you we were proud to have you in the family, either, but we are!" He sighed then and turned back to lean his arms on the top railing. "I just wish I could say the same about Steven, my baby girl is heartbroken!"

"Where is Steven anyway?" Queried Rodney. "I expected him to be with 'em."

"God only knows,...she says he's off somewhere looking for work!... But, between you and me, I don't expect him back this time."

"It's happened before?"

"Twice,...she says! But he always came back....He's been gone for six weeks now, without a word."

"Sorry to hear that, John."

"So am I!" He sighed, and then reached a kerchief from his pocket and wiped his forehead. "It's hot as the Devil out here, son, let's go inside."

CHAPTER ELEVEN

Friday, August, 31,...Cantrell and Mitch were watching the soldiers from the dark of a pariially-opened door, while the other men were crouched at the dingy windows.

"What th' hell are they doin', Jarvis, homesteadin'?...Can't see anything out there!"

"Don't get yourself all bent out of shape, son, we'll know before long!...They appear to be waiting for someone else to arrive."

"You can bet on that! They'll be comin' from this side, too."

"All the more reason to be patient!...Is everything ready to go?"

"Saddled, packed, and ready,...took care of it th' minute you woke us up."

"Then if we have to run, we'll have the time, stop worrying!"

"How'd you know they was here, anyway,...can't see nothin' out there?"

"A horse squealed!...Now relax, Mitch,...I'm surprised you didn't hear it, it was loud enough?"

"Wasn't expectin' to hear anything!...What is it, anyway, the middle of th' night?"

Cantrell sighed heavily. "I'd say it's going to be pretty close to dawn by now, otherwise they would be setting up camp, and they don't have a fire!...I would guess that they are waiting for that Surveyor fellow."

"Again,...how many times they gonna servey that thing?"

"Takes a lot a planning to build a bridge, son,...and that old river is pretty wide at this point!,...now be quiet, we could have a long wait!"

*   *   *

Connie woke up to stare at the familiar dark ceiling for a minute then yawning, rolled over to find that she was alone in bed,…and curious, she sat up and moved her legs off the side of the bed, felt for her moccasins and slipped them on before getting up to don her wrap and hurry out into the kitchen.

"OHHH!" Gasped Mattie as she quickly turned around. "You startled me, honey." She chuckled then, still stirring the mixture of flour, salt, and water in the large crock bowl she held cradled against her. "Why are you up so early?"

"Oh, I don't know, Mama Bailey,…I woke up, and Billy was gone,…so here I am!...Have you seen him?"

"Lands, yes!...He's out on the front stoop drinking his coffee, honey,…said he felt bad, and couldn't sleep. You ready for some coffee, too?"

"Yes, ma'am, but I have to go out first." She grimaced jokingly, and hurried out the back door, and the outside facility, as Mattie dumped the dough onto the floured kneading board and began working it with her hands.

Mattie looked up as she came back, and still smiling, watched her Daughter in law pour her coffee.

Connie smiled also, when she caught her watching her. "I'll be in to help you in a minute, Mama Bailey, I want to check on Billy." She hurried off down the hall and out to the porch, finding him in Doc's old rocking chair with his feet atop the railing.

"What are you doin' up, honey?" He smiled, and removed his feet from the railing.

"You weren't in bed, and I was worried,…it isn't like you."

"I know,…I couldn't sleep."

"You told Mama Bailey you felt bad, what's wrong?"

He sighed and looked back in the direction of town, able only to see the dark, bulky shapes of the buildings against the coming dawn. "I don't have a clue, honey,…I woke up with a strange feelin', that's all,…a sort of,…urgency, I guess!...Anyway, when I heard Mama in th' kitchen, I got up!"

"What do you think it might be,…a nightmare?"

151

"Not that I recall, no....But," He sighed again. "I don't know!...I feel like somethin's gonna happen, honey,...and I think it's got to do with th' town, why, I don't know!...But something's tellin' me to keep an eye on it."

"Then tell me what it feels like?"

"Honey, it's crazy,...but I feel like I got air in my chest, and I can't exhale it!...Like what I felt almost every day, when I was huntin' Willy that time!" He sighed then and drained his cup. "I need more coffee!" He gripped the arms of the chair to get up, but stopped when Connie touched his arm.

"Take my coffee, honey." She said. "I want to get to the bottom of what you're feeling." She gave him the cup. "Now, go on."

He sighed again. "There's nothin' else to tell you, baby,...I just have a feelin' somethin' gonna happen in town today,...that's all I can figure out!"

She turned to look at the dark outline of buildings then, and hugged his arm against her. "You've got me worried now, too!" She sighed. "What makes you think it's going to happen in town?"

"My neck tingles while I'm watchin' it, and don't ask me why,... but, I've grown to trust it!"

"Is it that Cantrell man, you've been so worried about,...do you think they're going to raid the town?"

"Now, that never crossed my mind!...But it is a possibility, I guess.... One thing, I've learned,...if it can happen, it sometimes will!" He took a swallow of the coffee then, and gave her his empty cup.

"Well," She sighed, and then straightened up. "I have to help Mama Bailey with breakfast, are you going to be all right?"

"I'm fine, honey, you go ahead, call me when it's ready."

*   *   *

The day was dawning clear, and hot and by daylight, the dry southwesterly wind picked up again, gusting to speeds of from ten, to thirty miles per hour, seeming to shift to the southeast periodically. However, once it blew across the swift current of the Red, it seemed to ricochet off some invisible wall to blow much cooler air back at the deserted buildings.

They were able to see the soldiers now as they sat on the ground eating their cold rations, their mounts' reins clutched in their hands.

"My neck's killin' me!" Complained Mitch. "Why don't we just pot-shot 'em and leave, Jarvis?"

"Mitch, you know we can't do that,…I want no more killings on my conscience!"

"Yes, sir, I know that,…I'm just mouthin' off, I reckon….But what's to keep us from leavin' anyway, we could climb that tree-lined hill in back, and hit th' road a half-mile from here,…they'd never see us?"

"You already answered that!…There may be more soldiers on the way. Now relax, son,…all we can do is wait them out!…You wouldn't want all this waiting to be for nothing, would you?…We have to stick to the plan, to be successful!"

"I know you're right, Jarvis, I'm just restless,…somethin' like a cornered wolf might be."

"We all are, son. But patience always pays off in the end, even for a wolf."

*   *   *

"That was good, Mama." Sighed Billy as he pushed the plate away and reached for tobacco and papers.

"Yeah, Grandma, that was real good!" Grinned Willy. "Can I have some coffee now?"

"I'm sorry, baby." Sighed Connie. "I forgot your coffee." She got him a cup and poured his coffee before refilling all their cups.

"You ever think of quitting them things, son?"

"Quitting what, Doc?"

"Cigarettes!…You remember old Luke Henshaw, over at Gresham's Livery?" And when Billy nodded. "He smoked them things like a tree on fire, all his life,…I know, I treated him for what everybody thought was a bad cold, even me!…But we just couldn't get rid of his symptoms,… because it wasn't a cold, or pmeumatic congestion that kept him from breathing, nor was it a sore throat that made him caugh all the time!… It was the cigarettes, son. Old Luke had developed a cancer in his lungs, and it killed him!…He wasn't five years older than you are."

"I don't know, Doc." He shrugged. "I hadn't thought about it!…I like th' taste,…and it's about th' only thing that'll relax me."

"Well, you should think about giving them up!"

"I might do that!" He grinned. "But not today."

"I didn't expect you would." He sighed. "Now, what about this,…omen, you seem to have,…about something about to happen?"

"Omen, what's that?"

"An omen,…a premonition,…your feeling of doom, a look at the future, impending danger!...There's other names for it in the Medical Journals. Anyway, my Daughter in law said you had a bad feeling about today?"

"Woke up with it this morning." He nodded. "I went out on th' porch and looked toward town, and it was like every nerve in my body was on fire,…I had pressure in my chest, the hair on the back of my neck stood up,…I don't know!"

"And you have had this before?"

"Lots a times." He grinned. "And usually for a reason!...That's why I pay attention to it,…it's saved my life before."

"What do you think it is, Doc?" Urged Connie.

"Me,…I haven't the foggiest, darlin',…Psychology is a whole different medical term. Science is only now beginning to study it!...The mind is the most complicated area of human anatomy,…and to a common M.D., something unimagined….But I would venture to say that William has a gift that only God can explain! He is an extraordinary young man, with abilities that are beyong most men!" He drank a swallow of coffee then, and smiled when he looked at them.

"But that's a good thing!"

"Doc," Said Billy, and shook his head. "I don't know what you just said, but it don't feel like a gift from God,…more like a curse from th' Devil!"

"Nonsense,…be proud of it, my boy, because there is nothing wrong with you!...You have a talent,…say, a protective nature that most don't have. You recognize what your feelings are telling you, and look for the probable answers!...Almost like a Doctor would do."

"Well, a Doctor, I ain't, neither!" He chuckled. "And, you know what you ought a be, Doc,…one a them head Doctors,…what are they?" He looked at Connie as he spoke. "Honey you read about all that stuff, what's th' word I'm lookin' for?"

"I'm sure I don't know, honey!"

"The word is, Phychiatrist!" Laughed the old Doctor. "And like I said, science is just beginning to study the emotional minds of men. Of which,…even if I was a young man again, I would run from!…There were those, as far back as the Seventeenth Century, who studied that sort of thing, mostly in Europe someplace….But it probably drove them all insane!"

"Well, thanks for th' diagnosis, Doc!" Laughed Billy. "Now that I know there's no cure, I feel better."

"I thought you would!…You are fine, William, healthy, strong and able, and we all love you terribly."

"What more could I ask for?" He smiled across at Connie's smiling face, then at the children, and they were all watching him intently. "Now, I'm worried!"

*   *   *

Rodney pushed his plate away, and with a satisfied sigh, reached for a thin cigar and lit it.

"Do you have to, Rodney?" Urged Melissa, and cut her eyes at her mother.

"Oh, I'm sorry, Mother Gabbett, I clean forgot!" He pinched it out, then used the table knife to cut the burnt end off, reached a spoon of milk-gravy and smothered the ashes.

"Thank you, Rodney." Smiled the older woman.

"I'm goin' out to watch the horses, Mama." Said the seven-year old Benny, after wiping his mouth.

"Me, too!" Cried Cindy. "I want to see the horses."

"I'll look after her," Nodded Benny, and then looked at Rodney. "But I wish Willy was here, Uncle Rodney, when is he coming?"

"Today, or tomorrow, Benny." He smiled then as Benny nodded and left the kitchen. "He's sure growing, Sabrina."

"I know." She replied, getting up to help with the dishes.

"Let's us take our coffee to the sitting-room, shall we?" And with that, both got up, took their coffee and left the kitchen.

"Sabrina sure ain't herself." Commented Rodney as he sat down. "Maybe she knows something, she's not telling you, John?"

"I think you're right,…I think she knows Steven won't be back!…I think he left her. That, or she's really worried about him!…She says she left a note where they would be, but he won't come for them….And that's quite okay with us, I might add!"

155

"Yes, sir, I know it is."

"Looks like you'll be with us another day or so, as well, and that makes us even happier!"

"Thanks!...Billy would a been here by daybreak, if he was coming."

"I've been hesitant to ask you about something, Rodney." Sighed Gabbett. "Seeing as I know nothing at all about Indians, except that I've always been afraid of them, what, after all the stories I've heard!... But,...how are you all getting along with them up there,...aren't they hostile?"

Rodney grinned then, and shook his head. "Not in the least, John. You will find hostility in the Nations, but most of that is from the Comanche, or maybe the Apache,...and there's a few others....But they're all in the western parts of the Territories....My Deputy is a Choctaw Indian, he's also the Chief of Police, of a very able Choctaw Police Force, I might add....You'd never meet a finer man than Peter Birdsong, in fact,...He saved our lives once!...You know,...you and Mrs. Gabbett should come visit us, John, there's plenty of room."

"I would like that,...and I will discuss it with Myrna."

"Yeah, well, do it tonight, John. You give me an answer before we leave, we'll set a date, and come get you, how's that?...And by the way, Sabrina and Benny as well!"

"A deal!" Smiled Gabbett. "I'll do that."

"Good!"

"Will you show us that hidden valley, Lisa told us about?"

"I can arrange that,...what did she tell you?"

"Just that it was very old, and untouched!...Would that be where your gold mine is?"

"I'm afraid not." He lied. "But that's a secret, John, one that only Billy and myself know about. If word of it ever got around, it would put us, and our family in danger."

I can understand that,...my God, some of the evils that men do!... Who's watching your holdings while you're gone?"

"Peter's police are there, his office is with mine, in one end of the Trading Post."

"It's hard to believe that some of these tribes have chosen to live in peace with us,...I knew the Cherokee pretty much had already, but I wasn't sure about the Choctaw?"

"Well, don't get me wrong, John,...none of them actually trust the white man that much, and that includes the Choctaw, Billy and I had to earn their trust, believe me!...But once we did, we were all like brothers."

"That's remarkable....And you're right,...I think I would like your Peter Birdsong."

*   *   *

Jim Stockwell wiped his mouth with the table linen and moved his plate back then placed coins on the table, got up and walked out onto the crowded boardwalk where he immediately began speaking to people that greeted him. Stopping at the top of the steps, he rolled and lit a smoke as he watched the buckboard traffic along South Main, which was heavier at this hour than it would be in the heat of noontime.

He quickly reached and grabbed his hat as the wind gusted down the wide thoroughfare, and then exhaled the smoke before turning to walk back toward the middle of town. He was just turning the corner on the square's south side when Glenn called to him, stopping him in front of the Farmer's Market and Grocery, and watched as the Deputy climbed the steps to the boardwalk.

"Hi, ya, Marshal." Grinned Glenn as he avoided a couple of men and stopped in front of him. "You had breakfast yet?"

"Just left Calina's, why?"

"Nothin', I was gonna join ya."

"Anything goin' on in town?"

"Normal, as usual, Jim." He sighed. "Almost boring!"

"Just th' way I like it!"

"Yeah, me, too, I guess!" Confessed Glenn. "Say,...you goin' to th' dance tonight, Marshal?"

"Not me, Glenn,...I can't dance a lick!"

"Is it okay if I go,...Lily wants to go,...and I'm on duty tonight?"

"I guess so,...I'll watch things till you get back!...Where is it, anyway?"

"Usual place,…McGleason's barn! It's getting' bigger ever year, too, had folks dancing in th' street last year!"

"Yeah, I remember!…Just don't drink too much, Glenn, I expect you to relieve me at the office!"

"Not to worry, Marshal."

"Then you go ahead and go, Glenn….Tell ya what, I'll ask th' wife, she likes listenin' to th' music, and with the kids gone, she might want a go….If she does, can I get you and Lily to pick her up, and bring her home?"

"Be glad to, Marshal,…well, see ya, Jim, let me know."

Stockwell watched him work through the shoppers and disappear around the corner, then walked on down the boardwalk, only to stop again when loud cursing was heard through the swinging doors of Myers' City Saloon, prompting him to push through the swinging gates.

Andrew Myers and his stepson were in a heated argument near the end of the long bar, and when Myers saw him, he took the young man by the arm and pointed toward the room. Young Taylor Pounds scowled darkly at Stockwell as he grabbed the broom and began sweeping the floor.

"Hello, Marshal!" Grinned Myers as he walked up. "What'll it be?"

"Thought you didn't open till noon, Andy?"

"I'll make an exception!"

"No thanks, Andy. I heard part a th' argument, and thought I'd check it out. Anything wrong?"

"No, nothing new!" Sighed the middleaged man, looking back at his stepson. "It's that shiftless stepson of mine,…he ain't worth spit, never was!…Hell, he's half drunk right now." He looked back at Pounds angrily. "He's been getting into my private stock of Brandy, Marshal,…I don't know what to do about him, to tell you the truth!…I can't kick him out, Mary Beth would throw a hissey!"

"I could arrest 'im, Andy, throw a scare into 'im?…Might straighten 'im right out!"

"As much as that would please me," He sighed then. "No,…I'll handle him, Marshal."

"Okay, Andy." He nodded. "But you know where I am."

"Yes, sir, I do, thanks, Marshal!"

He stopped on the boardwalk again to scan the large square. It was almost full with buckboards, and medium sized wagons, their teems of mules and horses all enduring the coming heat and hot wind with drooping heads. Many of them had families just deboarding to tie the animals to heavy blocks of wood they had brought along for the purpose,...and with parasols spread, quickly made their way to the shade of the boatdwalks and trees that lined the off-streets.

Still others were placing wooden pails under the spouts of the square's two watering troughs, and filling them, only to carry them back and place them on the ground for the horses before going about their shopping. People were crossing the wide expanse on foot in all directions to get to where they were going, and he shook his head as he watched, because he knew that by noon, the square would be nearly empty.

*   *   *

It was almost eight-thirty before the civilian Surveyor arrived across the river and unloaded his instruments from the pack animal, and fifteen minutes afterward, his counterpart arrived on the Jonesboro side,... along with six additional cavalrymen, all dismounting to assist the Surveyor with his equipment.

"How long's this gonna take 'em, I wonder?" Breathed Mitch.

"They weren't here very long the first time." Returned Cantrell, his voice almost in a whisper. "Maybe it won't take them long....How far is this, Clarksville again?"

"A good twenty miles as th' crow flies, maybe farther'n that!...We don't leave pretty quick, we won't get there till dark."

"Then we'll just have to reopen the bank!...How far is the bigger town, you spoke of?"

"About th' same, Jarvis, more southwest."

"Okay,...if these bluecoats aren't gone by noon, we'll leave anyway. We can stay in the wilderness, away from the road."

"I don't think so, Jarvis,...there's a swamp between here and that Tradin' Post, I went to. We'll need to use th' road, at least till we get to the cut-off!"

"If that's the case, we'll do it, be patient."

159

"I don't know, sir," Breathed Mitch as he eyed the soldiers. "Maybe we ought a forget about that bank and strike out on our own,...this whole thing is becoming too complicated,...givin' me a bad feelin'!... What do ya say, Jarvis,...let th' boys go now, we can always find us a coach to rob?"

"I have never deterred from a plan of action, son,...that would be like swimming half way across that river out there, only to realize you can't make it across....We'll stick to the plan."

"I trust your wisdom, Jarvis, you know that!...But we never stayed this long in one place before,...something's bound to go wrong!"

"We've been wrong for the past ten years, Mitch, and me for much longer than that!" He sighed then. "And someday, we'll pay for it!...It's our destiny, son, and we'll have to face it!...But not without a plan, and not by changing plans in midstream."

"Yes, Sir!" He became silent then, angry for the first time in ten years at his Mentor, and worked hard at forcing it out of his mind,... finding it easy to do, because he knew Cantrell was right.

Cantrell pulled his watch to check the time. "Two more hours, Mitch, and we can go!...They're driving the stakes in the ground, it won't be long now."

"That only brings up another question, Jarvis,...which way will they go, and where?...There's got a be a larger force camped somewhere close, that, or there's a Fort near by?"

"I think all of them are from that Fort Towson, you spoke of."

"Maybe you're right." Sighed Mitch dejectedly. "Got a be a bridge, Ferry, or somethin' west a here."

"I'd say so, son,...and I am not reprimanding you, so don't get so angry at my logic, it hasn't let me down yet!...I value your input, too, so don't stop giving it!"

*　　　*　　　*

Jim Stockwell was dozing, slumped back in his armchair, his feet propped on the roll-top, absently fanning himself with an old wanted poster when the Sheriff walked in. Startled, he quickly pulled his feet from the desk and sat up,...and recognizing Gose, grinned and wiped his face with the damp bandana while the Sheriff caught his breath.

"Seat yourself, John." He grinned. "This is a rare occasion, man, what brings you out in this heat?"

Gose came on to the spare chair and sat down heavily. "If I'd remembered how many stairs I'd have to climb, I wouldn't have come at all!" He panted. "They're a killer on a hot day!...I don't know," He said, wiping his own face and head. "Just a mite bored, I guess,...a little restless, too."

"Makes two of us!...but you ain't gonna climb three flights a stairs for nothin', so what's up?"

"Bill Upshur!" He sighed. "I've been thinkin' about our conversation the other day....You know, I didn't leave Paris till the Summer of sixty-nine, and I say that because I remember when he came home!...And if I remember it right, some said the law was after him! I was also in the square that day when, then, Deputy Taylor shot Ben Lang!...I also heard part of the Sheriff's conversation with Bill Upshur, before he was shot!...And I distinctly recall hearing Ben Lang call him a killer, hell, the street was full of folks that heard it!...And I hate to say it, Jim,... but there was a man that could handle a gun, Ben Lang shot Deputy Taylor before he could pull his gun."

"Well, you see, that's what I was talkin' about, John!...I didn't live in town in them days, I only heard about all that, but when I asked about it, nobody knew anything,...course it was a month after th' fact, and about th' time I went to work for Sheriff Taylor. Anyway,...when I finally got th' nerve to ask him about it, all he told me was that Ben Lang was the leader of the gang that Murdered Billy's family! He also told me some about when he met Billy, and His wife, but not much more than that!" He reached to roll a smoke and light it. "Awww, hell, like you said,...I guess it didn't interest me all that much back then, but now,...I'm just curious."

"That goes with being a lawman, Jim." Sighed Gose. "But you got me to thinking about it. Anyway,...Deputy Taylor walked out into the street after he shot Lang, and explained to everybody there why he had shot him,...and that being the case, I didn't blame him for doing it!...So I went home....I knew all about Bill Upshur's folks being murdered, and I guess I figured, if Lang was responsible, he got what he deserved....I heard later, that Taylor had called a special town meeting that same day, and afterward,...nobody that had attended the meeting would talk about the incident in the street. Next thing I knew, U.S. Marshals were in town taking statements, and after they left, the whole affair was forgotten."

"You didn't go to the funeral?"

"That's another mystery,…the funeral was by invitation only!…Nobody, but those people who attended that town meeting was allowed in the cemetery.…Anyway, I didn't try to go, I was still a single man courtin' my wife,…what did I care about a funeral, never been to one in my life, except that one with Gus Thornton,…and I enjoyed it!…Did you go?"

Stockwell shook his head. "I didn't live in town,…I have been to th' grave site, though, and I've wondered a lot about it ever since."

"About what?"

"There's two graves there!…Ben Lang is in one, and a gunfighter in the other,…and here's what's strange about it all.…Ben Lang's headstone says, and I quote! "Here lies Sheriff Benjiman Lang, killed by a gunfighter called, Reb".…The other grave says, "Here lies the gunfighter, known as Reb, killed by Sheriff Benjiman Lang in a duel.", and you and me both know that Marshal Taylor killed Lang,…does any of this make sense to you?"

Gose lowered his head then nodded. "I'm afraid it does, now!…And knowing the circumstances, I now know what happened, too!…Jim, our Mister Bill Upshur, is the Reb!…The town faked his death, old son!…They broke the law, killing him, and his reputation!…I would a thought Marshal Taylor would have told you about that, you being friends and all?"

"He never did." Said Stockwell, shaking his head in wonderment. "But why didn't Bill Upshur kill Lang,…it's obvious, he was faster?"

"Because Bill Upshur was unarmed, Jim, I was there, I know!…Ben Lang was going to murder him, right there in the streets of Paris!"

Stockwell's eyes grew larger then. "That's got a be it, John,…and if it is, I can't say I blame him for not tellin' me!…And you know somethin' else,…I think you and me had better end this investigation right here, and now!…After all, you said yourself, there's some things that are better left alone,…and this is definitely one of 'em!"

"When you're right, you're right, Marshal!…This confab never took place."

*   *   *

"All right," Said Cantrell as the soldiers mounted up. "They're leaving,… and it's almost twelve noon!" He stood and faced the somber looking crew then. "We leave here in fifteen minutes, Gentlemen,…I want to give the soldiers time to get off the road. The way I figure it, they will head west through the timber after a bit, and I want to give them time to do it!"

"Mitch and I will leave last, you will all leave two abreast, and a few minutes apart!…You'll go out the back and up the hill into the timber,…Mitch says there's a bog not more than a half mile out there, so when you reach it, turn west back to the road and head south!…Once you reach the cut-off to this Shockey's Prairie, ride into the timber and wait for the rest of us. We'll cut across country from there, this town of Clarksville is thirty miles away."

"Those words never sounded so good, Boss!" Voiced Morgan White, and his comment was quickly chorused by the rest of them.

"Your dynamite still dry, Morg?' Grinned Mitch.

"Bet your ass it is, ready and able!"

"Good!" Returned Mitch. "That bank will likely be closed when we get there, if it is, we'll have to reopen it."

"Men," Said Cantrell then. "I want this last job done with precision. I do not want any killings, and I do not want any of you killed. Once we meet at that crossroad, we will ride at a gallop when possible, we have thirty miles to cover, so stay alert, and organized!" He turned back then to stare out at the river, and after several minutes, turned around and nodded at them.

"You men pair up now!…Morg, it's best, you and Billy Jack go first, to scout for those soldiers." He looked at his watch again. "Go now!"

They all watched impatiently as the two men led their mounts out into the sunlight, mounted and quickly spurred them, squealing up the side of the hill behind the old saloon.

"We got two spare horses now, Jarvis, what'll we do with 'em?"

"Take the rifles and saddlebags, son,…leave the saddles here. We'll take the horses as far as the cut-off and turn them loose….Next two men go, now!" He ordered then turned back to peer out through the open

163

door to scan the shoreline across the river from them as Mitch went to gather the dead men's gear.

"Rifles and saddlebags are stowed on my horse, Jarvis." He said as he returned.

Nodding, Cantrell sent another two men in pursuit of the others,… and a couple of minutes later, another two. "Okay," He said, turning toward the last three. "You three go together, and take the two loose horses with you,…turn 'em loose at the crossroad!" He checked his watch again, and after a couple of minutes. "Go now!"

CHAPTER TWELVE

August, 31, twelve, fifteen P.M....Taylor Pounds was twelve when his mother married Andrew Myers. She had been serving drinks in his City Saloon since the allotted, expected time of mourning for her husband's untimely demise,...and young Taylor had become more defiant and uncontrollable ever since. Andrew Myers had convinced her that the boy needed a father figure in his life, and believing him, had agreed to marry him.

The wedding had been six years ago now, and though Taylor was still mourning the loss of his father,...he had been complacent enough, had even been willing to work by sweeping the saloon's floors every morning. He was even satisfied with an allowance of half-wages. At the age of sixteen, Myers raised Taylor's salary to a dollar a day, and began training him to tend bar, but by then, Young Taylor was already becoming disgruntled and defensive,...and dissatisfied with being paid the going rate of pay for a working man's salary. Instead, he had began arguing that he deserved part of the profits as well, because he and his mother were now part of the family, also making them half owners of the saloon.

Taylor's demands, at times bordered on outright abuse, but never to the point of actually trying to hit his stepfather,...and now, two years later, the arguments continued. Myers had said no to these demands countless times over the past two years, and each time it was brought up, there ensued the loud arguments. The good part of this was that they never took place during business hours.

Taylor Pounds, however, allowed his losing the argument to escalate into frustration,…and a rising hatred of his stepfather, and his saloon of which, he continuously believed he should be half owner in due to his status as Myers' only heir,…aside from his mother, of course!...But he also knew that his mother had resigned herself to being a housewife now, and hardly ever came to the saloon any more. Therefore, she didn't count in the equasion.

The futile arguments always fell on his stepfather's deaf ears, and this infuriated Taylor even more, and to the point of drinking his stepfather's private stock of Brandy. At first, he used the liquor as a crutch to shore up his bruised ego, but in time, because he liked it,… and now, because he needed it!

Today had been no different, they'd had their usual argument,… only this time, the Marshal had heard it,…and already having had his morning Brandy, and feeling the effects of it, became even more upset when Myers had gone to talk with the lawman. He believed his stepfather was telling the Marshal everything, and in his fevered state, became even angrier, believing it was no one's business, but his own.

Over the next few hours, he finished his sweeping and cleaning, and while Andy Myers went about his preparations for opening. He strode angrily out of the main room, and into the large storeroom in back where, in a childish tantrum, he threw the broom against the wall and watched it ricochet onto the keg of coaloil, thinking it would serve his stepfather right, if his precious saloon were to burn to the ground!

With a verbal, "Son of a Bitch!" he went to another door, retrieved his stashed bottle of stolen Brandy and went inside to drown his troubles where, cursing again, he tilted the bottle and drank from it before laughing out loud. 'God', he thought, wouldn't it be something to laugh in his stepfather's face while his precious saloon burned?...Yes, he thought, and drank even more of the liquor, it most certainly would!... And why not, he decided after draining the bottle, he'd already made up his mind to leave this one-horse town?

He threw the empty bottle against the wall and strutted back into the main storeroom, stood for a moment to look toward the saloon's main floor, and not seeing his stepfather, stared at the keg of coaloil for another moment before walking to stand over it, and then,…after another look toward the saloon, he squatted and removed the plug, and then stood back to watch the flammable liquid slowly spread over the dry planking as he backed slowly ahead of it's progress toward the alley door. Stopping there, he reached behind him and opened the door, took a match from his shirt, hesitated for a moment then snickered and struck it to quickly toss it to the floor as he pulled the door closed behind him. He heard the unmistakable swoosh as the oil ignited, and laughing again, began running west along the weed and debris infested alleyway.

*   *   *

Andrew Myers was busy wiping dust from bottles as he stocked the mirror-backed shelves behind the bar with different shaped bottles of liquor, using these more for decoration than for drinking, as they were all imported, and very expensive. But he would serve drinks from them, if a customer was willing to pay more for it. Sighing, he took a step backward to look at it, and satisfied, turned and began wiping dry the many shot-glasses beneath the counter as he thought again of Taylor, and wishing him and the boy got along better. He could understand his feelings about it, he had no father, his mother had remarried, hell, his whole world had changed!...But he couldn't give in to him, neither, in spite of how much he had grown to love Taylor's mother!...Taylor was too impatient, all he had to do is work hard, and wait,...he would eventually make him part owner, if only he would change his attitude.

He had just finished the glasses, and was wiping down the long countertop when he heard the unmistakable combustion, and for a fraction of a second, the blossoming heat generqating from it robbed the entire room of it's oxygen, causing him to momentarily gulp for air,... and in that fraction of a second, realization grabbed at his consciousness and he screamed,"FIRE!...FIRE!" and ran out from behind the bar. With only a glance back at the roaring inferno, he ran and threw open the swinging doors, rushing out to collide with pedestrians on the boardwalk.

"FIRE!...FIRE!" He yelled at the top of his lungs. "SOMEBODY HELP ME!"...And by then, dark, thick smoke was boiling out of the saloons door. Screams immediately erupted from the women along the walkways, men began yelling as both them, and their women and children began running wildly along the walkways, also shouting fire.

Some were jumping from boardwalks to the ground, and all running madly for their wagons, or horses. Men were already running from the hardware store with wooden buckets, and in a matter of seconds, a dozen men had formed a bucket-brigade and were splashing water onto the saloon's front, and through the doorway.

In a matter of maddening moments, traffic in the square was a melee of squaling animals, screaming women and cursing men as the traffic jam ensued, all trying to leave the crowded square at the same time. Smoke was already swirling thick in the square, only to rise and be whisked away by the brisk winds aloft as the flames quickly engulfed the saloon's interior like a hungry Devil, consuming the dry wood and combustible materials in seconds, broken bottles of liquor adding even more fuel to the flames. The tremendous heat blew glass windows out over the boardwalks and street as they shattered, and in mere moments, the flames were eating upward to consume the business housed above it on the second floor.

Eating through the thin walls of the saloon, the fire seemed to leap onto the adjoining market, quickly igniting the dry lumber, and then to race upward to consume the business above that,...and doing the same to that store on the other side to quickly roar upward into those second and third levels. People were exiting out of those upper floors to rush pell-mell down wooden staircases to the alleyways, only to be pushed, or overrun by others in their haste, some were jumping from upper windows onto the boardwalk's awnings to drop to the ground in a heap. Ankles, legs and arms were sprained and, or broken in the frenzied attempts to escape death by fire.

In a matter of only minutes, half of the south side of the square was an inferno of flames, aided by the strong, hot south winds that gusted and carried embers and licking flames across the square and onto other buildings along the west side. More bucket-brigades were formed, and the valiant men and women were passing buckets of water along long picket-lines to be thrown uselessly onto the boardwalks and storefronts, as it was just too hot to try and go into the buildings. Men were kept busy pumping water from the cisterns into the watering troughs, but not fast enough, as buckets were dipping out the water faster than it could be pumped in.

Pedestrians were still running wildly along the streets screaming fire, and in minutes, every Church in town began ringing out the alarm, as the thick, black smoke billowed it's gassious way across the square, and the town,...blown downward by the gusting wind, only to rise and be carried northward. Explosions shattered the afternoon as oil drums ignited, liquor bottles blew. Exploding ammunition and gunpowder adding a dangerous tone to the disaster as flying lead searched for prey in the streets,...and through it all, men and women alike were valiantly working to fight the spreading flames.

Only minutes had elapsed before the volunteer fire department was on the scene, and with only the small, seemingly inferior steam pump, quickly attached the large fire hoses to cisterns on the corner of the square and began pumping streams of water onto the blaze, which had already torched the dry wood of other buildings along the west and east side of the square. The roaring flames were already licking at the walls of the Peterson Hotel on the west corner of Grand and Wall, the fire crackling and popping like musket-fire on a firing line, and was loud enough to send fear through the hearts of the most brave,...and that, blended with the constant rumbling roar of the firestorm it's self, was something most wouldn't easily forget!

*   *   *

Twelve-thirty P.M.....Billy, Connie, the Baileys, and the children were all sitting idly in the shade of the Bailey's front porch, all periodically wiping their perspiring faces in the noonday wind and heat. All of them had become curious at the feeling Billy had about impending doom, and had decided to join him in his vigilance,...and were all watching the heat-shimmering buildings of town when Billy suddenly stood up.

"You hear that?" He asked, and then went down the steps into the yard.

"Hear what?" Queried Connie as she joined him.

"Listen!...Every Church bell in town is ringing,...and I smell smoke!" He pointed then. "See it?...Something's on fire in town!"

"My God, it is!...look Doc, Mama Bailey!" She pointed toward town as well, and all of them walked out into the yard to look.

They saw the dust from wagons then, and watched as they materialized, hearing the cracking of whips, and cursing as the drivers urged the running teams faster along the rutted road, dust billowing up behind the bouncing wheels in a reddish cloud as they drew closer until finally, the careening buckboards were racing by as they continued west on the Bonham Road.

Billy ran to the picket gate, slung it open and ran out into the road, swinging his arms as he moved in front of one of the wagons, and finally stopping the frenzied team by grabbing the bridal harness and hauling back on the reins as he turned their heads toward him.

"What th' hell are you doin', man?" Yelled the farmer, quickly reaching to hold his wife as she was almost thrown from the wagon.

"What's happenin' in town?" Asked Billy loudly when the wagon finally stopped. "What's burnin'?"

"Whole God damn town, Man!" Gasped the man. "Everything's on fire, now get out a th' way!" The man used his whip and the wagon bounced on it's way again.

He released the reins as the whip was used and stepped back toward the fence, still staring at the distant, billowing smoke from town. By then, they were all worriedly watching the blowing smoke, and were still able to hear the very audible sounds of Church bells as the gusting wind carried both the sound and choking smoke north, and westward.

"They'll need some help!" Said Billy loudly as he came back into the yard. "I have to go!"

"I'm going with you!" Yelled Connie.

"No, you will not go with me!" He said sternly, stopping her to stand and gape at him.

"But, Billy,…I can help, too!"

"You'll help me more by staying where I know you're safe!"

"She can go with me, son!" Said Doc quickly. "I'm going to the hospitol, Lovejoy will need some help!…Send the injured there!" He turned and went up on the porch, and then into the house for his bag.

"Okay!" Said Billy, nodding at her. "You go with Doc, but stay away from town!"

"Don't worry about the children!" Called out Mattie,…"go!"

"Be careful, honey!" Gasped Connie, and came to quickly kiss him on the mouth.

"I will,…now come on, you can help me with the horses." They ran for the barn and quickly swung the door open. He grabbed the nearest saddle and hastily saddled one of the captured mounts, and between them both, had Doc's horse harnessed to his buggy and waiting when he came into the barn.

Connie kissed him again. "Be careful, Billy!"

They all mounted, and Billy spurred the horse into a run ahead of them,…and was in a hard gallop past the oncoming escaping traffic toward the smoke and fire impaired town of Paris,…and at that point, he could see the licking flames above the buildings as he reined the horse in, and around the road's traffic at a hard run.

*   *   *

Rodney pushed his plate back and sighed mightily. "If I'm here much longer, my horse won't be able to carry me."

"I'm full, too, Uncle Rodney!" Voiced Benny.

"Me, too!" Giggled Cindy, not to be outdone.

"Well, I'm for going outside and walking some of it off!" Grunted Gabbett as he scraped his chair back.

"Amen to that!" Nodden Rodney as he followed suit, and immediately followed his father in law out through the sitting room and out to the front porch where he reached for, and lit his thin cigar, before stepping out onto the steps to peer up at the sky.

"Sure is hazy out, John,…do you smell smoke?"

Mister gabbett walked out beside him and also began searching the hazy sky. "That is smoke, Rodney," He sniffed the air again, and shook his head. "Something's burning, that's for sure,…but where, I don't see anything?"

"Got a be a grass fire somewhere, or timber. The winds out of the South, so it's got a be toward town."

"Could be something in town." Said Gabbett.

"It's an awful lot a smoke, if it is,…or something real big!" He stood for a minute to watch in the direction of the smoke's travel then looked at the older man.

"John, if that's grass fire, it could be headed this way,…I'd best go see about it!" He started down the steps then.

"I'll go with you!" Prompted Gabbett, quickly falling in beside him.

"Not a good idea, John." He argued as they walked toward the corral. "I'd rather you be here,...you might have to get every one to safety."

"You're right, son,...I didn't think about that!...What will you do, if it is?"

"Won't be much I can do, as dry as it is,...I'll check out some a the farms in the area, try to get some help, if that's what it is,...there's another ranch east of here, too!"

Coming to the corral, Rodney opened the gate and quickly grabbed the halter of the horse nearest to him, and led it into the barn. It took only a short time to saddle the animal and when done, he pulled himself into the saddle and paused to look down at Gabbett.

"Tell Lisa where I've gone, and not to worry,...but you might want to keep an eye on that smoke, and be ready to move....I'll be back, if there's nothing to worry about!...If there is, I might be a while!" He reined the horse around and gigged it into a trot across the yard and once on the road, reined it into the grass on a more direct, southerly route in the direction of town.

*   *   *

Cantrell and Mitch led their mounts through the rear door of the old saloon and into the sunlight, where they mounted and silently spurred their horses up the slightly steep incline into the thick timber aboue them,...and for the next half mile or so, fought briars and thick foliage as they made their way through the trees.

"Here's where we go west, Jarvis." Said Mitch as he stopped his horse. "Swamps not ten feet in there, can't ya smell it?"

"That I can, son, let's go." He urged his horse through the trees in wake if those that went before them, and was soon riding down an embankment onto the Jonesboro Road, where they immediately turned south.

They held the horses to a steady, mile consuming gallop along the unused road, and an hour later were pulling up at the Snockey's Prairie cut-off to watch the other eleven men ride out of the timber toward them.

"Sky don't look right, Jarvis." Commented Mitch as he looked up. "It's not as bright as it was,...and I think I smell smoke."

"You're right." Agreed Cantrell, also looking up. "Could be a grass fire,...or timber,...nothing we haven't seen before!"

"Could be worse than that, that town's over that way!"

"Somethin' on fire, Boss!" Yelled Morg as they urged their horses up onto the road. "Billy Jack thinks somethoin mighty big is burnin' off yonder!"

"If that town's on fire, it could be easy pickings, Jarvis!...Won't nobody be armed, be too busy fightin' fire,...what do ya think?"

Cantrell sat his saddle and gazed up at the sky. "Yes, it would, Mitch,...but it could just as well be a forest fire between here and that town!"

"Well, it's your call, sir....I know we'd be changing your plan, and you don't like doin' that!"

Sighing, Cantrell continued to stare at the smoke darkening sky, and knew that if he changed his plan of action, things could go wrong for them! But he also knew that Mitch was right,...a burning town was easy to raid, because the people there would be scared, exhausted and for the most part, unarmed!"

"Jarvis?" Urged Mitch restlessly.

Cantrell cleared his throat then. "Okay, Gentlemen,...we are changing the plan,...and I have never done that before. But that smoke is liken to a town on fire and if it is, our job will be easy!...It also means that anything could happen, a changed plan sometimes courts disaster, so keep your eyes open, and your wits about you,...and my rule still stands,...no killing!"

"If I'm wrong, and it is only a grass fire, we can still turn east to the smaller town, hide out for the night, and hit the bank tomorrow!"

"Thought we was gonna open it tonight!" Voiced Morg.

"That was the other plan," He sighed. "But we'll see." Without waiting for further reply, he spurred his horse through the milling men and galloped on up the weed-grown road, with Mitch and the others in his wake.

*   *   *

One O'clock P.M.,...Billy held the frenzied horse to a hard run as he entered the town limits, and already seeing hoards of residents, and business owners along Bonham Road as they feverishly carried out their precious belongings and placed them in waiting wagons and carriages, loading them down in preparation for escaping the gorging flames. People were running down the street, away from the fire in the square, and just as many were were rushing toward the disaster area,…whether just to look, or to help fight.

He slid the frightened horse to a sliding stop alongside Doctor Lovejoy's black buggy, and amid the heavy smoke and screaming pedestrians, leaped from the saddle and spooked the animal, stampeding it back down Bonham Street in the dust and smoke. Seeing the Doctor come out of his office and cross the boardwalk with large valisses, he climbed the steps to intercept him.

"You need help, Doctor?"

"No,…this is pretty much everything,…I'm going to the hospitol!… Have the victims sent there, please." Without another word, he climbed into the buggy and whipped the horse into a run toward the corner, turning north on Wall and out of sight.

Looking back across the wide street, he saw Stockwell, and the Judge run out of the Court building and along the boardwalk toward the corner and yelled at them, stopping Stockwell who waited for him on the walkway.

"What th' hell happened, Jim?" He yelled breathlessly.

"Don't know!…We just now heard the commotion. The Judge told me the bells were goin' off.…We're just goin' to help, if we can!"

Nodding, he watched Stockwell run after the Judge then began entering the shops and stores along the busy street himself, helping those he could to carry their belongings out, before moving on to the next. By the time he made it to the square, dozens of people were already overcome by the thick, blowing smoke, some bent over hitchrails caughing and gagging, while others were being helped to wagons waiting at the North side of the square to carry them to the hospitol.

He spotted those fighting the fire then and began trotting across the square toward the bucket brigade, and fire engine, but had barely started to run when he was overcome by the gassious smoke and intense heat, having to stop and gasp for what little air he could drag into his lungs. Taking the bandana from his neck, he made his way, instead, to the watering trough, dipped the scarf in it and tied it around his lower face,…but before starting across the square again, he saw several men staggering toward him, each trying to help the other, and falling to their knees in their efforts. He quickly ran to help the nearest two men back to their feet while they continued to gag, and caugh and at that moment two wagons came into the square from North Wall, and the men leaped to the ground to help him.

In a matter of only minutes, he had helped load as many as a dozen smoke inpaired, and partially blistered men into the wagons and helplessly watched the wagons take them away toward the Hospitol, several blocks away.

Men were falling out everywhere and by now, swirling smoke and ash had become so thick, that he could not even see the south side anymore. The gaseous smoke played no favorites, nor did the blistering heat,…and heat exhaustion was taking its toll on those trying valiantly to fight the fire. These were being replaced by others almost as quickly as he could help the ailing into the waiting wagons,…and it was then that he resigned himself to that task completely. He began making his way into the smoke in search of those that could not make it back on their own, and began to help them across to the wagons, having to rewet the bandana several times and rinse his face and burning eyes.

The roar of the fire was deafening at times, as it continued to spread. The sharp cracking of splintering timber as walls crashed down,…the impacts throwing even more embers and burning wood into the gusting wind to be blown onto other buildings along the east and west sides, starting even more fires and creating even more bucket brigades to try and fight it. More and more people were succumbing to the intense heat and smoke, and these were being carried bodily across to the hospitol wagons, and still, the licking flames continued to spread. The entire west side of the square was a roaring inferno by now, due to the fiery debris being carried on the wind.

There came the loud crash of brick and wood then, as the walls of the Peterson Hotel collapsed, sending spirals of acid smoke, fire brands and ash skyward, only to be whisked away and fall on yet other buildings and residential dwellings along Grand and Bonham streets. The Farmer's and Merchant's building was now in flames as the fire had broken through the hotel's outer walls, and allowed the flames to span Wall street as the fire leaped and roared its way onto every building alongside, and those between Grand and Bonham,…

and in only seconds everything was burning. The fire was devouring everything in sight, and had already leaped across Bonham. The large clothing store on the corner of Wall and Bonham was in flames, as well as the temporary Courthouse, and Civil Court building, housing the offices of Judge Bonner and Marshal Jim Stockwell, three stories up.

The heat had become so intense on the brick, and rock structure that the outer walls simple crumbled, or turned to powder, and then imploded in on themselves….Having been so busy helping others, Billy had not seen Judge Bonner being carried by two men and placed in the wagon, nor Stockwell, as he was helped into one of them, as he was having a very bad time seeing anything at all now. His eyes were on fire and watering profusely, and to the point that he was costantly rubbing them as he continued helping others to the waiting wagons.

Kegs of gunpowder began exploding in the gun shop, next door to the Court Building, as well as the stock of ammunition,…and the combined concussions was deafening and caused the very ground to shudder as the blasts hurled metal, lead, and burning material onto those buildings and people within a hundred yards of it,…and they were being maimed and burned mercilessly. The fiery debris littered the buildings and homes along and behind Bonham Street, quickly engulfing the dry wood and leaping from building to building, and from building to house.

Buildings and homes east of the square were now in flames, and after two hours of battling the out of control wildfire, the valliant steam Pump ran out of water, as one by one, the cisterns went dry, leaving the men no choice but to abandon the long stretches of played-out hose to the fate of the fiery furnace. The Firemen, and those civilians still able to walk on their on began an agonizing retreat north along Wall, and Main Streets, while still others went south along South Main, and South Wall,…the fire had not touched that part of town, except for those buildings and homes in close proximity to the square. Everyone was then forced to stand aside, caughing and crying, but all watching the ageless Monster devour their already "Depression devastated", and beloved town.

*   *   *

Rodney knew the town was on fire after he had ridden for several miles through timber and plowed ground, and was dumfounded as he sat his saddle, able to see the spiraling flames and debris above the distant rooftops,…and the pain in his gut and heart was overwhelming. Everything was on fire, it appeared, except for those houses, or businesses too remote to be affected,…and the sight of it all was maddening, as well as diffucult to comprehend.

He thought of Billy then. They were at Doc's house, and the fire looked to be burning along Bonham Road. Oh, God, he thought, and wondered if they were all okay? He kicked the fidgeting animal in the flanks, reining it more to the South and headed for the distant Bonham Road. It seemed to take forever as the horse carried him through brush and wild briars, but he kept the frenzied animal at a run, dangerously jumping fallen logs and ducking hanging branches to finally ride out of the trees and down a descent to The Goodland Road. Stopping abruptly, he barely avoided contact with a loaded Spring-Wagon and its occupants then urged the animal across and back into the grass and planted fields,…and fear was a growing dread as he pushed the animal over the uneven terrain.

*   *   *

Jarvis Cantrell, and men were still galloping their horses briskly along the Jonesboro Road and by now, he was sure the town was the source of the smoke. He was even able to see the leaping, distant flames over the treetops of the forest between them and there. He watched the smoke for another minute then turned and motioned Mitch alongside.

"How much farther, Mitch?" He yelled.

"I don't know!" He shouted back. "Could be ten miles!…We can cut across, if you want?"

"Too risky!…Let's pick up the pace a bit!" He spurred his horse to a faster gallop then, and all of them began using their spurs, settling the animals into a steady, hard-paced run in pursuit of Cantrell.

Cantrell began watching the weed-grown road ahead of the horses bobbing head, and was thinking of the decision he had just made. He knew something like this could bring the Army out in force again, not counting lawmen from other towns in the area. If they were going to have a chance at taking that bank's money, it would have to be done with quick, methodical precision, otherwise there would be too many guns in town to deal with,…they would be cut to pieces! He was also taking a gamble that the money was not already in ashes as well. But he also knew that those iron safes were usually insulated against fires and such.

But still,…he had changed his plan in mid-stream, something he had never done before,…and that could spell disaster for all of them. But, he thought, as he watched the billowing smoke above the line of trees again. To change his plan again, just might be even worse! The way he saw things now,…it was too late!…They would have to go through with it.

The thought of dying anywhere else, but his beloved Utah had never crossed his mind before, and he wondered about that?…Oh, he knew he was going to die, sooner or later, and he knew he would not be in Utah when he did,…but it seemed different now, for some reason!… He suddenly found himself thinking of the family he once had, of how peaceful and serene his life had been before they,…! He shook his head then to clear away the thoughts. That was then, and this is now! Setting his jaw, he watched the narrow wagon-path go by beneath the horse's hoofs, suddenly hardening himself to what they were going to do.

"Horses are getting' winded, Jarvis!" Shouted Mitch as he pulled alongside again. "We keep this up, they'll falter, for shore!"

Nodding, Cantrell slowed his heavily breathing horse to a walk. "Time is not on our side, Mitch!" He said, still watching the smoke. "In a wind like this, that fire is going to travel over that town in nothing flat….It's also going to bring folks from every town around here to help fight it,…maybe the Army, too!…We waste too much time, we won't be able to do our business before they recooperate!"

"I know, Jarvis,…but if we're afoot, we won't get there at all!"

"Five minutes!" Nodded Cantrell.

*   *   *

Almost totally exhausted from the unbearable, blistering heat, and choking smoke, Billy leaned for a moment against the boardwalk at the corner of Wall to watch the raging flames devour the stores and shops,not thirty feet away from him, as the fire began gorging it's self along Wall Street. Store after store was crackling under the roaring flames, and all the while, a gusting, steady southern gale blew ash and burning embers even farther north, and west, igniting every building, house, barn, and tree in it's path. He was caughing with almost every breath he took, and his already overly weak eyes were constantly burning from the acid fumes in the thick smoke.

Weak from exhaustion, he moved the few feet to the boardwalk steps and sat down, removed the sweat-soaked bandana from his nose and mouth then removed the eyeglasses from his blistered nose and tried to clean them. His shirt was sweat-soaked as well, and blackened from the blowing soot and dust, and wiping his face and eyes, he donned the glasses again and watched the licking flames across from him, the blistering heat almost unbearable.

He heard the horse squealing then, and got up to watch as the hospitol wagon careened toward him from the direction of North Main Street, the driver hauling the team to a halt at the corner. He got Billy's attention and pointed into the smoke. When he looked, he was able to see three more victims of heat and smoke exhaustion staggering toward them,...and both him, and the driver ran to help them back and into the wagon, then he stumbled back a step as the driver climbed to the seat again,...and without a word turned the screaming horses around and used the whip, sending them racing for North Main Street again.

The smoke was not as thick as it was, he noticed, because now, he was able to see almost the whole square. Tears filled his burning eyes as he sadly surveyed the burning, charred remains of the town that had adopted him twenty-one years ago, and almost broke down and cried. Except for partial pieces of wall, piles of brick and burning debris, the entire south square was totally flattened into a smoldering, charred, blackened landscape of ruin. Every building there, and almost all those on the west, and east sides were gone, as well as everything for as far as the smoke allowed him to see,...there was nothing but burning debris everywhere he looked! The only building not in ruin along the east side, was Bratcher's original bank building on the south corner.

The once elegant Peterson Hotel was gone, with nothing but partially erect, and crumbling sections of thick brick walls left standing. The Farmer's and Merchant's Building, bank and all, was now history. From there, and for blocks along Grand Avenue was flattened, or on fire, buildings, houses, the Catholic and Episcopal Churches, and from there west and north, nothing was left untouched by the hungry flames. Homes, and businesses farther out on Bonham, as well as several streets northward, and everything in between were burning, still being fueled by the strong winds.

Hearing distinct cracking of timber somewhere to his left, he moved out into the square, and still wiping at his eyes,...blinked away the teardrops to see the old abandoned Courthouse in flames at the northeast end of the block. And caughing again, he bent and placed both hands on his bent knees, and watched the flames shooting from the many windows, fed by the wind, and old discarded wagons, unwanted furniture and items being stored there. He caughed again as he saw the wagon returning then turned to stare for a minute at what used to be Jim Stockwell's office building,...and briefly wondered if him and the Judge had gotten away unhurt.

He shook his head as the wagon stopped beside him and climbed up to the seat. "Get me out a here, will ya?" He said hoarsely.

"Is that everybody?" Queried the driver, turning to look the square over. "Who's that over there?"

He looked up to see the group of people returning to the square from along South Main Street. "Checkin' th' damage, I guess,...They're okay."

*   *   *

Rodney pulled the winded horse to a stop at the picket fence, seeing Mattie and the children on the porch, and quickly dismounted as Willy and his siblings ran out to meet him.

"You kids okay?" He asked breathlessly.

"We're okay, Uncle, Rodney!" Said Willy. "We're worried about Mama, and Daddy, they went to fight the fire!" He sniffed then as tears filled his eyes.

"Oh, Rodney!" Cried Mattie as she came to the gate. "I am so glad to see you."

"Where's Billy, Mattie?...And where's Doc, and Connie?"

"Lord, honey, I don't know where William is, he flew out of her toward town several hours ago, God knows what's happened to him!... Connie is with Walter at the hospitol, unless it's on fire, too!...Find

William, honey, and please check on Walter, and Connie,…I'm so worried about them?"

"I'll find 'em." He said then turned to stare at the still-burning devastation for a moment before looking down at the children.

"Don't worry, Will, you neither, kiddos,…I'll find Mom and dad!… Stay with Mattie now." He nodded at the old woman then turned to leap back astride the horse, spurring it into a hard run again.

Fear and worry was strong in his heart and mind as he rode, and it became much worse as he neared the town's limits. Everything was either burning, or was charred and smoldering. Flames were still leaping skyward as the few remaining shops and houses caught fire, the wind sweeping flames and embers back and forth across the road in front of him. The thick, acid smoke burned his eyes and cut off his breath at times as he fought the terrified horse, to keep it on a direct route into town. He was just entering the business district, and slowed the animal to a prancing walk in front of what was once, Connie's Café, now only a smoldering memory, and with the only thing left upright, being the old blackened remnant of a kitchen stove.

Sighing, he spurred the skittish animal on toward the square, eying what was left of what used to be his town. Nothing was left, on either side of the street, he was on, nor the one next to it, or the next over from that. Bonham, and Grand was like a war-zone, nothing was left on his right, or left, only remnants. He stared at what used to be the Farmer's and Merchant's Bank building, thinking he could see the large, brick enforced iron safe standing alone in the debris.

The new rock and brick, Civil Courthouse lay in ruin, it's walls all but crumbled, and leaning precariously. Judge Bonner's office, and that of Stockwell's was totally gone. The square was a devastation of horror as he rode out into the debris littered emptiness,…nothing was left unburned on three sides of it, with only a few stores on the north side left standing, and showing only minimal damage. The choking smoke, though not nearly as thick, still swirled across the wide expanse of empty square, only to quickly be carried away by the gusting wind,… but at times, obscured the small steam pumper left unattended in front of the Peterson Hotel, it's large hoses all burned.

He saw the several onlookers then as they wandered aimlessly in their grief, and urged the horse toward them, pulling up to stare down at their wide-eyed, soot-blackened faces.

"Mister Sykes?" He asked as he stopped beside one of the men. "Is that you?"

Recognition was slow to come to the older man, but he suddenly reached up and squeezed Rodney's leg. "My, God, it's good to see you, Marshal Taylor!" He looked around then and waved his arm. "Look at it, Marshal,…it's gone, all of it!" By then, others had come up to surround Sykes.

"Was anybody hurt?" He queried. "Anybody die in the fire?"

"We don't know, Marshal, it all burned so quick, we,…we couldn't stop it!"

"That's right!" Yelled one of the women there. "We couldn't stop it,…but I know who started it!…It was that Heathen stepson of Andy Myers, that's who!…I seen 'im runnin' down that alley behind the saloon just before the fire!"

"Which way?" He asked.

"That way!" She pointed. "West!…If you don't find th' little Bastard, we will!"

"We'll hang th' Son of a Bitch!" Shouted another man.

"We'll do worse than that to th' Fucker!" Shouted yet another.

"That's enough of that sort a talk, now.…Leave that to me!…Have you seen Marshal Stockwell, or th' Sheriff?"

"Seen th' Marshal about two hours ago." Said someone else. "He was helpin' th' Judge into a wagon. Th' Judge was bleedin' pretty bad, looked like!"

"What about Gose?"

"Last I seen him, he was helpin' folks out a th' hotel,…that was some time back, too…What are we gonna do, Marshal, we ain't got nothin' left?"

"Rebuild it!,…Make it better." He said sternly. "Any of you seen Billy Upshur?"

"Yeah," Nodded Sykes. "But I didn't know it was him, till just now. He was helping folks into the hospitol wagons."

"Thanks, Mister Sykes.…Now, you folks shouldn't be here,…go somewhere till th' smoke clears." He reined the snorting horse around and galloped across the square, and then along North Main Street toward the hospitol several blocks away.

*　　　*　　　*

Billy allowed Connie to help him out of the sweat encrusted shirt, and after pouring water into a basin, he proceeded to wash the grime from his face, and picking up the bar of lye-soap dunked his head in the water and washed his hair and upper torso, taking care not to scrub his almost blistered skin too hard.

"My, God, Billy,...you are red as a beet!" She exclaimed worriedly. "Are you all right, Sweetheart?"

He finished toweling his head and face then sighed heavily, and caughed a couple of times before nodding. "Other than my guts bein' ripped out, I'm okay....It breaks my heart, honey! You ought a see it out there." He pulled the Union-top up as he spoke, and ran his arms into the sleeves.

"Looks like Vicksburg did, after th' shelling." He buttoned the front of the unions and sat down while she hurried to dump the pan of dirty water. He watched her go then sighed again as he surveyed the over-crowded room, seeing both, Doc, and Doctor Lovejoy working feverishly on the many cuts, bruises, burns and broken bones. Several nurses were busy dumping dirty, bloody water, and bringing clean water back,...others were boiling water and sterilizing medical utensils. Victims of heat, and smoke inhalation were lying on cots and tables along every square foot of the large floor, and all were caughing and gagging with every breath.

He saw Marshal Stockwell and Sheriff Gose across the room watching, as the staff-Doctor set the leg, and arm of Judge Bonner. Horace Bratcher, his coat and shirt barely clinging to his sagging shoulders, sat in a chair against the wall, elbows on both his legs, with his head cradled in his open hands. He was shaking like he might be crying. His clothing was soot-blackened as well, and his heart went out to the man, who was the very backbone of Paris. So many good people were hurt today, spiritually, mentally, and physically,...they lost everything they had!...Sighing again, he looked up as Connie came back, and smiled weakly at her.

"Thanks, honey."

"For what,…I love you, silly!…Oh, look, there's Rodney!" They watched as he came into the room to look around and then waved as he looked their way.

He quickly maneuvered his way toward them with a smile on his face. "Thank God, you're both okay!" He blurted, coming on to hug Connie, and to shake Billy's hand. "Are you okay, man,…your face is beet-red?"

"It was a hot fire!"

Amen to that!…I just saw what was left!…It was bad, wasn't it?"

"You wouldn't believe how fast it went, Rod, there was no way in th' world to slow it down!"

"Yeah," He nodded, and looked around the large room. "I talked with Mister Sykes, and some others in the square just now." He said, looking back at him. "A woman there said she saw Andy Myers' stepson running from the rear of the saloon just before the fire started."

"Think he done it?"

"It's a good possibility, and I think he likely did!" He nodded. "I see Jim, and John Gose over there, I'm gonna go tell them about it!…Be right back."

"Wait, Rod,…did you go by Doc's?"

"My first stop." He nodded. "They're all okay, just worried sick!…I wish I'd got here sooner, Billy." He shrugged. "But from th' ranch, it looked like a grass fire, I spent over two hours looking for that before realizing it was Paris!…I never saw nothing like this before!"

"It still burning?"

"It's burning it's self out, I think, houses are too far apart out of the town limits." He grinned then. "You look like some Rodeo Clown, Billy,…you ain't burned too bad, are you?"

Just blistered some, I'm okay."

"Good, be right back." He left and worked his way toward the other lawmen.

Billy watched him for a minute then scanned the room again in time to see Doc pull the sheet over one of the victims. "Looks like somebody didn't make it!" He sighed then and frowned at her.

She shook her head sadly. "That was, Charles Ellison, I think Doc said….He was unconscious when they brought him in!…Doc seemed to know he was going to die, poor man!"

"What happened to him?"

"Too much smoke, I guess." She replied. "Doc said it could also be a heart attack. He didn't seem to be hurt in any way!" At that moment, Rodney came back.

"What did they say, Rod?"

"Gose had already talked with Andy Myers, says he pretty much suspected the same thing,...and so does Jim, he caught the two of 'em arguing this morning."

"They gonna look for 'im?"

"Said he was, soon as they're sure the Judge is okay."

"What happened to th' Judge?"

"Seems him and Jim went back for some of his important papers when the building caught fire....Jim said the ceiling fell on 'em."

"Lucky as hell!" Commented Billy. "Both of 'em."

"Amen to that!"

"What about Lisa, and Cindy,...are they okay?" Queried Connie.

"They're at the ranch,...at least, I hope they are!...John will take care of them."

"You forgot your gun, too!" Stated Billy. "Ain't like you."

"I was in a hurry!...Why, we gonna need it?"

"Gonna be some lootin' after all this, Jim's gonna need some help!"

"Never thought a that!...Well, I can go get it, my horse is outside, want me to swing by and get yours?"

"No,...I think we'll borrow Doc's buggy in a bit, I'll get it myself. I need clothes anyway....I'll be here when you get back."

"Be back in a couple a hours then." He turned and left.

"I brought you a shirt, Billy." Said Connie, reaching behind her for the folded garment. "One of the nurses found it somewhere,...but it's your size."

"Thank her for me, honey." He pulled on the shirt and buttoned it up before stuffing the tail into his pants.

"I'm going to see if I can help Doc now, honey." She said. "He looks exhausted!...We can go back later, okay?...you just relax and rest for now, okay?"

*   *   *

185

As the thirteen riders came to the Clarksville Road, Cantrell held up his hand to stop them, and they sat their saddles to study the dozen or so wagons bordering the lane, on both sides…and the families that were standing in them to watch the smoke from the town.

"Must a been a bad one." Commented Mitch. "Well, this bunch has seen us now, so what do you think,…we still on?"

"That is the plan!" Returned Cantrell, looking at the haze over the town. "We have about a mile or two to go yet,…and a lot more people are gonna see us!" He turned to the men then. "When we get to the town square, half of you circle to the right, the rest stay with Mitch and me, and that includes you, Morg….If anybody is there, and I'm sure there will be, herd them all up together in one spot and cover them. We'll only have a few minutes to blow the safe,…providing we can get to it!…Let's go!" He spurred his horse onto the road and headed for Paris at a gallop.

They had only covered a half mile or so when they began seeing the few remaining, intact houses, and were also seeing pedestrians grouped on the road in places to watch the smoke, dispercing them as they rode past. Some were walking toward town, but all scattered off the road to allow them to pass,…and a few minutes later, they were in the outskirts of the smoldering destruction. Some houses were still burning, while others were just a mass of charred, smoking rubble. People were crying brokenly as they searched for salvageable relics in the smoking ashes, others were just hugging each other in frustration,…and holding on to their children,…and this scenario was everywhere they looked. Loose livestock was roaming aimlessly on and off the roadway, horses, cattle, goats, and even poultry,…and all scattered as the gang of men galloped by.

Cantrell held his hand up again as he stopped just short of the smoldering square to survey the devastation.'Whole damn place burned down!" Breathed Mitch. "It's as bad as I ever seen one."

Nodding, Cantrell motioned the men in closer. "Sammy, Dutch, Curley, Milton, you, too, Burle,…you five circle off to the right when we go in. I can see people in the square there, so keep 'em together…. The rest of you, all except you, Morg,…the rest of you come in behind us. Once I find out where that bank was, you can take that small group yonder to join the others….Okay, now walk your horses in."

They entered the square from the southeast corner, and the first five men broke right, as ordered, pulling their guns as they did, and quickly, and quietly began herding the frustrated civilians to the middle of the large square, while Cantrell led the others along the south side, where he stopped beside two men and a woman as they watched what was happening.

"Good afternoon, Gentlemen." Voiced Cantrell, tipping his hat. "You, too, Madam!...Now,...would one of you Gentlemen be so kind as to tell me which of these charred remains was the bank?"

"What do you want a know that for, Mister,...who are you anyway?"

"My name is Jarvis Cantrell, Sir!" He smiled then. "And I am here to save the bank's money from being burned!...Now please, Sir, point it out for me?" He drew his pistol as he spoke. "Haven't you had enough trouble for one day?"

The man's eyes widened slightly when he saw the gun, and then quickly nodded toward the end of the square. "On th' corner there." He said. "Other side a th' street."

"Thank you so much!" Smiled Cantrell. "Now, if you will, please join your friends out there,...and I have to say this,...cooperate, and you won't be hurt!" He nodded at the remaining five men then, and they immediately began using their horses to force the three toward the other civilians.

"You heard the man, Morg,...I can see that safe from here!"

CHAPTER THIRTEEN

"How's th' Judge doin', Jim?" Queried Billy as he came up to join him and Gose.

"Oh," Gasped the Marshal, quickly turning around. "Hey there, Billy." He shook Billy's hand, as did Gose. "Judge has a busted arm and leg,...but he'll be okay, damn ceilin' fell on us,...got my arm, too!"

"Is it broke,...your arm, I mean?"

Stockwell shook his head. "Bone's cracked,...Doc Lovejoy's gonna put a cast on it later."

"That's good, man." He looked back at Gose then. "How are you, Sheriff?"

"Mister Upshur, under different circumstances, I'd be very well,... all I feel like doing right now, is bawling!"

"Yes, sir," He nodded. "Me, too....Well, give my best to th' Judge when he wakes up." He grinned and went on to sit down beside Horace Bratcher then.

"You okay, Horace?"

"Hell, no!" Groaned the banker hoarsely as he looked up, and then, as he recognized Billy, he straightened in his chair. "Forgive me, William, I didn't know it was you,...I was lost in my misery!" He sniffed then and wiped at his eyes. "I'm not okay, no....Just look at these folks here, William, after having to scratch shit with the chickens for four long years, just to keep what little dignity thay had left,...and for what?...Just to lose everything they had in one afternoon,...their jobs, homes, dignity, everything!"

"That's what I wanted to talk to you about." Said Billy, scanning the overfilled room again. "I've been here for a while now, watchin' th' goin's on, and I spent that time thinking....I heard what you did to keep folks afloat these past four years,...and they wouldn't a made it without you!"

"Well, I can't do it again, William,...there's not ten thousand dollars in my vault, not cash money, anyway."

"Yes, sir,...but, I think you can do it again! You still got a bank, your building is still there!...That means you still got a place to do business."

"Are you going somewhere with this, William?...Cause if you are not, I am lost."

"I am!...I want you to rebuild Paris, Horace,...and I want a help you.....I have one hundred and forty pound of pure gold dust at my disposal,...and every ounce of it is yours, if you're up to th' job again?... It can help feed these folks, maybe keep 'em in clothes while they rebuild,...help with th' building supplies, too!...What do you say, sir,... have you got th' energy to do it again?"

"A hundred and forty pounds,...wh,...?"

"No questions, Horace!...You can't tell anybody, ever!...And that, Sir, is the only repayment I'll ever ask for,...just keep our secret!"

"You have to be joking, William,...son, in the first place, no one gives that much gold away for nothing,...and in the second place,...I am an honest man!...I have to know it is legal before I can accept it!... And I'd like to know why you're doing it?"

Billy lowered his head for a moment then nodded. "Rodney Taylor and me have a mine in Indian Territory, Horace,...it's all legal, and aboveboard, you can believe that!...And as far as why?...I'll try to explain it th' best I can." He grinned then, and shook his head.

"It's simple, Horace,...I want a do this, and so will Rodney, when I tell 'im. Besides, we're not givin' it to just you, it's for everybody that made Paris what it was.....This is my home, too!...You, and these folks saved my life nine years ago,...I owe them, you, and this town everything!...Now,...have we got a deal, or not?"

"Of course, we do, and God bless you, William, And Rodney, too!"

"No, sir,…You are th' savior here here, not us, remember that!…It's you that held this town together for four years, and now, you'll help rebuild it!…Knowin' you, it'll be built better, too!"

"Oh, yes, William!…No more wood structures on that square, you can believe that!" He sighed then. "But even with your generosity, my boy,…I'm afraid we'll fall terribly short of the funds needed."

"How short?'

"Well, I don't know,…but I can see it costing several hundred thousand dollars, before it's done!…Of course,…the Government could also grant us a large loan, once they see our efforts paying off,…and they will see it, thanks to you boys."

"Well, if it'll help, I know some Choctaw Indians that'll haul all th' rock in here that you want, and the price will be very reasonable. They can furnish lumber, too. You put th' money where it's needed, Horace!… You've got th' bank, a safe to keep th' money in, and th' heart to get th' job done!"

"And I'll do it, too, William!" He grinned, shaking Billy's hand. "Should I keep you informed on the progress?"

"Why,…Th' gold, and th' job is yours!…You just open that bank for business on Monday mornin', and we'll deliver your gold."

"Thank you, William."

"I didn't do anything, Horace, Rodney, neither, remember that." He shook the banker's hand again. "Monday mornin', nine o'clock!"

"Nine O'clock." Nodded Bratcher.

Nodding, Billy had just gotten to his feet when the muffled explosion echoed toward them,…and like it was yesterday, the explosion from eight years ago was happening all over again!

"Wha,…what on God's earth, was that?" Exclaimed Bratcher, also getting to his feet.

"That was your bank-vault, Horace, just stay here!" He quickly made his way back to Stockwell and Gose, who were also watching his approach, as well as the front door, both unsure of what they had heard.

"I need a gun, Marshal!" He said quickly, and when Stockwell only frowned at him. "Come on, God Damn it, didn't you hear th' blast?" When he said that, the Sheriff bolted toward the front door with a curse.

"We heard it, I think,…But, what was it?"

"Bratcher's bank vault, now who's got a gun I can use?"

"Rufe's in bed over there, his gun's on th' floor!"

"I see it, now go after Gose, tell 'im to grab a wagon, I'll be right behind you!" He watched Stockwell run after the retreating Sheriff for a moment then ran and grabbed the Deputy's gun and holster from the floor, and was buckling it around his waist as he maneuvered his way toward the door,…but then stopped when he heard Connie call to him. "Stay with Doc!" He shouted, waving her back then hurried out the door. He crossed the porch to jump from the top step into the wagon's bed as Gose whipped the team into a dead run back toward the square, and several minutes later were hauling them to a halt amidst a crowd of excited civilians.

"They robbed Bratcher's safe, Marshal!" Yelled a man breathlessly. "We thought they was gonna kill us!"

"They went west!" Yelled another man, pointing wildly. "Hurry!"

"Hold on here!" Shouted Gose. "One at a time!…Who robbed the safe?"

"It was Jarvis Cantrell, Sheriff!" Said Curtis Sykes, shoving his way to the wagon. "He told me his name!"

"They went down the Bonham Road, Sheriff!" Yelled a voice from the rear of the crowd, and when Gose shook the long reins to turn the team, Billy stopped him.

"Hold it a minute, Sheriff." He leaned closer to Curtis Sykes then. "Mister Sykes,…Rodney Taylor will be here in an hour or so, tell 'im where we're gone!" And when Sykes nodded. "Let's go, Sheriff,…no, wait, there comes Cletus!" Gose pulled the wagon across the square to intercept the Telegrapher.

"Hey, Mister Upshur, Sheriff, Marshal, what happened here, I heard another explosion?"

"Never mind, Cletus!…Can you still climb a pole, man?"

"Well,…not as fast as I used to!"

"Well, go climb one right now, get word to Honey Grove, tell 'em th' Jarvis Cantrell gang just robbed th' bank's safe!…Tell 'em they're headed their way, and to head them off, you got that?"

"You bet'cha!" He shouted as Gose whipped the team into a hard run again.

Almost losing his balance a time or two, Billy finally managed to sit down in the bed of the careening wagon, pulled the new Colt, Peacemaker pistol and checked the loads before putting it away again to watch the roadside destruction,...and the soot-blackened victims of disaster as they searched the remains of their homes. He noticed that only the women were crying, and holding on to their children in desperation, while the men only stood and stared at what they had worked so hard to build,...stared in futility and at times, angrily kicking at the smoldering debris.

He saw the smoking ashes of his wife's Café, and felt the loss as he remembered what it was like just to be there, and he knew she would be devastated. They were finally out of the remains of town, and coming up on Doc's house, and he was able to see Mama Bailey and his children on the porch, and all watching the wagon go by. He didn't draw attention to himself, however, not wanting to further worry them, and then they were past the house, and bouncing toward the community of Honey Grove, some twenty miles distant.

Jarvis Cantrell, he thought, shaking his head while he settled his hat back on his head. Who would have believed it?...Rodney was right,... they had to have been held up at Jonesboro all this time. They must have seen the smoke, and knew what it was.....Easy pickings, he thought grimly, taking advantage of the situation!

We'll have to see about that, he vowed, hoping Cletus was able to send that message. If the Sheriff of Honey Grove had the nerve to to do his job, they could possibly sandwich the gang between them, force them to leave the road,...and maybe catch them napping.

What he needed was the Roan between his legs, he thought drearily, but he didn't,...so now, he would just have to hope for the best,...and a little luck wouldn't hurt!...And speaking of horses, he thought, and then moved forward enough to touch Gose's arm.

"Best rest th' team, Sheriff, else we'll never catch 'em!"

Nodding, Gose slowed the winded animals to a walk along the semi-rutted road. "How far ahead do you think they are?"

"Fifteen, maybe twenty minutes!" Returned Stockwell. "We ain't gonna catch 'em in this wagon, anyway. Hell, they're gainin' on us with every second!"

"We might!" Said Gose. "If Daniels gets his ass in gear, he can head 'em off!"

*   *   *

Cantrell raised his hand to stop them, and then slowed his badly-winded horse to a walk as he scanned the wooded countryside,...and sure that he had seen something he liked, stopped and reined his horse around toward them.

"Gentlemen, you did very well back there,...thank you!...But now, we must find a place to hold up in until we can split up the money,... of which,...I must say, is not as much as I hoped!...Never the less," He sighed, staring back the way they had come.

"We are taking you men too far away from your objective, Arkansas is back the way we came."

"So, where do we do all this, Boss?" Queried Billy Jack, also staring back down the road. "Not here in th' road, I hope,...they're gonna come after us."

"No,...not here!...Look around you, Gentlemen,...do any of you see someplace we could hold up?" And when all of them began standing in their stirrups to search the roadsides, he shook his head. "Look closely, men,...there's a barn, off there a ways." He nodded his head northward. "See it?" And when they finally all acknowleged. "If you didn't see it, they won't, either!...That's where we'll do it,...I don't see a house anywhere close by, so it should be safe enough."

"I don't know, Boss!" Said Morg worriedly. "Them people all live here, they might know about this place!...They could be after us right now."

"Come on, Morg, you saw the devastation in those people's faces, they are a beaten people. There was no lawmen around, and no horses anywhere, that I could see!...By the time the authorities are notified of what happened, our trail will be cold!...Besides,...They may know about the place, but if they're not looking for it, they won't see it, not tonight anyway....Out of sight, out of mind, Gentlemen!"

"Makes sense to me, boys!" Grinned Mitch. "If they're after us, it'll be dark before they get this far!"

"They still got telegraph wires!" Said Billy Jack. "And we're wastin' time in th' middle of th' road, like this,…somebody's likely to come along any time."

"Okay, you're right!" Said Cantrell. "One of you boys sling a rope over that telegraph wire, and pull it down then follow us." He reined the horse around and led the way down off the road, and up out of the ditch into the waist-high grass and trees, and all of them galloped off toward the distant barn in the trees where, five minutes later, they were stopping in the doorless opening of the old barn.

"There was a house here once!" Commented Cantrell as they walked their horses into the barn's darkness. "Close as it was, I'm surprised it didn't burn the barn, too."

"Big house from the looks a that charred ground." Added Mitch as they entered the semi-darkness. "Wait, Jarvis,…we need to clear th' place of snakes." He gave his reins to Cantrell then gave the order to police the area,…and by then the other rider had joined them.

Cantrell sighed worriedly and turned to look back toward the road. He was not at all sure they were out of the woods, and regret was heavy on his mind again. If they didn't make it, he was sure that it would be because they changed their plans. He did not like playing anything by ear, not without disgussing it first!…But he had, and now, he was worried. He knew their survival would depend on how long it would take one of those civilians to find their Sheriff, and then it would depend on how much that Sheriff cared about doing his job?"

He'd forgotten about the Telegraph, too!…And that thought sent a chill over him.…Chances are, they had already sent the alarm ahead of them. Sighing heavily, he turned back to watch the men as they worked. Maybe it would be better all around, if they were found, he thought sadly,…none of them had a future any more,…just more of the same, and he was tired of it,…every gut-wrenching, heartbreaking part of it!

Going to Mexico with Mitch and starting over was a great idea, he thought.…But he had no thoughts that they would ever make it, he just didn't tell Mitch, not outright, anyway. Mexico was a dream, and he knew it!…So was a ranch, and cattle,…but none of it would erase the memories of who he was, or of what he had become,…and especially what he had done! Everything was too vividly implanted in his mind!… He couldn't sleep a full night without dreaming of his horrible deeds, his transgressions against God!...Like Lucifer, he had fallen from God's grace, and condemned to hell!...They would all be better off dead!... And dead, is what they would be, soon enough....Morg was right in his fears, he thought, because he knew they were already coming,...he could feel them!

"It's okay now, Jarvis!" Said Mitch, coming to take the reins. "There was only five or six of th' devils, but they won't be botherin' us."

"All the discomforts of home!" Sighed the aging leader as he walked across the dead hay and manure.

"Yeah," Agreed Mitch. "That saloon was a better place, that's for sure!...It's getting' dark fast, too,...do we chance a fire?"

"Sure,...if you want to be be seen!...And for what?" Sighed Cantrell. "We've got no supplies....No, we'll sleep here tonight, and split the money in the morning....Besides, my old bones can use the rest,...I'm tired."

"Yes, Sir,...I know you are. You go make your bed, Jarvis,...me and th' boys'll watch th' road for a while before turnin' in."

*　　　*　　　*

It was coming up on six-thirty when they saw the group of riders coming toward them, and Gose pulled the wagon off the road and stopped, unable to identify them as yet,...and all three of them were standing in the wagon's bed as the posse stopped beside them.

"Hi, ya, Charlie." Nodded Gose as the Honey Grove lawman urged his horse in closer.

"John?" He reached out and shook Gose's hand. "And Jim Stockwell,...ain't seen you in a spell." They shook hands and he looked back at Gose. "Heard you had a fire, your way,...a bad one!...Sorry to hear it, man."

"Yeah, thanks, Charlie." Sighed Gose. "Don't guess you ran into Cantrell back there anywhere?"

"Saw two wagons on th' road, nothin' else!' He sighed, shifting his weight in the saddle as he eyed Jim, and then Billy. "How have you been, Marshal?"

"Tolerable, Charlie, that's about all."

"What's wrong with your arm?...Th' way you got it stuck in your shirt, looks like you're playin' with your tit!"

"I wish I was." Grimaced Stockwell. "Ceilin' in th' office fell on me, arm's busted, not clean through, though,…just hurts like hell!"

"Sorry to hear it."

The Sheriff looked at Billy then. "Do I know you, Sir?"

Billy shook his head. "Never been to your fair town,…name's Upshur!…Chances are, you knew my ex-foreman, though,…Sam Mullens?"

Charlie nodded. "I knew 'im, good man,…likeable fella." He turned back to Gose then.

"John,…all I can say is, they must a took off cross-country somewhere.…We been watchin' everything on both sides all the way here, didn't see a damn thing, except them two wagons."

"Any place they could hold up?"

"Maybe a farmhouse," He said, lifting himself in the saddle to scan their surroundings. "They're scattered everywhere out there."

"That's why I don't think they left the road." Sighed Gose. "I think they're close by, somewhere!"

"Well," Sighed Charlie, looking around again. "If they are, they still had to get off this road somewhere along th' way.…Be hard to track, too, dry as it is,…and definitely not in the dark!"

"It is too dark to see." Agreed Gose. "What do you think, Jim?"

Stockwell sat down again. "Damn if I know!…There's a dozen roads criss-crossin' this one along th' way, they could a took any one of 'em!"

"Guess you're right about that!" Agreed Charlie, turning in the saddle to look back at his men. "Jesse,…come on up here!" And when the Deputy urged his horse alongside.

"Jess, you worked on farms all over this area.…If you was a gang of men on th' run, where would you hold up?"

"I wouldn't, Sheriff,…I'd split up and take my chances!…But,…if I was gonna hold up somewhere, I'd do it where nobody could see me,… and right now, only place I can think of, is the old Jamison Place. Their house burned down two years ago, and they just picked up and left.… Ain't nothin' there but a barn!"

"I remember that,…anywhere else?"

"Nothin' close!…But that's th' place I'd look!" Said Jesse, turning his horse and rejoining the others.

"There you have it, Sheriff." Grinned Daniels. "Jesse don't say much, but he knows what he's talkin' about, when he does."

"Where is this barn?" Queried Billy. "There an easy way to it?"

"Barn's off in th' trees , north of us there!" Nodded Charlie. "The road in is about a quarter mile back,…want a check it out?"

"It's your call, Charlie,…your jurisdiction." Replied Gose.

"It's your bank they robbed, John, that gives you jurisdiction!"

"Then let's, by God, go see!"

"Wait a minute, men!" Urged Billy. "If they're there, they'll hear us, and likely see us, as light as it is,…especially this wagon!…We can't just go bustin' in on 'em, believe me,…they'd cut us to pieces!"

"What do you suggest, Billy?" Queried Stockwell.

"Wait till they're asleep,…maybe midnight, then go in real slow, and quiet!"

"And if they're there, what then?" Asked Gose.

"We surround th' barn while it's dark….If there's a guard, it'll be just one man, and we can handle him!…Then we wait till daylight and take 'em!"

"A sound idea," Nodded Gose. "And if they're not there, we can cut our losses and go home, I guess!"

"You and Billy's th' only ones with a home to go to, John!" Sighed Stockwell.

"I didn't mean it like that, Jim, no offense, man,…your wife okay?"

"Helpin' out at th' hospitol, she's okay,…and I knew what ya meant, John."

"Okay then." Sighed Charlie. "I guess we all agree, we wait till Midnight…So, where do we wait?"

"What's wrong with right here?" Asked Billy. "Noise from a wagon can go a long ways. Besides,…Marshal Rodney Taylor will be here in a couple a hours."

Who?' Queried Charlie.

"Marshal Taylor." Replied Stockwell. "My old Boss, you know 'im!"

Nodding, Charlie turned in the saddle and motioned Jesse forward again. "Jess, you three tie off on th' wagon here, we'll be here a while!…John, it okay we wait in th' wagon?"

"Sure!...You might as well be as uncomfortable as us, Charlie."

*   *   *

Connie saw Rodney as he entered the hospitol and hurried to meet him. "I'm so glad you're here, Rodney," She gasped. "Have you seen Billy?"

"I just rode in, did something happen?"

"All I know is, him, Jim and that Sheriff ran out of here in a hurry,... and Mister Bratcher told me his safe was being robbed!...That was two hours ago, Rodney, and I'm worried!"

"So am I,...don't worry, I'll go see!...You got a way home?"

"I'll go with Doc, please hurry?"

Nodding, he left, running across the room and back outside, leaving her wringing her hands in expectation.

He crossed the porch anf leaped from there into his saddle, leaned down and pulled the reins free of the slip-knot then spurred the animal toward town in a run.

Several people were still in the large plaza, with more trickling in from the off streets, and as he stopped and reined the horse across to the bank's remains, he saw Curtis Sykes waving to him and stopped. ""Mister Sykes, you seen Billy anywhere?"

"Sure did, Marshal, he told me to tell you what happened....Him, th' Marshal, and th' Sheriff took off after th' Jarvis Cantrell gang, they robbed th' bank's safe yonder!"

"Cantrell,...you sure about that?"

"Man told me his name, Marshal, had a dozen men with 'im, ta-boot!...And you'd best hurry, they ain't gonna catch 'em in no wagon!"

"They're in a wagon?"

"It's all they had!"

"Thanks, Curtis." He spurred the horse back across the plaza and down the Bonham Road at full gallop, scattering another mob of people in the street as he did,...and dread was like a weight on his chest as he held the animal to that pace. He wasn't worried about Billy taking care of himself, but the three of them would be no match for that many men!...He suddenly hauled back on the reins, sliding the horse to a squealing halt in the street, as one of John Gose's deputies suddenly ran out in front of him waving his arms frantically.

*　　　*　　　*

Billy rolled a smoke, and cupping his hands around the flaring match, lit it, taking the stimulant into his lungs, and just as suddenly began caughing. He caught his breath and put the cigarette out as he breathed deeply and stared up at the brilliant night sky.

"What was that all about?" Asked Charlie, causing Billy to look at him. "Don't you smoke?"

"I thought I did." He sighed. "Spent th' afternoon breathin' it,... guess that enough!"

"You fight th' fire, did ya?"

Billy shook his head in the pale moonlight. "Helped folks to th' hospitol's all."

"You say Sam Mullens works for you?"

"My Foreman,...or was!...He's got a cattle spread down along th' river now."

"Then, you're a rancher?"

"Farmer....Ross Sizemore runs th' place for me."

"I know Ross, too, I think....What brings a civilian out chasin' a gang of outlaws, Mister Upshur,...seems to me, you'd want a leave that to th' law?"

"Don't question his reason, Charlie, you have no idea!" Said Stockwell. "He's here at my request."

"I meant no offense, Jim,...Mister Upshur. Just makin' conversation."

"None taken, Sheriff." Nodded Billy. "A good lawman's always curious, it's 'is job!"

"Yes, Sir,...I'm sorry to say, it is!...I'm surprised, too,...ain't been nothin' happen in Honey Grove in so long, I sometimes forget I am th' law!...This little manhunt is a welcome exercise, too!"

"Well, don't get too relaxed, Charlie." Muttered Gose. "Jarvis Cantrell ain't nothin' to joke about,...he's a calculating killer, so's his men. Smart as hell, too, else the Army would a had him a long time ago!"

"I know that, John, I got th' wire....Forgive me men, I don't mean to be bustin' your chops like this, after what you been through today....

We could see th' smoke and haze all th' way to Honey Grove,...must a been real big!"

"Ain't no town left, Charlie." Said Gose. "Damn fire must a burned fifteen acres, took most everything everybody had,...and then this Cantrell, son of a Bitch comes along and takes the rest of it!"

"I'm sure sorry for you folks, John, I truly am!"

"Thanks, Charlie,...we are, too!...Don't know what some a them folks are gonna do, come winter time, what with no money to rebuild!... It's a total loss, all the way around!"

"What about insurance, John, Insurance Company was right there?"

"It burned, too!...Don't know how far-reaching they were. Anyway, nobody could afford that stuff, Charlie, damn premiums was more than most folks earned in a month!...Oh, I'm sure the Post Office carried it, Telegraph, too, and Horace Bratcher, maybe!...The rest, I don't know. If they do, it won't cover their losses....Town looks like Lawrence, Kansas after Quantril rode through it!"

"I didn't know you fought in th' war, John?' Said Stockwell. "Who was you with?"

"I don't talk about that, Jim,...but I was there!"

"I was at Vicksburg!" Added Billy. "Sort a resembles that, too."

"I was expectin' you to have more men with you, Charlie." Said Gose.

"Not many willin' men in Honey Grove, John,...Jesse here's the only real Deputy, I got....Martin, and Kenny help me out from time to time....Oh, yeah,...I took th' liberty of sendin' wires on to Wolfe City, and Ladonia about Cantrell,...Bonham, too, in case they got through us."

"How'd your fire get started?" Asked Jesse suddenly.

"Arson." Said Gose. "We know who did it,...we'll deal with it later."

"Paris was bustin' at th' seams, I'll tell ya that!" Added Charlie.

"It will again, too!" Stated Stockwell. "might take a couple a years, but we'll rebuild it."

"I thought you had a pump engine, didn't that help?"

"Ran out of water,…and as high as the wind was, we had to let it burn itself out!…Now, I don't want to discuss th' fire anymore, okay?" Growled Gose. "It's done, and gone!"

"Let's talk about Cantrell then." Returned Charlie. "What exactly is th' plan here?…We take th; road in, and wait till daylight, I got all that,…but what then?"

"It's your idea, Billy," Said Stockwell. "You do have a plan, don't you,…I mean, aside from what you already said?"

"With seven men, eight when th' Marshal gets here?…My best plan would be to surround th' barn, like I said before, two men in back, two on each side. I plan on sidin' th' Marshal in front.…Then, we'll call 'em out, give 'em a chance to give up!…If that don't work, we'll think of somethin' else. But th' plan is up for grabs, Gents, you got a better one, I'm listenin'!"

"Hold on!" Voiced Stockwell, and when they all grew silent. "We got a horse comin' in!" They all got to their knees then, and palmed their pistols while waiting, but as they waited, one of the horses snorted loudly, stopping the rider in the road several dozen yards away from them.

"You might as well come on in and identify yourself, Pilgrim." Said Gose loudly.

After a moment, the rider urged his horse in closer to them and stopped again. "Name's Morgan Storm,…now, who's asking?"

"Name's John Gose, Sheriff in Lamar County. Sheriff Charlie Daniels, and Marshal Jim Stockwell are also here,…now state your business!"

"Jarvis Cantrell is my business, sir!"

"You a Bounty Hunter?"

"I am not, no, sir. I work for the state of Utah!"

"And that makes you, what,…a lawman?"

"More like a Government Agent!…I have been looking for this man for a very long time, now."

"How did you find us, how'd you know we was here?"

"Telegrapher, in that town back there told me. You'd be surprised what a little money will buy."

"Then, what do you want here?" Voiced Charlie, somewhat defensively.

"I am here to offer my help, sir,…you are outnumbered!"

"What happened to goin' someplace you never been?" Queried Billy.

Storm was silent for a moment. "You have me at a disadvantage, Sir, who are you?"

"Every road's a muddy one!" Returned Billy.

"Bill Upshur!" Said Storm. "Yes, sir, it was, as a matter of fact!…How's the store business?"

"Light down, Morgan, join us in th' wagon, we'll talk about it!"

"Good enough!" He said and dismounted to tie his horse to a wheel before climbing in. "Let's see, now.…there's three lawmen, Bill Upshur, and a Deputy or two, I presume?…You seem to be missing one, Bill Upshur, where is Marshal Taylor?"

"He'll be along in a while. I got a say, this is a switch, Morgan. You had us thinkin' you was just a common gunfighter, why th' secret?"

"No offense, Bill,…just part of my cover, that's all!…Now, what about Cantrell, do you know where he is?"

"Do you have any credentials, Mister Storm?" Asked Gose. "All we got is your word here, and we don't know you from Adam!"

"I carry nothing with my name on it, Sir. I have no wallet, no pictures, and no family to miss me!…I do not lie, except to get what I need,…and I never stop something when I start it,…unless it's over!"

"I trust 'im, John." Said Billy with a sigh. "And we just might need his help before we're done here."

Gose was silent for a minute. "Okay,…if you say so!…But I'm gonna watch 'im."

"That's fair enough!" Chuckled Storm. "Now, would any of you be hungry?…I stopped at that little diner in town before coming out. I have biscuits and ham, biscuits and sausage, and biscuits and bacon."

"Mister Storm, you just earned my trust!" Laughed Gose.

*   *   *

Mitch heard something in the dark behind him and whirled, his hand snaking for the gun on his hip.

"It's Morgan, Mitch!" Came the voice, stopping his draw.

"Now, that's dangerous, Morg!" He sighed, sliding the weapon back into the holster.

"Yes, sir, I know it is,…but if I wanted you dead?"

"I know, Morg,…I thought you sacked out?"

"Can't sleep, Mitch,…I got a bad feelin' about bein' here."

"How's that?…Nobody seen us leavin' the road, Morg,…and this place ain't seeable at night from there, so what's th' problem?"

"We ain't safe here, boss!…Th' law's out there somewhere, and they know we're here!…I can feel it!"

"I'm a bit uneasy myself." He sighed. "But I think it's because we stayed too long in that fuckin' saloon,…that, and ate all that damn fish! My friend, that would make anybody edgy!…Don't worry about it, man, Jarvis ain't worried."

"No, he prob'ly ain't worried, Mitch,…I ain't never seen 'im worried!…Th' man's got nerves of iron, but sometimes I think he don't really care, one way or the other!…And I don't know what I'm talkin',… it's just a feelin'!"

"He ain't been wrong yet, Morg, and I trust that old man with my life!…He'd die for us, too,…and you know that!"

"Yes, sir, I do!"

Come daylight, we'll split that money, and you can be on your way. We ain't twenty miles from Indian Territory here!…When you leave, all you got a do is cross that old Red River, turn east, and go straight into Arkansas."

"Well, I'm of a notion to leave tonight, Mitch,…without th' money!"

"Suit yourself, Morg, nobody'll stop you!…But what about the other men,…they find you gone, they'll think you're tryin' to get to Arkansas ahead of 'em…. They'll be gunnin' for ya, man!"

"Yeah, that's for sure!…Hell, I ain't leavin', Mitch,…I just wish we hadn't stopped here, that's all!"

"Don't worry about it, Morg, I've only seen movement on th' road one time tonight, four men headin' back th' way we come, nothin' from the other direction."

"Can't see th' road at all, now." Said Morg.. "We don't know what's waitin' out there!…Okay, Mitch," He sighed, throwing up his hands in defeat. "I'm goin' to bed."

"Wake up J. P., will ya,…I'm sleepy, too."

*   *   *

Billy was dozing when he felt someone touch his arm, and was instantly alert.

"It's me, Morgan," Came the voice. "We got a horse coming in at a gallop."

"From where?"

"Behind us."

"That'll be Marshal Taylor, I reckon." The moon was high by this time, and they could vaguely see the oncoming rider, and the sound of running hooves woke the other men as well,...and they were all watching as Rodney stopped the winded horse beside the wagon.

"What took you so long, Rod?"

"Stopped a couple a times!...John, you and Jim awake?"

"We're here, Marshal."

"John, one a your deputies flagged me down coming out a town, said him and Glenn found Taylor Pounds hiding in the brush of a vacant lot west of town. But, when they tried to take 'im to the hospitol under arrest, they were jumped by an angry mob and barely got away."

"Lynch mob,...God damn it!...If it ain't one thing, it's another, where are they now, Marshal?"

"Said he was locked in a tool shed at the burned-out Episcopal Church. He also said people were still looking for them, and as much as they didn't want to hand Pounds over, they would not want to shoot somebody who had just lost everything they had,...not to save the man that took it from them!...That's a quote, John."

"Take one of our horses, John." Said Charlie. "They're fresh."

"I can't leave now!" Breathed Gose. "Jim, you go, you're hurt anyway."

"Nothin' wrong with my gun arm, John." Said Stockwell. "But I doubt I can handle a runnin' horse that far in th' dark, with just one good arm!...You're elected, my friend, and you need to go, there's been enough trouble in Paris."

"You're right, of course!" Sighed Gose.

"Take my Sorrel, John." Said Charlie. "He's stronger than the others."

"Shit!" He cursed, and angrily climbed down from the seat to tromp to the rear of the wagon and untie the Sorrel horse. "You men be careful, you hear?" He mounted the horse and spurred it to a run on the moonlit road.

"Tie your horse and climb in, Rod." Said Billy. "While you're at it, say hello to Morgan Storm."

"Morgan Storm?"

"It's me, Marshal," Chuckled Storm. "Good to see you, too."

"Who else is here, I don't know about?"

"Charlie Daniels, Marshal."

"How are you, Charlie?" He shook his hand and peered at the man next to him. "That you, Jesse?"

"It shore is, Marshal!...Martin, and Kenneth's here, too."

"Men?" He said, shaking their hands. "Good to see you....Okay,...I can see that Cantrell ain't in custody here," He grunted and sat down to lean against the sideboard. "So, where is he, and why are we just sitting here?"

"We don't know where they are, Rod, they're not on th' road, or Charlie would a seen 'em....Jesse seems to think they might be held up in an old barn about a quarter mile north of us."

"And?"

"And we're waitin' till midnight to go in." Said Stockwell. "We're goin' in on foot."

"That's good thinking, maybe they'll be asleep or something. So, what time is it?"

Billy pulled his watch and held it up to the moonlight. "Eleven-ten."

"Okay." He sighed then leaned forward to look at Storm and hold out his hand. "Mister Storm, it is good to see you again,...but you are the last man I'd expect to find on our manhunt."

"I could say, you're right, Marshal....Good to see you, as well."

"So, why are you here?"

"He's after Cantrell, Rod." Sighed Billy.

"And, no,...I'm not a Bounty Hunter." Chuckled Storm.

"I'll tell ya about it later, Rod."

"Do I want to know?"...Okay," He sighed. "We are gonna walk up to that barn, right?"

"That's th' plan, yeah." Said Billy. "If we're quiet enough, maybe we can surround th' barn,...call 'em out at first light."

"Where do we leave the wagon and horses while we're doing that?"

"Off th' road in th' trees somewhere." Replied Billy. "Jesse, how far's that barn off th' main road?"

"I'd say a quarter mile, trees all th' way up."

"Then it's settled." Yawned Rodney. "If I can stay awake that long."

*   *   *

Twelve forty-five a.m. found them staking out the animals in the line of trees some fifty yards off the main road, and surrounding the unused wagon-road leading to the barn. When they were ready, Billy decided to go over the plan again, telling Charlie to take his three men, and Stockwell, and watch the rear, and both sides of the barn,...then they started up the road, one behind the other for silemce-sake. A half hour afterward, found Billy, Rodney, and Morgan Storm slipping quietly through the brush and trees until they were finally able to see the entire front of the doorless structure,...as well as the man hunkered down in the opening.

"Is he asleep?" Whispered Rodney as they crouched behind an out-cropping of brush and foliage. "I could go take 'im out right quick, what do you think?"

"They ain't ameteurs, Rod,...they're used to things like this!... Prob'ly used to getting' out of 'em, too. We wait for daylight!" He looked across at Morgan Storm then. "You okay with that?" And when the gunman waved his arm in the darkness, all three of them found a semi-comfortable place to sit, and settled in to wait for daybreak.

Leaning against a tree, Billy could watch the man in the doorway through the foliage, and he did appear to be fast asleep. He could also see the rifle in his hands,...and knew it would be easier if they could disarm him and slip inside. But he also knew that men like these carried a built-in sense of danger, and could react accordingly....They would have to wait for light, and then call them out, and not knowing how many men Cantrell had was another problem, because if they were to ride out of there in force, most could get away,...and that's exactly what they would do, if they knew they were out here. Cantrell was no fool, he was sure of that,...and he must be guilty of what they said he did, to have a Government agent tracking him down....If that's what Storm really was?...Morgan Storm could be nothing more than a Bounty Hunter and gunman, except for the fact, he was too immaculate looking, and at ease when talking with lawmen.

He cast a look at the gunman, who was steadily gazing at the sleeping man in the doorway. But, he thought as he watched him, that could just mean he was good at his job! He glanced at Rodney then, and grinned,...he was already asleep, his head hanging to one side of the tree and almost resting on his shoulder. Sore neck, come daybreak, he thought, and then yawned his self.

His eyes popped open when the thrown twig struck him, and he looked to see Storm nod,...and looking at the sky, could tell it was close to dawn. He reached out and shook Rodney awake then moved around the tree, stood up to stretch, and then to relieve him self,...and then grinned widely as Rodney did the same.

Crouching, he moved back around the tree, and was squatting there when another man came to the barn's entrance, stretched his arms above his head then shoved the man over with his foot, spoke to him when he woke up then both went back into the barn.

Rodney came back to squat beside him then. "You about ready, Rod?" And when he nodded. "You're th' law, call 'em out!" He looked at Storm then. "You ready?"

When Storm nodded, Rodney moved back around the tree and got to his feet, and while he watched the barn, cupped his hand to his mouth and shouted.

"JARVIS CANTRELL!,,,THIS IS UNITED STATES MARSHAL, RODNEY TAYLOR, AND YOU ARE SURROUNDED!...COME OUT WITH YOUR HANDS UP, ALL OF YOU!" He quickly squatted as a man suddenly appeared in the shadow of the open doorway and fired at them, taking a sizable chunk of bark from the trunk of the old tree as the sudden, deafening explosion echoed away. But, just as the man fired, he was knocked away from the door's frame as he was also shot.

Billy looked in time to see Thorn lower his pistol, and was impressed.

*   *   *

Mitch quickly grabbed the wounded man's collar and drug him away from the door, and after checking his pulse, looked at Cantrell and shook his head

"God damn it!" Hissed Morg. "I knowed they was out there, Mitch, I told you they was out there!"

"Shut up, Morg!" He snapped. "They want us, they'll have to come through that door, now get your rifles and be ready, we ain't dead yet!" And while they scrambled to follow orders, he moved across to squat beside Cantrell. "What do you want a do, Jarvis?"

"John Paul was a good man, Mitch!" He sighed. "If I had not changed our plans, he'd still be alive!"

"Everybody dies, Jarvis, you know that….And it ain't your fault!… Now, come on, Sir, what do we do here?"

"YOU HAVE ONE MAN DEAD, CANTRELL!" Came the loud voice from outside. "COME ON OUT OF THERE!…NO NEED FOR ANY MORE KILLING HERE!…COME OUT, I'LL SEE YOU GET A FAIR TRIAL!"

"And a fair hangin'!" Snapped Mitch. "Come on, Jarvis, get us out a here?"

"All right!" Replied Cantrell, reaching to stuff the money back into the saddlebags. "Tell the men to get mounted,…you, too. Son."

"No, Sir!" Gritted Mitch. "If I leave here, you go, too!"

"Okay, son." He nodded. "Okay,…but we'll go last, you and me. Now, get these boys mounted,…but first, help me up from here!"

Mitch pulled him to his feet, and then gave the order to mount up.

"Now,…tell them to lay down on on them saddles when they leave, and once out that door, to scatter and ride like hell. It's the only chance they've got!"

"And we'll be right behind 'em, right?"

"Of course, Mitch, now do it, son, go on."

"I'll get our horses ready, Jarvis, you tell 'em what to do!"

With guns ready, Billy, Rodney and Morgan Storm rigidly watched the barn's open doors, and as the minutes dragged by, Billy suddenly knew what Cantrell was planning.

"They're gonna run for it, Morgan." He said suddenly. "Rod, be ready!"

"Maybe I can change their minds." Rodney cupped his mouth again and yelled. "CANTRELL, IF YOU CAN HEAR ME, LISTEN!...RUNNING WON'T WORK, WE'LL JUST SHOOT YOUR HORSES, SO DON'T TRY IT!...THESE DEPUTIES ALL HAVE RIFLES, YOU WON'T HAVE A CHANCE!...COME OUT AND GIVE YOURSELVES UP, MAN, YOU AIN'T GOT A CHANCE!" Movement at the barn's side caught his attention then. "There comes Charlie and Jesse up the side there, they're ready, looks like."

*   *   *

Mitch watched them ready their horses. "Keep 'em quiet, men!" And once they were ready and all had mounted, he walked between their horses and looked up at them.

"We won't be seein' each other again, men, so good luck to ya." He shook their hands then and moved back to allow Cantrell to walk among them.

Cantrell looked at each of their faces and smiled. "You have been the very best a man could ever ride with,...and I thank you, one and all for your loyalty,...and to apologise to you for this!...Turned out, I lead you into a trap, and I am sorry." He cleared his throat then.

"Now, when Mitch tells you to go, I want you to bust through that door like a bunch of wild Indians, and scatter like the leaves of fall. Lay down on your horse's necks and ride like hell!" He backed away from them then to watch as they palmed their pistols,...then turned and nodded at Mitch.

"Go!" Yelled the second in command,...and with shrill, rebel yells, all ten men spurred their screaming horses into a jumping run, boiling out of the old barn in a yelling, shooting melee of desperation, and all scattering in different directions as the hot, summer morning erupted in thunderous, echoing gunfire! Men and horses alike could be heard screaming as the shooting continued, the deputies, as well as Stokwell and Daniels running after them on foot, and shooting as they ran.

Both, Billy and Rodney fired quickly as the first horsemen burst through the dark opening, but not expecting them to be hanging off the sides of their horses and firing back, both missed hitting anything, but air,...and then had to duck for cover as returning lead began searching for them. Storm had managed to fire twice, also missing on his first shot, but hearing a horse squeal as it was hit by his second. The animal stumbled, but regained it's footing and raced on into the dark undergrowth with the four deputies in pursuit.

Billy, and Rodney got to their feet and started to run after them, but by this time, were afraid to fire for fear of hitting their own men. As they started to run, Storm quickly rushed to cut them off.

"Wait!" Said the gunman, stopping them. "Cantrell ain't with them!"

They crouched again to stare at the dark opening.

"What makes you so sure?" Urged Billy.

"He's smarter than that!" Returned Storm. "We chase after his men, he leaves in the opposite direction."

Rodney shrugged, and all three of them backed up into the shadows again to wait.

*   *   *

Both, Cantrell, and Mitch listened to the deafening barrage as they watched the lawmen give chase past the open doorway, all firing wildly as they ran, and after giving them sufficient time to get far enough away, mounted their already skittish horses and walked them to the doorway, where Cantrell stopped him.

"We walk our horses out, and around the barn, son." Sighed the older man. "If luck is with us, we can disappear in the trees before they even know we're gone. You ready?"

"Always." Nodded Mitch, and they both rode out into the morning light, paused for a second to peer in the direction of distant shooting,... and was about to rein their animals around to the side of the barn when the three men stepped out of the trees to confront them. Pulling up quickly, they stopped the horses, and Cantrell quickly reached out to grab Mitch's left arm as he was about to pull his gun.

"Don't, Mitch!" He hissed, causing the younger man to hesitate, and then let the gun slide back in the holster. "There's a time for everything, boy!"

"It's over, Mister Cantrell!" Said Rodney loudly, as he held the pistol trained on them. "I'm Federal Marshal Rodney Taylor, and you are under arrest,...now dismount, please and drop your weapons!"

"Get off your horse, son!" Sighed Cantrell, and they both reluctantly dismounted to move in front of their horses and face their captors.

Billy watched them get down and come forward,…and believing Rodney had the situation in hand, holstered his pistol to watch.

"Drop your weapons!" Ordered Rodney again. "Do not try anything foolish!"

Nodding, Cantrell looked around at Mitch. "Go ahead, son, do what he says."

"No, sir,…I can't!" He whispered. "Not till you drop yours."

"Mitch,…do what I say, boy,…you don't deserve this!"

"What th' hell are you gonna do, Jarvis?"

Cantrell sighed then looked back at his captors. "I'm tired, son." He said, and looked back at him. "I'm going to end it right here."

"We're waiting, Mister Cantrell!" Voiced Rodney again. "Drop the guns."

"FUCK YOU!" Yelled Mitch, suddenly going for his gun, but as he cleared the holster, his eyes widened, and he was suddenly thrown back into his horse, then to fall in a lifeless heap beneath the pawing hooves of the animal.

"NOOO!" Yelled Cantrell as he watched his adopted son go down,… and he quickly went to his knees beside him. "You weren't meant to die, son!" He sobbed, his tired frame shaking as he wept.

Morgan Storm released the grip he had on his own gun, letting it slide back into the holster as he watched Billy holster the Peacemaker, and he stared at him in awed wonder for a second before looking back at Cantrell.

"There was no need for that, Cantrell, it is over!" Urged Rodney, still shaken by the suddenness of the gunfire, of which he had been unprepared for. "Drop your weapon, sir!"

Cantrell pushed to his feet, and with one last look down at Mitch, turned to face them again. "I won't do that, Marshal!" He said flatly. "Don't get me wrong here, boy.…I know I could never hope to outdraw the young man next to you there, nor you, you have your pistol in hand!…But, sir,…I will have my say, first!…Oh, you can shoot me, but you'll have to kill me, otherwise I'll kill one of you, and I'm tired of killing!" Tears were still running down his cheeks, as he looked at each one of them, and the bore of Rodney's drawn pistol loomed large and dangerous.

"One of you is an Assassin,...my Assassin!...I know this, because I've been expecting you,...and I can feel your presence!" As he talked, he was eying them closely. "It is not you, Marshal,...and I do not believe it is the young man next to you!" He smiled sadly then, and shrugged. "Come on, Marshal,...to disarm me, you'll have to shoot me, and I know you do not want to do that,...so put your gun away, please?...I'm not going anywhere,...and I wish to face my Assassin!"

"Go ahead, Rod." Said Billy in a low tone. "See where it's goin'?"

Rodney slowly lowered the gun, taking it off cock before holstering the weapon. "All right, Cantrell, say what you're gonna say,...But then, I want your gun, Sir,...it is over!"

"You are right, Marshal, it is,...and I thank you, sir." Nodded Cantrell, and then he looked across at Morgan Storm, staring hard at him for a second. "I am certain I don't know you, sir!...Are you the one they sent to kill me?"

Storm stared back at him for a minute, and then slowly moved forward a few steps. "Yes, sir, I'm afraid I am!"

Both Rodney, and Billy stared in disbelief at Morgan Storm. The man had lied to them a second time, and just like before, they had believed him.

"Hold on here, Morgan!" Said Rodney quickly. "I won't allow this!"

"You can't stop it, Marshal." Returned Storm. "You'll never take him alive, anyway!"

"He's right, Marshal." Smiled Cantrell. "Today, I pay for my crimes,...and I will admit to you,...and in the presence of God Almighty, that I am bitterly sorry,...for everything!...And just so you'll know, both of you. This man is an Assassin!...He works for the Mormon Church,...and one just like him murdered my entire family!...They made me what I have become, Marshal!...They are fanatics,...and this man does their bidding!" He looked back at Storm then.

"Are you the one who murdered my family, sir?"

"Come on, you men!" Argued Rodney. "You don't have to do this!...Storm, you shoot him, I'll arrest you for murder, you got my word on that!"

"Let 'em alone, Rod." Said Billy sternly.

"No, sir!" Returned Storm, after Rodney's outburst. "I did not kill your family!"

"I thank you for that!" Cantrell drew then, the pistol coming into his hand with a fluid motion, and he fired at almost the same instant as did Storm, the slug's impact pitching him backward to fall across Mitch's body,...and then he was still.

As the thunderous retorts of gunfire echoed away, they both looked at Morgan Storm, with Rodney pulling his gun again as he turned,...but he stopped when they saw the gunman slowly picking himself up off the ground,...and holstered the gun again.

Storm unsteadily straightened himself, stood erect and looked at them while holstering his own weapon,...then he suddenly grinned slightly and sank to his knees, only to fall on his face in the dry grass.

"What happened here?" Yelled Charlie Daniels as him and his deputies ran toward them. "You men okay?" He stopped then when he saw the bodies, and stared in disbelief. "They bluffed us, didn't they?" He sighed.

"Bluffed us, too!" Said Rodney as he looked at Billy. "All but Morgan Storm,...he got 'em both!...We didn't expect 'em to draw on us like that, we had 'em cold!." He sighed then. "Guess Storm knew 'em better than we did."

"Son of a Bitch!...Got him, too, though,...that's too bad!"

"What about you, Charlie, you get the rest of 'em?"

"All but three!" He nodded. "We got four men dead back there, three more wounded, two dead horses,...and three that got away!...They are long gone, too!"

"You did good, Charlie, all of you, and we appreciate it!...Think you could send Jesse back to get the horses and wagon, we'll have to carry the bodies back?" He waited while Charlie left to give the order, and nodded his head again as he watched Jesse, and another deputy trot off down the overgrown road then sighing, waited for Charlie to come back. "Who's watching the wounded?"

"They ain't goin' anywhere, Marshal, all three shot in th' legs!...
Besides, th' Marshal's there."

"Good,...I wondered where Jim was?"

"He done good, too,...some a them slugs was his!"

"Well, you're sure gonna get credit for what you did today, your
deputies, too,...and I thank you very much!"

Daniels moved in closer beside him then. "No need for that,
Marshal,...it ain't like I've got the most excitin' job in town!...But I was
wonderin',...." He peered up at Rodney then. "These old boys must a had
a hell of a bounty on their heads, 'specially Cantrell,...did they?"

"Come on, Charlie,...I wouldn't know that!" Frowned Rodney. "If
there is, I'll make sure you get your share."

"It's not that, Marshal....What I mean is this,...If there is one, you
can add our share of it to th' building fund, it's th' least we can do!"

"Why thank you, Charlie, you had me worried for a minute!"

Nodding, Charlie looked down at Storm's body. "Ya know,...I guess
there might be somethin' to bein' a gunfighter, at that!...Because if he
hadn't a showed up last night, them two might a killed you both!...It's
a shame, though, he was a likeable fella."

"Yes, he was!...Charlie, when the wagon gets here, have your
men load the bodies on it, will you, wounded and all,...and there's
another one in the barn there!...I'll want the weapons, knives, wallets,
everything!...you did manage to stop their bleeding, I hope,...the Army
wants 'em alive?"

"They'll make it to th' hangman's rope, Marshal, don't worry."

"We'll need those loose horses, too, by the way....And I appreciate
it, Charlie!"

"Sure thing." He turned to watch Billy and his other deputy as
they removed guns and personals from the bodies of Cantrell and his
lieutenant, and when they were done. "Come here, Kenny!" And that
brought the deputy running.

"Yes, sir, Charlie, what'll it be?" He asked, dropping the holstered
guns on the ground.

"There's a dead man in th' barn, drag his body out here,...and see
if they left anything, Then you can go back and relieve th' Marshal, tell
'im to come on in! Catch 'im up a horse, if need be,...and Kenny, catch

up all th' horses and wait for th' wagon, th' Marshal wants th' bodies loaded, weapons, too!"

"What about this one, Marshal?" Queried Daniels, looking down at Storm.

"Load him, too,…he was nothing but a Bounty Hunter, Charlie,… everything he told us last night was horse shit!…He was a gunfighter, though, got 'em both before he went down!"

Billy brought the two men's personal belongings and gave them to Rodney as Charlie walked away to look at the bodies.

"That old man nearly whipped ol' Storm, didn't he?" He shrugged as he looked down at the body. "Surprised 'im, too!"

"Weren't no winner, that's for sure!…By the way, Billy," He said, toeing the body over to remove the belt and gun from the gunman's waist, then straightened and gave it to him. "Happy Birthday,… whenever!"

Billy took the Silver-plated Remington from its holster and hefted it a few times before shaking his head. "This is an expensive piece of artillery, Rod,…all that Silver, carved, Ivory handles….But I never did like a Remington revolver,…don't fit my hand like a Colt. This one's a little too gaudy for my taste, too, and a little too heavy,…but you know what?" He nodded toward Chariie Daniels then, as the Sheriff was leading the dead men's horses back.

"Old Charlie there was a big help today, somethin' like this wouldn't hurt him none."

"I think you're right,…good thinking!" Grinned Rodney. "But first," He flipped open the gate and checked it for empties. "Just to be sure!" He grinned. "Hey, Charlie!"

Daniels stopped in front of them then bent to wrap the animals' reins around a broken, dead branch before giving them his attention.

"Yeah, Marshal?"

"I don't know about any reward that might be coming, course, I'll honor your request about that!…But, we figured that a thanks for your help, just was not enough!…So, here is a token of our appreciation!…. Thanks for your help, Charlie." He gave the holster and gun to him, then looked at Billy and grinned again.

"That is one fuckin' beauty, Marshal,…you sure about this?" He took the pistol from the holster and worked the action before holding it out in front of him.

"It's plated with pure Silver!" Added Billy. "Got real Ivory handles ta-boot!...A very expensive revolver in anybody's book!"

"And it's no doubt, one of a kind, too!" Said Rodney.

"Well, hell, yeah,…I'd be a fool to turn somethin' like this down!... Where'd it come from?"

"From him!" Grinned Rodney, and nodded at Storm's body.

"Well, hell, yeah!...Thank 'im for me, will ya?" He grinned and looped the rig over his shoulder while he unbuckled his own and let it fall around his feet,…and still grinning, buckled the new one around his waist and tied it down, just as the wagon and horses arrived….And nodding at them, he picked up his old rig and went to hang it on the horn of Jesse's saddle,…then climbed into the wagon and directed the deputy to head back for the bodies.

Billy walked over and took the horses' reins from the deputy, and led them back, tying the animals to a low-hanging limb, all except Morgan Storm's horse, that one, he led back in beside Rodney and grinned. "I will not ride back in that damn wagon, though….Besides, it's a pretty good-looking horse!"

Rodney laughed, and shook his head. "I just noticed it, Billy,…you got somebody elses gun on, don't ya?"

"Jim said it belonged to somebody named Rufe., one of his deputies, I think" He nodded and pulled the Peacemaker from the holster. "Pretty good gun, too,…a little awkward, and th' barrel's too short,…but I like th' balance,…and it's a fairly new model….But I like mine better!" He grinned, holstering it again. "Can't beat a Colt Conversion, Rod!"

"Amen to that!"

Billy dropped the horse's reins and went back to Cantrell's horse to retrieve the saddlebags, and after checking the contents, brought them back to Rodney. "Horace Bratcher's money!" He said laying them across the lawman's shoulder.

They waved goodbye to Charlie Daniels, and his deputies as Rodney reined the heavily-loaded wagon back out onto the road, and then stopped to watch them gallop away leading seven of the captured horses.

After waving one last time, Rodney grinned and slapped the reins on the team to send them home.

The rear of the wagon hosted the dead men's bodies, and that of Morgan Storm,…with the silent, closemouthed wounded sitting just behind the wagon's seat. The bodies of Mitch, and Cantrell, were draped across their own mounts and were in tow behind the wagon, along with Rodney's.

"How's the arm, Jim?" Queried Rodney.

"Hurts like hell, Marshal,…but as satisfied as I am right now, I can hardly feel it! We caught th' Jarvis Cantrell gang, can you believe that?…Somethin' no other law enforcement was able to do, not even th' Army!…But we did it!"

"We sure did." Agreed Rodney. "You did your job very well, too!… And that should tell you something, my friend,…it should put all your feelings of inferiority to rest, once and for all!…Because they're unfounded!…And here's a secret, Jim!…There ain't a lawman anywhere that don't second guess his self, or thinks he's wrong when he makes a judgement. That ulcer you say you've got, was not caused by th' job, you did it to yourself, and I got a feelin' you can cure it now, too!"

Thanks, Marshal,…I just might do that!" He sighed and looked up at Billy. "How do you like Storm's horse,…he sure is a goodlookin' animal?"

"I like 'im,…damn good horse, too!"

"You gonna keep 'im?"

"Why, you want 'im?…He's yours when we get to Doc's!"

"Hey, I'll take 'im, too,…and thanks!…Don't know where I'll keep 'im right now, but I'll take 'im….Got two more out there somewhere, if I can find 'em. Had 'em stabled over at Gresham's Livery." He sighed then. "Hell, McGleason's gone, too,…no tellin' how many horses burned to death."

"They got 'em all out, Jim." Said Rodney. "They had plenty a time."

"You might have to hunt 'em down!" Added Billy. "But they didn't burn." He grinned and looked up at the sky then. "You notice anything, men?"

"What?" Queried Rodney. "Besides being hot as hell?"

"No wind!" He said, matter of factly.

"Hey, you're right!" Laughed Stockwell.

"Why not," Returned Rodney. "It did it's job, don't need it any more!"

"I don't know, Jim," Said Billy, reaching to roll a smoke. "You might check with Doc about boardin' th' horse there for a while, I don't think he'd mind."

"No, no," Came Rodney. "Bring 'em out to th' ranch, if you want to, Jim, put 'em up in the pasture."

"Yeah, thanks, Marshal, I might just do that,...once I chase 'em down!...Got a find me and Lily a place to sleep, too."

"You can stay at the hospitol, Jim," Nodded Rodney. "For a while, anyway. A lot a folks will!"

"And don't forget your cast today!" Grinned Billy.

"Not to worry about that!" He twisted around to peer back at the wounded men then. "They're bleedin' again, Marshal,...think they'll make it?"

"Men like that don't bleed to death!" Grinned Billy. "They're too mean!...Well,...if you two don't mind, I'm gonna stretch this old stud's legs a bit!...I'll leave 'im at Doc's front gate, Jim, Rufe's gun, too,...and don't forget to thank 'im for me." With that, he tipped his hat, gigged the horse into a lope first, and then into a brisk gallop down the wide, partially rutted road in the direction of Paris.

CHAPTER FOURTEEN

It was late afternoon when Rodney and Jim stopped for the horse and gun, and Billy came out to meet them as they stopped,...as well as everyone else,

"Hi, Uncle Rodney." Voiced Willy, and as usual, the greeting was echoed by the other two as they ran to the gate.

"Hey, kiddoes!" He grinned. Hello, Connie, Doc,...Mattie,... everything okay here?"

"We're all on the mend, son." Nodded Doc. "Physically, at least. Looks like you all had a full day as well?"

"We sure did, Doc!" He grinned. "And I'm damn glad it's over!"

"It's such a God-awful shame!" Said Mattie sadly, as she surveyed the bodies. "Just look at them, Walter,...such a waste!"

"Yes, old Darlin', it is!" Soothed Doc then reached and wrapped an arm around her shoulders before looking back at Rodney.

"You'll find some extra company in town when you get there, Rod,...Doc said a troop of cavalry's there."

"Cavalry?...They didn't waste any time!"

"They got here late yesterday." Said Doc. "They're bivouacked on the square. Got the whole town locked down solid."

"Well, that's Jim's and John's company, not mine!"

"Thanks a lot, Marshal!" Laughed Jim as he started to climb down.

"Keep your seat, Jim," Said Billy, quickly reaching to untie the horse from the fence. "I'll get 'im for ya." He tied the animal to the wagon, behind the rear wheel, and then came back to look up at Rodney. "Get down for a minute, Rod, I want a talk to ya." Rodney nodded and climbed down, and once away from the wagon.

"What's up, Billy....Something wrong?"

"No, nothin' like that!...Do you think you might renege on half of your father in laws gold?"

"Well, yeah, no problem,...what's up?"

"I want a help these folks rebuild Paris, Rod,...I owe 'em that!"

"Oh, no, my friend,...we owe 'em that!...It's my home, too!"

"Thanks, Rod....Anyway, I told Horace, that if he would open his bank for business on Monday, that you and me would bring him a hundred and forty pounds a dust, to use where he needs it."

"Say no more, Billy, it's done. He's still got most of his important papers, and we got his money back!...He gonna help 'em rebuild?"

"Chompin' at th' bit, last I seen 'im!"

"He will, then!"

"Oh, if you see Cletus, tell 'im thanks,...he had to climb a pole to send Charley that wire."

"I'll do it,...now, what say we all get together at the ranch tomorrow for a cook-out?"

"It'll have to be after Church tomorrow, Connie and Mama both insists we all go to Church!...Say, two O'clock?"

"Two, it is,...see you there, all of ya!"

"We'll be there, count on it!"

*   *   *

The wagon was met at the outskirts of town by mounted Soldiers, and they were escorted from there to the square, where they saw several officers coming out of one of the smaller tents to wait for them. Sheriff Gose hurried out of a larger tent on the north end of the plaza, and was with the officers as Rodney stopped the wagon.

"I've been worried sick about you, boys." Panted Gose. "I see you got 'em,...is that all of 'em?"

"All but three, John,...get some help for the wounded, will you?"

"We'll handle that, Marshal!" Said the officer as he approached. "Some of you men, on the double!" He yelled, and when they arrived. "Get these corpses out of here, and cover them with something,...you other two help the Medic with the wounded!" When he was done, he came on to shake Rodney's hand, and that of stockwells'. "I am Captain Silas Mayberry, Gentlemen,...am I to understand these are what's left of the Jarvis Cantrell gang?"

"All, but three, yes, sir." Nodded Rodney. "That's Cantrell over his saddle back there. The other one might have been his second in command, I don't know!"

The Captain peered at the corpses as they were unloaded and laid side-by-side in the square and covered with blankets. "It would have been commendable if you had brought in Mister Cantrell alive, Marshal,... was that possible?"

"No, sir, it was not!...I gave him several chances to surrender."

"Too bad!" He sighed, looking back at him. "In some ways, that man was worse than Quantril!...He was a vicious, cold hearted murderer, and I would have loved to put him on trial in a Military Court!...How did he die, sir?"

"In a duel with a Bounty Hunter!...He wouldn't give up his gun, and drew on us without warning....I'll have you a full, in depth report on Monday morning, Captain, early,...and Captain,...their belongings are in the floor of the wagon there."

"Very good, Sir,...and thank you again!" He turned then and went to watch as Cantrell's body was laid out then had a soldier retrieve the contraband from the wagon.

"Sorry, John." He sighed, and climbed down to the ground. "You need some help, Jim?"

"I'm okay." He said, and climbed down beside them. "Three men got away, John." Said Stockwell.

Rodney reached into the wagon for the saddlebags and gave them to Gose. "They boiled out a that barn all at one time, John!...All of 'em laying down on their horses necks and shooting at us,...and then they all scattered!...Charlie, Jim here, and Charlie's deputies began firing as they came out, and so did we....Anyway, Jim, and the others ran after them on foot. We started to do the same thing, but Storm stopped us, and he was right, too, because Cantrell didn't come out with the rest."

"And Storm shot 'em?...I thought he was a Government man?"

"He lied, John,...He was just another Bounty Hunter with bad judgement!...When Cantrell drew on us, they were both killed!"

"Son of a Bitch!...I was starting to like that man."

"How about Taylor Pounds, you get here in time?"

"Uhhhh," He nodded. "Barely! I had to threaten a mob of people, but I got away with it!...At least till next election. I got him locked in a storeroom at the hospitol for now. Cletus wired th' Circuit Judge for me, he'll be here in a day or two."

"What about th' Judge, John?" Queried Stockwell.

"He'll be stove up for a spell, Jim, but he'll make it okay."

"Well, men," Said Rodney. "If you don't mind,.I'm going home!... John, if you'll take over here, I'd appreciate it, it's been a rough two days!...And Jim could use a ride to the hospitol, he was in some pain on th' way in, and John,...I have no idea who this wagon belongs to."

"I do." Nodded Gose. "I'll see they both get to the hospitol."

He shook the Sheriff's hand, and then Stockwells. "Don't forget your horse, Jim." He went back and untied his own horse, turned it around and mounted, and nodding at them, reined the animal on around to scan what used to be his town, then urged it to a gallop back toward Wall Street, and the Goodland Road.

*   *   *

Doc, Mattie and the kids were grinning widely as the old Medic reined the team into the large yard and immediately, Benny and Cindy ran around a corner of the house yelling.

"Hi, ya, Benny!" Shouted Willy and jumped to the ground in a run and as usual, Christopher, and Angela were right on his heels as all five of them made a running dash for the corral. Billy and Connie rode the their horses in beside the buggy, and Billy dismounted to help her down as Rodney rounded the house to hurriedly help Mattie from the carriage.

"Thank you, Rodney. "She smiled, and then wiped perspiration from her brow with a kerchief. "My Goodness, it's so hot!"

"Yes, Ma'am, it is!" He grinned. "Now, come on, I'll show you inside, it's cooler there." He took her arm and walked her up the steps to the porch. "Go on in, Mama Bailey, the gals are in the kitchen."

"Thank you, honey." She opened the screened door and went in as he turned to descend the steps and shake Doc's hand.

"Good to see ya, Doc!" He shook Billy's hand and hugged Connie. "Go on in, Connie, they're all in the kitchen."

"What are you doing back there, Rod?" Inquired Billy, looking toward the side of the house.

"Sweating,…can't you tell?" He grinned, holding up his arms to reveal his sweat-soaked underarms. "Come on, me and John are roasting a side of beef,…I left him turning the spit!"

They followed him around the house and into the back yard where both of them went on to shake John Gabbett's hand.

"Good to see you, Doc,…you, too William!" He grinned. "There's a couple of chairs there, have a seat."

Rodney went to spell the older man, telling him to sit and visit for a while.

"William," He grunted as he sat down. "You boys had a busy day, yesterday, I hear?"

"Reminded me of th' war." He nodded.

"I'll bet it did." He sighed. "I don't know if I can even bear to go to town right now!…It's heartbreaking."

"That, and then some." Replied Doc. "My Connie, and me didn't get home till after midnight Friday night,…must have had a hundred people burned, or suffering from smoke inhallation. Don't think I ever saw so much pain and suffering."

"It's a miracle there weren't more deaths." Sighed Gabbett.

"It is, that!" Agreed Billy.

"Rodney told me of your plans to help rebuild, William." Smiled the older man. "And I think it's wonderful,…that gold will go a long way, and Horace Bratcher is just the man to get it done!"

"Amen!" Said Doc. "Maybe, this time, they'll build with brick,… or maybe rocks. Anything that won't burn so fast.…We lost the whole town in less than four hours, John,…four, short hours,…and a lifetime of labor and love, went, poof!" He took the Kerchief from his pocket and loudly blew his nose.

"I'm sorry, Doc." Soothed Gabbett. "I shouldn't have started that conversation, I know you helped build Paris."

"Nonsense,…I'm a little sentimental, that's all. I'm fine now."

"Then, how about some cool tea to drink, I've had a jug sunk in the well since daybreak this morning?"

"No, no!" Argued Doc, wiping his forehead with the kerchief. "I can wait....That side of beef smells like it's done, by the way. Looks like it, too!"

"You're right, Doc!" Grinned Rodney. "All that's left, is the carving."

*   *   *

Horace Bratcher wiped his forehead with his bandana and stared down at the box of papers and deeds still waiting to be categorized and filed away, and was already tired after having spent all day on Sunday readying the bank building for doing business,...and while soldiers continued to help townspeople and laborers in their effort to clean up and haul away the debris to a landfill, he had also enlisted their help,...as well as a makeshift boom with a block and tackle and by mid-afternoon had the large, and very heavy vault resting in it's previous spot.

He also had to enlist help from the Blacksmith to remove the twisted door from its hinges and haul it away to be repaired. A job that took the Smithy all night long,...with the help of several brawny Privates, to complete the repair and reinstall the thick, heavy door,...a job that had been completed only a half hour ago.

So now, sighing heavily, he stifled a yawn, and with one last look at the box of papers, sat down heavily at his oaken desk and pulled his pocket watch, thinking that William and the Marshal would be arriving with the gold at any time now and afterward, he was going home for a nap! 'I'm too blamed old to stay up all night like this', he thought, then yawned mightily again, unable to stop it. He replaced the watch and stared out through the window at the activity in the large square and smiled tiredly. 'It will be done', he thought, seeing the loaded wagons crossing the square. The entire square would be cleaned in a month's time, at this rate,...and the building would begin,...and as tired as he was right now, he was looking forward to it! Sighing, he checked his watch again, and had no sooner put it away, when he saw them riding in,...and he was standing behind his desk to greet them as they lugged in the two heavy valises and set them down.

"Boys," He sighed, looking down at the bags. "I hope I can live up to your expectations!"

"You carried this town on your back for four long years, Horace." Said Billy with a smile. "Whipped a Depression damn near all by yourself,...and I'm sure you did without things you needed to do it!... We're just makin' th' job a little easier this time."

"God willing, I'll do it, too, you have my word!"

"No need to go that far, Mister Bratcher." Smiled Rodney. "We're just curious how you're going to do it,...and keep our secret?"

"Awww, that's easy,...I'll make loans per usual, do the paperwork and everything, and when it comes time for repayment, I'll just mark the bills paid and give it to them!..."I'll wind up being a hero,...at you boys expense, I might add."

"And very much deserved." Laughed Rodney as he looked around the room. "You got the bank looking good, too!"

"Sticks out like a sore thumb in all this rubble, though." He sighed. "But it's a first step!...Gonna take a lot of paint to cover the soot, though, the outside walls look like a Pinto Pony!"

"You look tired, Horace," Said Billy. "You getting' any sleep?"

"Boys, as of this minute,...I have now been up for twenty-seven hours." He looked around the room then. "But it was worth it!...And when you leave, I'll put a sign on the door saying the bank will be open for business first thing tomorrow morning. Then I'm going home and sleep till then!"

"Then we'd better get this gold in th' vault while we're here, temptation, ya know."

"That,...I know very well, boys....Lets do it!"

It took only a few minutes to put the gold in the heavy safe, and once the door was closed and secured.

"We have to go now, Horace." Grinned Billy. "We're goin' home in th' mornin', early,...well,...back to th' mountain, anyway." He held out his hand and shook the banker's vigorously. "Good luck, Horace."

"Yeah," Added Rodney, also taking his hand. "And if you need anything, have Cletus wire me at Fort Towson, might take a week, but I will get the message."

"And remember what we talked about at th' hospitol," Said Billy. "About that rock and lumber."

"I remember....Thank you, William,...and you, too, Marshal,...I'll never forget this."

They both nodded and walked out, and down the steps.

"Looks odd without that old familiar boardwalk."

"It'll be there, by th' time we come back." He looked back at the bank then to see Bratcher standing in the door watching them,…and quickly walked back up the steps.

"You want that rock and lumber, send that wire, Horace. I can have a convoy of wagons on th' way in a matter of days!"

"Rod," He said as he rejoined him. "Let's go!...I can't stand to look at it any more. I want a go to th' mountain and sit on my own porch, sleep in my own bed, and forget about all this."

"Amen to that!...But good luck doing it!" Sighed the lawman as they scanned the charred remains around the once bustling town square. "Just look at it,…nothing left as far as you can see, just blackened remnants of someone's possessions."

"I don't see how th' north side escaped?"

"It didn't,…they'll be torn down anyway." Rodney reached the several-page report from his pocket when he saw Captain Newberry leave his tent to scan the square for a second before seeing them,…and they waited as he walked briskly toward them.

"I was wondering what was keeping you, Marshal?" He said with a nod.

"We were just coming to see you, Sir,…had a little bank business first." He grinned and gave Newberry the report. "You'll find that all in order, and to the point, Captain, beginning with when Billy here, and the Sheriff first heard the explosion."

"Thank you very much!" He replied, putting the papers inside his coat. "But, I would like to ask you personally about that Bounty Hunter?...I'm sure you covered that as well….But as yet, we have failed to Identify him." He turned then and waved his arm at the temporary poles, and wires leading to his tent."We have restored telegraph operations here, as you can see,…and by description, the War Department has successfully identified all but the one."

"He called his self Morgan Storm." Said Billy. "Said he worked for the Government, and that he tracked Cantrell for several years….But,… all that turned out to be a lie!"

"Well, I can tell you the Government hired no such man to do this!...But then again, who's to say?"

"No, no," Said Rodney quickly. "I think you're right, Captain. Cantrell seemed to be expecting him, because he called him his Assassin!...I don't think he knew him personally, because when he asked Storm if he was his Assassin, he admitted it!...Other than that, Sir, we don't know any more than you do, or why they chose to kill each other?"

"Come on, Rod," Chuckled Billy. "I don't think Storm meant it to turn out that way,...he died with a surprised look on his face!"

"Yeah, I saw that, too!" Sighed Rodney. "Guess he underestimated the old man!...None a that is in my report, by the way. I didn't think of it!"

"Well, this whole thing is a little strange." Sighed Newberry. "maybe his picture will help, we made tin-types of all ten before burial. Well, I thank you, Marshal,...you also, Mister,...I have forgotten your name, sir."

"Upshur,...Bill Upshur."

"Well, I thank you, the Army thanks you, and your Government thanks you!...And with that, I'll say good day!" He nodded at them and walked back to his tent.

"Seems like a nice sort." Grinned Billy. "But I still get nervous around soldiers."

"I wonder why?" Smiled Rodney as they both pulled themselves astride their horses and turned them around. "You really think Storm was an Assassin, Billy,...I always thought an Assassin was someone that committed murder without being seen,...he was open about it?"

"Assassin, Bounty Hunter,...same thing!...Hired killers, all of 'em... .I know, I was one!...I don't know, maybe he did work for that Mormon Church,...Cantrell was a Mormon,...is that right?"

"He was,...that wire said he was a Mormon Minister!...Not that it matters anymore, anyway, they're both dead!" They walked their horses past the Army tents and across the square, taking care to avoid the many pedestrians and soldiers crossing on foot as they hurried to help with the clean-up,...as well as the heavily loaded freight wagons on their way to the l;andfill.

"Looks like everybody's pitchin' in." Commented Billy. "Lord knows how they find the energy!...And look at that, Rod, can you believe it?"

They stopped the horses to watch the wagons roll into the square. There were at least ten such wagons coming in from South Main Street, all loaded with barrels of fresh drinking water, and food stuffs. "Now that's something to see, right there!...Look, here comes more of 'em."

There were even more wagons behind those first ten, and the soldiers were kept busy directing them to a staging area, these were loaded with food stuffs as well, some with large bags of flour, salt, sugar, wheat, and other ettable grains. Others had salt-cured sides of beef, and pork hanging from iron rods erected in the wagon beds, and left to swing to and fro with the wagon's movements. These were directed to one of the larger tents where soldiers quickly unloaded and carried them inside.

"Must be fifteen or twenty wagons there,...they're lined up down th' street there."

"Two of them are loaded with men, Billy, they'll have plenty of help now!"

"Got a be from Cooper, or maybe Greenville." Nodded Billy. "And there goes Horace to meet 'em,...he might not get any sleep today, neither!"

"Paris is in good hands, Billy."

"Makes a man proud to see good folks helpin' others."

"Amen, Billy,...Amen!...Let's go, I'm hungry!...By the way." He said as they walked their horses back toward Wall Street. "How was Church yesterday, I forgot to ask?...Where'd they hold Mass?"

"In front a th' Church, everybody brought their own chairs."

"An open-air Church Service. Lisa said the same about theirs."

*   *   *

They were all up before daybreak, and using lantern-light, Billy, Rodney, John Gabbett, and Doc Bailey were out readying the wagon for their trip home. Willy and Benny caught up the mules and led them out of the corral to be harnessed to the wagon, while Billy and Rodney caught and saddled their horses, of which were then secured to the wagon's tailgate.

"Breakfast should be ready by now, men." Grunted Gabbett as he got down from the wagon. "Let's get it while it's hot!" He took the lantern from Doc, who had been the bearer of light while they worked, and held it high as they all filed back into the house.

Once hands were washed, and they were seated around the large table, all joined hands while Doc gave thanks,...and then enjoyed a meal of roasted beef, eggs, potatoes, fried beans, large, fluffy biscuits, and grease gravy,...and not to exclude strong coffee, and fresh milk for the children.

"My, Lord, ladies." Grinned Billy. "Look at this spread!...This is liable to be a miserable trip, I can see that right now!"

"Amen to that!" Smiled Rodney, and they all burst out laughing.

"Well, you can take what's left with you, Mister Upshur!" Smiled Mrs. Gabbett. "And be miserable all the way home." They all began filling their plates then.

It was breaking day by the time the meal was over, and after a couple of Coffee refills, Billy sent Willy and Benny out to ready Doc's buggy for him, and shortly thereafter, they were moving their chairs back and leaving the table.

Connie and Lisa helped Mrs. Gabbett, and Sabrina pack a large basket with food for the trip, while the men, Christopher, Cindy and Angela all went outside to wait with the wagons,...and to watch the sun as it was just topping the trees to flood the yard with its yellow light.

The women joined them then, and as the sun climbed higher, the women and children were saying their emotional good-byes, then to be helped into the wagon,...and once done, Billy came to hug both Doc, and Mattie.

"We love you so very much, William!" Sobbed Mattie as she kissed his cheek. "God go with you all!"

"I love you, too, Mama,...we'll be back soon, okay?" He took Doc's hand in a firm grip. "Can you make it home okay, Doc?"

"Oh, sure, I can, son." He sniffed. "Don't you worry none about that!...You just be careful out there."

"Well, you don't worry about that, okay?...Take care of yourselves!... If you need me, have Cletus wire me, he knows where. I love you both." He nodded. "Be seein' ya." He turned and climbed to the seat, waved, as they all did then slapped the mules with the lines, sending them onto the wagon road at a fast walk.

It was an hour before Billy reined the mules onto the well-travelled Goodland Road and turned north and until then, not one of them had spoken a word.

"Well," Said Rodney, finally. "As anxious as I was to go home, I didn't think it would be so hard to leave!"

"Makes two of us!" Nodded Billy then breathed deeply of the still, semi-cool morning air. "Doc, and Mama looked old to me, this mornin', Rod,...It's hard to think they'll be gone one day!...Seein' his town burn like that, aged him, almost sucked th' life out of 'im."

"I could tell." Nodded the lawman. "He's a tough old man, Billy, don't write him off too quick, my friend....They're both still in pretty fair health, you know."

""I know,...I'm just sentimental....This thing took a lot out a me, too! It won't be th' same, neither, even after they rebuild it."

"Nothing ever is, Billy,...it's called progress, evolution, and the like!...The land changes with time, and so do people....Time changes everything!"

"Let's not go there again." He looked at Rodney and grinned. "I don't much like change."

"I have noticed that!" They both laughed then.

"How are you goin' to report all this to Judge Parker?"

"I'm leaving you once we cross the river, going on to Fort Towson... .I'll wire the Judge from there about the six Cantrell men, and of Major Wilkes' involvement,...and I'll tell him to expect the rest of it by mail."

"He gonna like that?"

"Of course not, he's too impatient,...but he'll get over it! After all, we did capture the Jarvis Cantrell gang!...John's gonna mail it for me this afternoon."

"How,...th' Post Office burned?"

"Not all of it!...Mister Craigo improvised, he set up in one of the unburned rooms. Business as usual!"

"Well,...whatever." Shrugged Billy. "Let's go home, and forget about it for a while."

"Amen to that!"

"Thanks ,…Adios!"

EPILOG

Taylor Pounds was held until the Circuit Judge arrived and ruled that a change of venue would be in order, as the Arsonist would not, and could not receive a fair and impartial trial in Paris. The trial was moved to Cooper, some twenty miles South where he was convicted and sentenced to four years. He was then sent to the township of Sulphur Springs to be held pending any appeals, and transport to prison.

Horace Bratcher, and the Council conducted their business from his office in the original Citizens Bank Building, with Bratcher taking on the job of overseeing the cleanup, and rebuilding process. The gold he had received was sent, by an Army escorted stagecoach, to the Federal Reserve Bank of Shreveport, and reimbursed with currency and coin.

Representatives were sent to Denton, Texas with questions for professional Architects, and Engineers on what type of buildings, and materials would be best suited to withstand disasters such as fire, and the elements?...They also requested building plans, and designs for such construction.....And then, the hard part began.

By 1885, a new, and more beautiful Paris, Texas would emerged to retain it's previously owned status,...but would burn again, a short thirteen years later.

Taylor Pounds somehow managed to escape the Sulphur Springs Jail, and was believed to have gone to the Indian Territory, and though pursued, did manage to ford the Red River and disappear, prompting an all-out search by Rodney Taylor, Peter Birdsong, and the Light horsemen,...but to no avail.

Billy Upshur, and his family resigned themselves to the, sometimes boring life at their mountain, having decided to be happy there, at any cost. Their trips to Paris became more frequent, and always in the company of the Taylors,...All were able to see Paris in it's different stages of rebuild,...and even bringing more of the precious metal to aid in the projest.

He had also decided, and did plant corn on part of the open, fertile prairie, and to continue using the remainder for hay. They also continued their periodic trips to the Denver Mint. As for that other thing, you know,...the big secret?...Well, that may not be over,...there is still a mystery shrouding that whole impossible thing,...who knows?"

Long live the Old West!......."Thank you."